A FORGOTTEN LOVE

Don's lips pressed tightly against hers and spoke of the happiness that would one day be theirs. Wrapping his arms around her lithe body, he held her with special tenderness for all the lost days. Joni melted against him as the unspoken promises overwhelmed her.

Looking into Joni's eyes, Don said, "There's one more thing that I should tell you. Before coming down here, I officially withdrew my name from the candidacy for the chief of staff position and for the ER chief spot. I don't want anything to come between us."

A FORGOTTEN LOVE

Courtni Wright

ARABESQUE
BET BOOKS

BET Publications, LLC
www.bet.com
www.arabesquebooks.com

ARABESQUE BOOKS are published by

BET Publications, LLC
c/o BET BOOKS
One BET Plaza
1900 W Place NE
Washington, D.C. 20018-1211

First Printing: November, 2000

10 9 8 7 6 5 4 3 2 1
Printed in the United States of America

One

The overhead fluorescent lights glared a blue-white as the emergency room staff rushed to care for the patients who filled the examining rooms and overflowed into the halls. Anxious friends and family crowded the waiting rooms and grabbed at the physicians' coattails as they hurried past. Joni, like the others in their white uniforms, smiled briefly and muttered words of comfort as she darted to see her next patient.

"City General, this is mobile unit three. We're coming in with a twenty-five-year-old female with multiple stab wounds to the abdomen and torso. Mobile two is right behind us with her girlfriend. Over."

The radio crackled loudly drowning out the sound of traffic. "Copy that, mobile three. We're ready. Out." Catching Joni's eye, Liz continued, "Dr. Forest, another ambulance is on its way. Mobile four is already bringing two more patients. Where will we put them?"

"We'll stack them up if we have to. There's probably a little space left along the walls," Joni replied as she surveyed the already bursting waiting room.

Joni Forest, M.D., rested heavily against the top of the nurses' station as she hurriedly scribbled notes on her last patient's chart. She was in charge of one of the busiest hospital emergency rooms in the state of Maryland. Even so, she never asked anyone to do anything that she would not do herself, including working grueling sixteen-hour shifts when the need arose. At thirty-five, she was one of the youngest senior staff members in the hospital. Despite her youthful appearance, medium build and complexion, and short, soft brown hair, Joni commanded respect.

"I hate Friday nights. They all think they have to be on the road at the same time. They can't wait to get home from work. Everyone's in a hurry to go to dinner, dancing, movies, clubs, and the theater. It doesn't do them any good to drive like maniacs. They only wind up here," Joni said without looking up from the chart she had just finished. The patient had died of a hopelessly lacerated liver caused by a rush-hour car accident. He had not even made it to surgery.

"Here, drink this. You've been on your feet for hours. This orange juice will give you a little energy," Randi Timberlake, the head nurse and Joni's best friend, said as she handed her a paper cup and a chart for a little girl who had been bitten by a rat.

"Thanks. This is just what I needed . . . the juice, I mean, not the chart," Joni commented as she turned toward the examining room.

"Only too happy to make your day," Randi called after her with a wry chuckle.

In examining room three, Patty Williams sat quietly sobbing on her mother's lap. Tears streamed from her big, blue eyes and her body trembled from the coolness of the emergency room and the trauma of the attack. Her blond hair and pajamas were covered in blood. Her mother's eyes nervously scanned the room as if on the lookout for another rat. Mrs. Williams smiled weakly as Joni entered.

"Good evening, Mrs. Williams, I'm Dr. Forest. I'd like to examine Patty's arm. Do you think you could set her on the table for me?" Joni requested in a soft yet commanding voice. Joni's short, wavy light-brown hair looked neat despite the long hours. Her brown eyes sparkled with determination. She had competed against older and more experienced women and many men for the position of acting chief of the emergency room.

"Doctor, it looks really bad to me. Do you think she'll be marked for life?" the mother asked as she lifted the five-year-old onto the examining table.

"I won't know until I've cleaned the wound a bit. How does your arm feel, Patty?" Joni asked as she lightly sprayed the area with a topical anesthetic. She could clearly see the outline of the animal's teeth and the broken, mangled skin. Already the area had swollen and turned an ominous shade of bluish-black. The nurse had done a good job of cleaning the site, but the blood still welled freely in each puncture mark.

"My arm hurts," Patty replied, swallowing her tears.

"What happened? Tell me about it while I look at your arm." Joni encouraged the frightened child in a gentle voice.

"I was playing in my bedroom. I dropped one of my doll's shoes on the floor. When I reached under my bed to pick it up, a big rat jumped out. It grabbed my arm and bit it . . . hard. It wouldn't let go. I tried shaking it off, but it wouldn't stop biting me. I screamed for my mommy. She came in and made it stop hurting me," Patty said, sobbing.

"When I came into the room, doctor, the rat had its legs wrapped around my baby's arm. It was clinging to her. I tried pulling it off, but it just clamped its teeth down harder. I didn't know what to do, so I carried Patty to the kitchen. I stabbed the rat with a knife until I finally killed it. That's the only way I could make it let go." Patty's mother finished the story, her face contorting as she remembered the horror of it.

"Did it bite you also, Mrs. Williams?" Joni asked without taking her eyes from the mass of bluish-black flesh that had once been Patty's forearm.

"No, but it bled all over everything. Blood was spurting out of every cut. I must have stabbed that thing at least twenty times before it finally died," Mrs. Williams replied with a shudder as she pulled her lightweight bloodstained sweater closer to her frail body. Both the woman and the child looked as if they had not eaten much recently.

"I'll order tetanus shots for both of you, just in case. Patty's going to need surgery on her arm, I'm afraid. The rat tore the muscle rather badly. I'll start the paperwork to transfer her to surgery right away. They'll take good care of her upstairs," Joni said as she quickly made a few notes in Patty's chart.

"Will it be very expensive, doctor? My husband just started working again, and money's kind of tight right now," Mrs. Williams offered. Her care-worn face, which might have been beautiful once, was lined from the constant battle to keep hunger and illness from claiming her family. Like many people who could feel poverty breathing down their necks, the Williamses would find the hospital bill to be yet one more hurdle to overcome.

A quick look at the woman's face assured Joni that she would heed her advice. "I'm sure social services will be able to offer some assistance. The most important thing right now is to restore the full use of Patty's arm. Without that surgery, she might experience stiffness and loss of mobility," Joni said as she walked toward the door.

"Thank you, Dr. Forest," Mrs. Williams called after her.

After placing the necessary call to the surgical department, Joni tried to escape to the physicians' lounge for a few minutes of rest. She had been on her feet since early morning and was ready to go home. Unfortunately, she still had to work until midnight to cover for a colleague who was sick with the flu. Right now, all she wanted was to sit with her feet up for a few minutes.

Just as she placed her hand on the doorknob, Randi shouted from the front desk, "Joni, sorry, but there's a gunshot wound in two that needs your attention."

Taking the chart, Joni said, "Do me a favor. Remind me why it was that I said I wanted to be a doctor."

"I think it was for the money, the glamour, the expensive car, and the luxurious house in the country," Randi replied with a chuckle.

"Well, I'm certainly batting zero. I'm not making any money to speak of, this is hardly glamorous, and I ride the subway when it rains or walk from my nice but not elaborate condo only a few blocks away from here. I messed up somewhere along the line," Joni retorted as she dodged a swiftly moving gurney and vanished inside examining room two.

A young man of no more than twenty wearing a black bandana on his head lay on the table. Blood completely soaked the right sleeve of his tattered, green T-shirt. He stared blankly at the ceiling as if his mind were miles away. As Joni entered the room, she noted that he did not appear to be in any pain. She was not sure whether his reaction was caused by the medication the attending physician had given him or by the booze that oozed from his pores.

"Mr. Martin, I'm Dr. Forest. I understand you've been shot in the right arm. The X rays show that you haven't suffered any bone damage. The slug passed right through without hitting anything vital. I'll stitch you up and have you out of here in a few minutes," Joni said as she took her position beside Billy Martin.

"Thanks, doc. I can't believe I walked into that one. I'm usually on my game, if you know what I mean. I'm always lookin' behind me, beside me, all around me. No one ever gets the jump on me. No one," Billy bragged as Joni opened the suture kit and began to stitch the clean entry wounds.

"Someone did tonight. What happened?" Joni asked as she made the first of many stitches.

"I guess I let my guard down or had too many beers. Next thing I knew some dude was all up in my face, pushin' and shovin' me. I don't take kindly to someone tryin' to make a chump out of me in front of my homies, you understand. So I asked the dude to meet me outside.

"From the way he dressed, you know, baggies, backward

baseball cap, leather jacket, tennis shoes, I could tell that he was about my build. I figured I'd be able to take him on with no trouble. Man, was I wrong. As soon as we reached the alley, the mutha pulled out a gun.

"Don't look so worried, doc. I don't truck with no guns. I'm a bare-knuckles man myself. I told him my preference. He said that was cool with him and gave the weapon to one of his boys.

"We squared off, you know, took off our jackets, got ready. My boys was standin' around in case anything got ugly. His boys was lookin' to keep things calm, too.

"Then, as I was walkin' toward him, he pulled another gun out of his pants pocket. Shot me right in the arm and laughed. Him and his boys laughed.

"I tell you no lie . . . my boys was scared. You see, we don't carry no weapons. Weapons'll get the cops on yo' ass real fast. We're knuckle men, you know.

"Anyway, we stepped back and let them leave the alley. The blood was runnin' down my arm pretty bad by then. All I wanted to do was get to the hospital and get myself patched up. There'll be another time and place for that guy. He'll come back and we'll be ready."

Shaking her head, Joni replied angrily, "Haven't you had enough? The next time he comes to pay you a visit that guy might kill you. This was simply a warning shot to scare you and to put you in your place. The next time, you might not be so lucky."

"That's the chance I'll have to take, doc. I can't have him walkin' into my hood actin' like he owns the place. We'll take care of him alright. We got his number now. We'll know what to expect when we see him again," the young man boasted.

"Well, I've finished. I'll send in the nurse with care instructions. Be good to yourself," Joni said with a sad shake of her head. Turning at the door she said, "Do me a favor,

Billy. Pick a night that I'm not on duty to tangle with that guy. I don't want to see you cut up or worse."

Chuckling as he pulled on his shirt, Billy replied, "You've got a deal, doc."

As she left the examining room, Joni stepped into the chaos of the emergency room at full tilt. Gurneys of newly arrived wounded lined the walls. The triage nurse had shifted around the charts so that anyone who could wait slipped further down on the list. Joni and her staff would have their hands busy with the gang-war victims for quite some time.

Looking at her watch, Joni saw that it was eight o'clock. Only four more hours before she would be able to go home. Forgetting the fatigue, she took the next patient chart from Randi, quickly darted past the waiting patients, wheelchairs, and supplies waiting to be stocked and entered examining room four.

As she slipped into a green disposable cover, checked the young man's eyes and breathing Joni demanded, "Bring me up-to-date someone."

"The patient is eighteen years old. He's suffering from multiple knife wounds, one of which appears to have punctured his right lung. His friends say that he's a heroin user and from the looks of his arms, I'd say they're right," responded a second-year intern.

"Thanks, Jeff. You're right about the lung. No breathing sounds. His arms are pretty well marked up. Any ID on this boy?" Joni asked as she pressed the patient's abdomen for rigidity and examined the other wounds.

"His buddies call him Woeto, meaning woe to anyone who crosses him. It seems they've seen the recent *Romeo and Juliet* movie. I don't know his real name. Apparently they at least remember a little from Shakespeare," Jeff replied with a chuckle.

"Woeto, can you hear me? This is Dr. Forest. We're going to transfer you up to surgery. You have a collapsed lung.

They'll take care of it for you," Joni said in a clear, loud voice.

Fixing his unsteady gaze in the direction of Joni's voice, the young man tried to speak but the tube in his throat made it impossible. He grimaced in pain from his assorted knife wounds.

"Do you have any family we should notify, Woeto?" Joni asked.

. Slowly the young man shook his head. Then he became completely still as if resigned to his fate. He appeared unconcerned about his surroundings.

"Has his blood work returned from the lab yet? I'm concerned about this lethargy. Anyone know anything?" Joni queried her staff.

Before anyone could answer, the door burst open and an angry, young man dressed in a dirty black sweat suit and sneakers entered. He brandished a long, thin knife similar to the kind butchers use for filleting fish. Without waiting for introductions, he pushed his way into the room.

"So this is where you've put this lying trash who killed my brother. I should have finished you off in the parkin' lot, punk, and I would have if the cops hadn't come. But I'll do it now. Better late than never," the guy growled in a deep, angry voice.

The young man on the stretcher at first looked perplexed and then shocked to see the other man approaching him. Then as recognition filled his drug-soaked mind, his facial expression changed to fear.

"Call security!" Joni shouted to the nurse standing behind the intruder.

"No need, I'll be gone before the cops can get here, and he'll be dead!" the man snarled as he lunged for the table.

Pushing Joni and the nearest nurse to the floor, the intruder lifted his muscular brown arm to strike the wounded man. As his arm came down, Joni kicked at his calf and upset his balance, causing the knife to miss the intended victim by barely a fraction of an inch.

"Damn you, bitch!" the man shouted as he slipped. His black eyes filled with rage as he looked at Joni who had scrambled to her feet. She backed away, but the intruder had already refocused on his target.

Joni watched as the injured young man quickly pulled a concealed knife from his trouser leg. He had attached it to his skin with tape. It glinted silver in the glaring lights. Holding it in his right hand and grimacing from pain, he waited until his attacker lunged again.

The older man clutched his knife with more determination, and he lunged again shouting, "Die, you son of a bitch!"

Without moving more than a hair, the young man raised his knife and braced himself for the impact. Two bodies connected with a sickening thud. The examining table tipped over and fell onto the floor. A loud clatter filled the room as the monitoring equipment landed in a heap. Screams from the horrified medical personnel added to the chaos. A moment later, it was over.

Slowly, Joni and her staff picked up the expensive monitors that were now only wildly blinking displays and useless wires. Moving carefully toward the men lying prone in a heap on the floor, she motioned to the security personnel to come forward. It would take several of them to lift the unconscious men and reposition the table.

Moving into position with his service weapon ready, the lieutenant carefully turned over the attacker until he lay on his back on a stretcher placed on the floor. The knife of the man he had hoped to kill protruded from a spreading red spot in his chest. Carefully, several security guards lifted him onto the examining table before placing the other young man on a gurney beside him.

Both men were bleeding profusely. Blood from their new wounds, the young man's original stab wounds, and the broken plastic bag containing the blood for transfusion spread over the floor in a slippery, sticky mess. Protecting themselves from blood-borne infections, Joni, Jeff the intern, and the nurses quickly worked to assess the new damage.

"No pulse, no respiration," Randi said as she checked the vitals of the attacker.

"Nothing here either. Time of death . . . 21:05," Joni replied as she listened to the still chest of the young man. His attacker's knife had found its mark between his ribs and punctured his liver.

"What a waste!" Jeff muttered as he pulled off the surgical gloves and gown. "Is this why we go into medicine . . . to try to save the lives of street thugs who wind up killing one another anyway?"

Joni sighed in frustration as she added her scrubs to the growing pile in the nearby hamper, "We did what we could for them."

Watching the others walk from the room filled with the aftermath of hatred, Randi slipped her arm around Joni's shoulder and said, "He's right. This was a waste of human life. I always feel sorry for the new doctors and nurses the first time they see something like this, but, unfortunately, they'll get used to it someday."

Joni looked at her friend with eyes that filled with hot tears and said, "Do we really? When? I still haven't gotten used to the sight of brothers killing brothers. It's this mindless street violence that's robbing us of black men. All the good ones are married and the ones that are left are either on drugs or in jail."

Slipping into the physicians' lounge before anyone could hand her another patient's chart, Joni sank into the worn upholstery of the familiar leather sofa. Wiping her cheeks with an angrily bunched-up tissue, she allowed herself to relax for a moment. Randi was wrong. Some things were just too terrible to become familiar. Waste of human life made her angry. Joni knew that if she practiced medicine for fifty years, she would never get used to the sight of people inflicting pain and suffering on each other.

Joni was so tired that her entire body ached. Easing her feet out of her shoes, she massaged her sore toes as she listened to the evening news. A late commuter train had derailed north of the city. Thinking of her overworked staff, Joni was grateful that City General was not the closest hospital to the site. They might experience some increase in patient load, but they would not bear the brunt of the accident. Rising and padding over to the coffeepot, Joni poured herself another cup of the thick, hot brew. She had promised herself that she would cut down on her consumption of City General's pathetic excuse for coffee. She knew that too much caffeine would make her jumpy. However, after working a twelve-hour day, she could not manage to keep her eyes open without the help of the strong brew.

Joni had been the acting chief of emergency services for six months and the grapevine said that the job would fall on her shoulders permanently in a few days. Her boss, Don Rivers, had initially taken a much-needed vacation. While he was touring Greece, he decided that he had endured enough of the demands of management, the lawsuits from patients, and the expectations of society. He had telephoned the chairman of the board and resigned, saying that he intended to make Greece his home.

Joni had heard through the hospital's extensive rumor mill that Don was happy with his decision. He was practicing medicine in one of the smaller towns in the suburbs of Athens, where his handsome, rugged looks, red-brown complexion, auburn hair, and outgoing personality had won him considerable attention. The weather was terrific, and the people were friendly. On nights like this, Joni envied him his move to paradise, but, despite the sore feet and aching legs, she would not give up the excitement and feeling of fulfillment she got from the emergency room for anything. Not even the blue skies and red sunsets of Greece could entice her.

Although initially, she had missed him terribly, Joni had worked hard during his absence to put Don out of her mind. They had started to drift apart long before he left. Neither of them could really commit to the relationship with the hospital and its responsibilities between them. Each had blamed the other for the missed dinners when they both knew that they were equally at fault for allowing work to separate them. After he left, she had turned all of her attention to the hospital and pushed thoughts of love into the recesses of her heart. Joni hoped that she could remain detached when she saw him again and that she would not feel that old flutter in the pit of her stomach.

Joni had wanted to be a physician ever since she was a little girl. From the first time she sat in the operating theater's balcony and watched her father repair the clubbed foot of a boy not much older than herself, she had dreamed of being not only a physician but a surgeon. Joni had felt so proud of her father that she had missed much of the procedure as the tears blurred her vision. While doing her residency, she had discovered that the excitement of the emergency room was the place for her. She could have the best of both worlds as an emergency room surgeon. Now that she had both, Joni longed for sleep.

Most of the time, Joni was too busy to listen to the gossip that circulated freely throughout the hospital. She hoped the one about the emergency room chief of staff position was true, but she was not counting on it. She would believe that at thirty-five she would become the head of a major hospital staff when the chairman of the board offered the position to her. For now, she was too tired to think about anything other than surviving another incredibly hectic night.

As Joni listened for a few minutes to the steady stream of voices in the hall and the constant drone of the hospital's paging system, she slowly began to feel guilty that she had taken a moment's rest when the staff was running from one patient to the other. Struggling to her feet, Joni decided to rejoin the staff in its effort to patch up the usual flow of wounded, sick, and dying that filled the emergency room.

Opening the door, Joni stepped into the fray. Almost immediately, Randi thrust a chart into her capable hands. Smiling she said, "I had planned to come in there after you if you hadn't emerged in one more minute."

"You know me too well. I can never rest for long with all this activity going on around me. Let's see what treat you have for me now. Is this correct? Do you really mean that I'm to see a pregnant nine-year-old?" Joni asked as she started toward examining room five.

"Be careful. Her mother is in there with her. She swears that her daughter only has an eating disorder and has simply gained a lot of weight. She says that the child doesn't know anything about boys. Considering the child's age and the mother's nervousness, I'd tread lightly if I were you," Randi advised with a knowing shrug of her shoulders. She had been the head nurse of the emergency room for two years and had heard and seen everything imaginable.

"If this chart is correct, she knew one about eight-and-a-half months ago. Call social services and ask them to send someone down here. No matter how this happened, this is a case for them. I guess there are no OBs on duty tonight? Call obstetrics and have someone stop by," Joni instructed and entered the room.

Smiling tiredly, Joni greeted the mother and daughter saying, "Good evening, ladies. I'm Dr. Forest. I understand that Melissa is here because of some stomach discomfort. Would you like to describe your symptoms to me, Melissa?" Joni asked as she perched on a short stool at the side of the examining room table.

"My stomach has been hurting all day. I think the pizza my mommy gave me for lunch made me sick," Melissa replied almost sheepishly.

"I'm very careful about what I feed my child, doctor. I don't think it's food poisoning, at least not from anything I cooked. What she eats at school, I don't know. She has gained a considerable amount of weight this year. She must be eating all sorts of junk when she's with her friends. Her nanny says that she never gives her any sweets," the mother interjected. She smoothed the child's hair back from her forehead.

Nodding in the mother's direction, Joni turned her attention to Melissa and asked, "Do any of your friends have the same symptoms?"

"No, I'm the only one. The others are just fine," Melissa responded as she gritted her teeth against the onset of another cramp.

Looking at the wall clock and placing her hand gently on Melissa's hugely distended abdomen, Joni felt the muscles contract for a little more than a minute. "When was the last time you felt one of those cramps? Have they all felt the same?" Joni asked as she noted the contraction in the chart.

"Oh, I guess I've had about five or six of them while I've been waiting to see you. This one was a little worse than the others. Am I getting sicker? I need to go to the bathroom bad," Melissa said. Next to her original notation, Joni recorded that Melissa had experienced others with increasing duration but of the same interval since arriving at the hospital.

"No, Melissa, I think things are progressing as expected. Mrs. Custer, if you'll step out of the room for a minute, I'd like to examine your daughter and ask her a few questions," Joni suggested as she motioned toward the door and the waiting room beyond.

"I think I'll stay right here, if you don't mind, doctor. Melissa is a minor, you know. I have every right to know everything about my daughter's condition," the mother objected pressing herself more firmly into her chair.

"Very well, Mrs. Custer. Nurse, if you'd position Melissa's feet in the stirrups, I'd like to do a pelvic examination," Joni instructed.

"A pelvic examination! I should say you will do nothing of the kind. My daughter is only nine years old. I have brought her into this hospital for mild stomach discomfort, not for you to inflict the indignity of a pelvic exam on her," the mother protested as she rose to her full height as the avenging angel standing beside her wide-eyed daughter.

"Mrs. Custer," Joni began, speaking in a slow, steady tone, "I have every reason to believe that the stomach cramps from which Melissa is suffering are labor pains. If that is indeed the case, I need to determine how soon we might expect delivery."

"My daughter is not pregnant, I tell you. She has never known a boy. She's just a baby! Nine-year-old children do not have sexual relations," the mother screamed as she pushed Joni away from the table.

"Mrs. Custer, statistically, children do begin having sex at your daughter's age. They don't necessarily understand the consequences of their actions, but they do engage in the act. However, if you think this is not possible in Melissa's case, has she ever told you that a male member of the family sexually abused her in any way? Has she ever mentioned that a neighborhood boy forced her to have sex with him? I'm almost positive that Melissa is pregnant," Joni continued as she stood her ground.

"Never. We live in a wonderful neighborhood. None of the boys would ever do anything like that. As for family members, well, I'm insulted that you would even suggest such a thing. My husband has been the perfect father to Melissa. He has loved her as if she were his own daughter. Nothing that sordid could have happened in my house," Mrs. Custer again stated vehemently.

At that moment, Melissa's tearful face contorted with pain. "It's tearing me apart. Stop the pain. I can't stand it any longer. Make it go away!" she screamed as her horrified mother looked on.

Stepping toward the table, Joni gently but firmly moved

Mrs. Custer out of the way and positioned herself at the end. As Patty helped place Melissa's feet into the stirrups, Joni slipped on rubber gloves and prepared to probe the girl's pelvic area.

Adjusting the drape that covered Melissa's abdomen and thighs, Joni quickly sat back. Looking at Patty and then at Melissa she ordered, "Don't push, Melissa. The baby's head is trying to come out. I need to make a little snip to help you."

Mrs. Custer fell into the chair in a hysterical heap. "The baby's head! That can't be. Who did this to my daughter?"

Quickly, Joni and Patty prepped Melissa for the imminent delivery. As soon as Joni made the little incision, the baby's head popped through the widening hole. Rotating the shoulders slightly, Joni prepared to catch the infant. As it slipped into Joni's hands, the baby started crying and kicking its little limbs.

Placing the baby on Melissa's stomach, Joni clamped and cut the umbilical cord. Then she suctioned the last of the mucus from the mouth and nose. Handing the infant to Patty and noting the time of delivery, Joni waited for the contractions to expel the placenta. Massaging Melissa's belly with the heel of her hand, she helped the sobbing child deliver the pulsating afterbirth.

Turning to Mrs. Custer, Joni said, "I'll arrange for social services to speak with you. I have to report this as a rape. If you know who did it, you should share the information with the police when they arrive."

"Mommy, don't hate me. Please, mommy, don't be mad at me," Melissa cried weakly. She had not looked at the baby. Instead her eyes searched her mother's contorted face for signs of the love she so desperately needed.

When Mrs. Custer did not move, Joni took the child's trembling hand in hers and said, "Your mother doesn't hate you, Melissa. At the moment, she's suffering from shock. Who is the father of the baby, Melissa?"

The child only stared at Joni and cried harder. Joni pulled Melissa into her arms and rocked her until her sobs turned to an occasional sniffle. She did not want the traumatized child to think that anyone held her responsible for what had happened to her.

When Melissa's trembling subsided, Joni explained calmly, "Melissa, the man who did this to you has taken something very special from you. He might have said that he was giving you a special present or extra love, but what he did was very wrong. None of this is your fault. You're a child. He's the one who did wrong. Tell me the name of the man who made you pregnant."

"I can't. He'll get in trouble. He'll leave my mommy. He told me that if I told anyone what he did to me, he'd leave us. He said my mommy would hate me if he left," Melissa cried softly into Joni's chest.

"Your mommy won't hate you, Melissa. You're her little girl, and she loves you," Joni replied. Her throat constricted with the emotions she felt for the child's lost innocence.

"My mommy loves him. She's always cooking special food for him," Melissa muttered, becoming calmer as she slowly unburdened her young heart.

"Did your daddy do this to you, Melissa?" Joni asked as she gently stroked the child's long, red hair.

For a while the only sound in the examining room was the soft sobbing of Melissa's mother and the hiccuping of the infant. Then very quietly Melissa replied, "Yes. He came into my room when mommy was asleep. He would wake me up at night. He put his hand over my mouth to keep me from screaming. He did not want me to wake up my mommy. He said that he wanted to show me that he loved me."

Mrs. Custer, who had been listening from her seat beside the examining table, rose slowly. Taking her daughter into her arms, she muttered, "I guess I knew all along. I just didn't want to face it. I love my husband and couldn't bring myself to think that he would do something this horrible. Yes, Dr. Forest, call the police. We'll cooperate any way we can."

"I'll arrange for Melissa and the baby to spend some time in pediatrics," Joni nodded to Patty who immediately left the room to call the police.

"Is the baby all right?" Mrs. Custer asked.

"He's a little small, but he appears healthy."

"Thank you, doctor," Mrs. Custer said automatically as she focused all of her attention on her exhausted little girl.

Returning to the physicians' lounge as social services and the police followed Patty into the emergency room, Joni sank into a chair at the messy table in the center of the room. Partially eaten doughnuts, peanut shells, half-empty coffee cups, and candy and gum wrappers littered the table, making it almost impossible for her to find a place to work. Holding the patient chart on her lap, Joni quickly wrote notes of what she had witnessed. She wanted everything to be on record when she transferred the nine-year-old and her infant upstairs. Social services and the police would need all the details, and Joni needed to vent the anger she felt toward the mother who would not see the pain and suffering of her abused child until it was almost too late.

Unable to stand the mess on the table, which reminded her of the family she had just witnessed, Joni found an overflowing trash can and slowly slid the debris of a long day into it. Then, taking a napkin from the doughnut box, she wrote in marker, PLEASE CLEAN UP AFTER YOURSELVES. I AM NOT YOUR MOMMY! After signing it, she taped it to the table and left the room to turn in her chart.

Joni was numb from fatigue and life. Her shift had finally ended, and it was time to go home. At least in the privacy of her condo, she could put her feet up without being disturbed, spread out her things without first having to clean up after others, and escape the sight of life's crueler side. However, when she was away, Joni's thoughts were with City

General. She worried about the patients and physicians who ministered to them. She thrived on the chaos and the energy of the ER and could hardly wait to return.

Two

Walking into the emergency room the next morning, Joni encountered the usual rush of humanity as the physicians and nurses worked to ease the pain of their patients. Families sat uneasily in the worn waiting room chairs as their loved ones waited in the examining rooms for someone to stop the bleeding, stitch the cut, or quiet the nagging cough. The familiar clamor made her feel needed and comfortable.

"Hi, you're just in time. I've got a good one for you in room three. You'll really like her. She's been calling for a surgeon ever since she walked in here," Randi said as she handed Joni the patient's file.

"Good morning to you, too. I hate it when you have that sarcastic tone in your voice and that wicked twinkle in your eye. That's when I know that I'm in for a particularly disagreeable task," Joni replied as she handed her friend the magazine she had purchased for her on the way to work. On the cover was a picture of the cast of *Cats* in full makeup.

Waving her on, Randi shouted, "Thanks. You see, we're always thinking of each other."

Pushing open the door, Joni found an elderly woman sitting stark naked on the examining room table with her gown in strips around her. She watched as the woman carefully picked up each strip of cloth and braided it into the long rope that dangled off the edge of the table beside her feet. The woman sang an indistinguishable song to herself as she worked.

"Mrs. Gardner, I'm Dr. Forest. I understand you've been asking for a surgeon," Joni introduced herself as she watched the age-spotted hands meticulously connect the strips and braid the flat rope.

"Yes, doctor, but call me Gwen . . . all of my friends do. I'd like for you to help me with this, dear. Would you hand me the little pieces of fabric? I won't have to stop my work if you do," Gwen said with a sweet smile.

"Certainly, Gwen, I'd be happy to help you, but the nurse told me that you needed a surgeon. What seems to be the problem?" Joni asked.

"Nothing. I feel just fine. I live alone and needed to hear a friendly voice. I can't go to the hospital in my neighborhood because someone would recognize me. They'd call my son to come to take me home. He'd like nothing better than to put me in a nursing home or to institutionalize me again. I just wanted some company. Last time I was here, I chatted with an internist. The time before that, I met a lovely pediatrician. I thought I'd like to meet a surgeon this time. How wonderful that a woman is making her mark in that field," Gwen replied with a proud smile.

"I'm also the acting chief of this emergency room. You got two-for-one this time," Joni added with a grin.

Handing Gwen another strip, Joni carefully studied the patient. Little brown spots colored her no-longer-ivory skin with freckles. Age and arthritis had gnarled her long, thin fingers. Gray had completely replaced the gold of her closely coiffed hair. Yet, despite the ravages of time, her crystal blue eyes sparkled with delight. The shadow of the youthful beauty lingered on her face.

Feeling Joni's eyes on her face, Gwen added, "You probably think I'm crazy, don't you, dear? Well, I guess I must be a little unbalanced to sit here making this rope of fabric from my hospital gown. I don't think I'm in such awful shape for an eighty-seven-year-old. I mostly take care of myself. I fix my own meals and never forget to turn off the stove. I gave up driving years ago because I just couldn't see as well as I used to. Now, I take cabs or walk everywhere and never get lost or forget where I live. I'm perfectly healthy. I simply felt lonely today."

Finding herself mesmerized by the fingers that should have been too stiff to braid the cloth, Joni sat quietly watching Gwen create the rope. "What will you do with your rope now that you've finished making it, Gwen?" Joni asked as she watched the last of the cloth strips vanish and join the others.

"I'll show you in just a minute, dear. I'll take a little of your thread and one of your needles, if you don't mind. I'll finish this project in no time at all," Gwen looked into Joni's eyes and smiled angelically.

Handing her the requested items, Joni watched as Gwen slowly and carefully wound the strips into a small circle. She stitched the rope together as she turned it in her skillful hands. When she had finished, she looked up and handed the gift to Joni saying, "There, dear, I've made you a little rug. It's only for decoration really. It's not large enough for any practical use, but it would look just lovely under a flowerpot or a vase of flowers. You could always use it in your dining room as a trivet to protect the table's surface from hot plates."

Turning the circle over in her hands, Joni marveled at the speed with which Mrs. Gardner had crafted her gift. "Thank you, Gwen, it's lovely. Now, what can I do for you?" Joni asked, skeptical about allowing the woman to leave the hospital without first visiting with psych services.

"Well, because I know you have to do something, dear, you can give me another gown. I've become quite chilly. And you can call your psychiatric department. That's what they always do at the other hospitals. I don't mind spending a few minutes more in conversation with strangers. I always feel as if I've made new friends by the time I leave the hospital."

"All right, Gwen, I'll do just that. Someone from psych services will be here very shortly. In the meantime, here's the gown you requested. Thank you again for making this lovely little rug for me," Joni replied as she helped Gwen slip into the new garment.

"Think nothing of it, my dear. Thank you for sitting with me," Gwen said as she fingered the fabric of the gown. It was covered in little flowers unlike the plain pink one from which she had made Joni's rug. As Joni walked from the room with the little rug under her arm, she looked back to see Gwen Gardner already ripping the hem of her gown into little strips of fabric.

"Oh, so she made you a rug, too. She was in here two weeks ago and made one for John. So far she has used up three gowns. I wonder who she'll ask for the next time she comes in. The people at Mercy said that almost all the doctors on the day shift got one from her. She works her way through the doctors on duty. I guess she'll start making them for the nurses soon," Randi explained with a laugh as she reminded Joni of her ten-thirty staff meeting with the hospital's chief of staff.

"Why didn't you tell me about her before I went in? You know that I have tons of work to do. But no, you let me sit there listening to her soothing voice. I could have sent for psych services sooner if I hadn't become mesmerized by the sight of her hands," Joni complained halfheartedly. She really could not summon the negative vibes it took to feel angry. She was very mellow from her time with Gwen.

"I thought a few minutes of relaxation would do you good. John felt so much better after spending his half hour with her that I decided that after last night you needed the same therapy. It worked, too, didn't it? Now, don't forget your meeting," Randi commented as she pushed Joni toward the elevator.

"It certainly was therapeutic. I could have used it last night, that's for sure," Joni agreed as she disappeared through the elevator door for the ride to the fourth-floor offices.

The tone of the meeting felt like the quiet before a big thunderstorm as Joni and the other doctors discussed the routine of running a big hospital with the chief of staff. After hearing the weekly reports from everyone, Bob Turner casually turned to the staff and said, "Let me remind you that I expect your budgets on my desk promptly at eight o'clock on Monday morning. You've spent a month on them, so this isn't an unexpected request. As you put on the finishing touches, don't forget that I've been directed by the chairman of the board to reduce spending. Yes, I know that we hear the same message every year, and each time we tighten our belts just a bit more. However, this time the directive carries more immediacy. I must ask each of you to do more than tighten your belts. This year, you must cut to the bare bone.

"I'm charging you with the responsibility of turning your departments into profit centers. You will need to minimize costly tests and procedures. No longer do we have the luxury of simply seeing ourselves as service providers to the sick. We must run City General as a business. Unfortunately, this will mean layoffs as well as reductions in services."

"Bob, in the ER we're already understaffed. If we cut back any further in either personnel or tests, I don't know if we'll be able to provide quality care," Joni argued as disbelief took hold of her. The task he had set before them was almost insurmountable. She could not possibly comply with his demands. Suddenly the little rug was not having its calming effect.

"Yes, I know, but there's always a little fat in even the leanest budget. You might think about hiring temps, combining positions, and looking for additional sources of income. I'm aware that this will not be an easy task. All of you have submitted preliminary budgets that show little excess. By Monday, I'm asking that you remove anything that is not absolutely necessary. The alternative, ladies and gentlemen, is for the board to sell City General to one of those large medical-care conglomerates. Our investors want the most bang for their bucks. The only way to give them what they demand is by reducing costs. They demand an increase in profits."

"Sell City General?" Eleanor Richardson from geriatrics

exclaimed. "That would be a dreadful mistake and a disservice to the people who count on us. We all have heard the horror stories about hospitals that have been bought by these conglomerates. The employees complain that the atmosphere changes radically under the new management. They feel as if they work on a production line rather than in health care. My friend told me that in a matter of weeks morale sank to an all-time low in her hospital. The board can't sell City General."

Bob replied, "The board will have no choice but to take drastic action if you don't come up with cost-containment measures for your departments. That's why it's incumbent on you division heads to reduce your budgets. The times have changed, and City General must adapt to them. We no longer have the option of ignoring the bottom line while providing care. We have to meld the two concerns if City General is to remain viable."

Smelling the stench of worry, Joni joined the others for the long walk to the elevators. Although no one spoke, she knew that they were thinking the same thing. The holiday season was only a few weeks away. She would have to fire a few of her staff right before Christmas if she could not think of another way to make the emergency room profitable. She dreaded the thought. Deciding to take the stairs, Joni eased into the flow of traffic in the hall. None of the other department chiefs seemed to see her leave. They were all preoccupied with figures and the dreadful reality that faced them.

Greeted with the bustle of the emergency room, Joni was impressed by its efficiency as soon as she walked into its crowded lobby. The two triage nurses quickly examined the incoming patients, assessed the seriousness of their illness or injury, and assigned patients to a nurse, physician's assistant, or doctor depending on the severity of their problem. While the patients waited, accounting clerks opened billing and insurance files on each new patient and checked for past medical treatment at City General. The physicians and assistants moved from one patient to the next with a minimum of confusion. The emergency room ran perfectly most of the time. Joni hated the idea of making a change in its operation.

As if sensing the change in her mood, Randi asked, "What's on your mind? What happened at the meeting?"

"Bob Turner gave the department heads an ultimatum. He said that we would either cut our budgets to the bone or the board would sell City General. If I can't find some way to reduce our expenditures on supplies and tests, I'll have to reduce personnel overhead and that means firing someone. This is definitely the part of management that I hate. I'm going to my office. Unless you find yourself critically shorthanded, schedule me out of the day's cases. I have to revise the budget figures by Monday," Joni said.

"I didn't know that there was anything left to cut," Randi interjected. "My nursing budget is to the bone now. I thought the emergency room budget was too."

"That's what I thought, but obviously Bob doesn't think so," Joni replied. "I know what he's trying to make us do, but that's the last thing I want to think about. I can't bring myself to cut staff positions. We're already overworked and understaffed. I don't think he understands the way we live. The emergency room makes a profound impact on the lives of everyone who works here. The board should spend some time with us rather than meeting on the fourth floor."

Randi chuckled dryly, "That would certainly be an eye-opener, wouldn't it?"

Shaking her head, Joni continued, "They don't understand that this is more than a job; it's a twenty-four-hour commitment. Even when we're not here, we're thinking about this place. I've seen marriages disintegrate because of the demands the ER places on the time of the medical staffs. Relationships sour due to neglect. Parents miss their children's ball games and plays because they can't get away on time."

"I guess that's why we all bond," Randi commented. "We learn that no one else would understand the way we live. We become one another's best friends in order to have someone who would understand the way we live."

"Well, I'll be in my office if you need me. I have to think of some way around what I see as the inevitable," Joni said.

"Okay, I'll see to it that no one bothers you. I'm sure you'll think of something," Randi replied.

"So much for the calming effects of this rug," Joni added as she slipped away to the silence of the office she inherited when Don Rivers had not returned from his vacation.

"Excuse me, Joni, but did I hear you mention personnel reductions?" Jim Toner, one of the ER's physician's assistants, asked as he stepped between her and the exit.

"Yes, but I don't think you have any need to worry, Jim," Joni replied with a smile as she tried to walk past him.

"Maybe I do and maybe I don't. I haven't been here as long as some of the staff and I'm a white male. I don't have laws to protect me the way some of the others have. I have to worry about cutbacks. I have a wife and kids who'll expect to have Christmas as usual this year. If you cut the budget and I get the ax, we'll have a very bleak holiday. It's not easy finding jobs in this town with all the hospitals suffering from the same or worse budget problems and cost overruns," Jim replied candidly.

Standing firm, Joni stated with authority in her voice, "First, let me assure you, Jim, that any reduction in force will be the last measure that I'll consider. I don't want anyone to be out of a job during the holidays or any other time. Second, I don't operate on quotas and resent the implication that I would protect women and blacks while throwing a white man to the wolves. If I had to eliminate people, I'd use not only seniority but performance as my guides. Race and gender would not come into the picture. Now, if you don't mind, I'll get to work on those figures."

"Joni, I didn't mean to hurt your feelings, but you needed to hear my reality. You're young and new in this job. This is the first time you've had to deal with quotas and head counts.

I saw what happened to surplus people at my other hospital, and I just had to have my say. It just looks to me as if the white male is becoming an endangered species," Jim replied without softening his approach.

"But you forget, Jim, that I've also encountered unfair treatment because of my gender, race, and age. I've felt the sting of prejudice, and I wouldn't do the same thing to someone else. You'll just have to trust me. If staff reductions become the only way to accomplish the mandated budget cuts, I'll fairly administer personnel rules without favoritism entering the picture. Thanks for bringing your position to my attention," Joni replied.

"Thanks, that's all I ask . . . fair treatment."

"That's what all of us should expect," Joni responded and walked down the hall. She did not blame Jim for being worried or for confronting her. She would have done the same thing if she felt her job was on the line.

Joni no longer saw the name DON RIVERS, MD, CHIEF OF EMERGENCY MEDICAL SERVICES as she entered the office. When she became the acting chief, she had dreamed of one day reading her name on the glass. Now, she was too busy to read the inscription.

The room had dull, industrial green walls, a scratched oak desk, a swivel chair that listed to the right, and three tall, locking file cabinets. A black leather sofa stood against the long wall. It had seen so much action that the seats and armrests had faded. The carpet had more coffee stains than pile.

One scrawny piece of ivy struggled valiantly to take root in an old pickle jar on the window ledge. Joni had hoped that its presence would brighten the room. Unfortunately, the sprig seemed to have succumbed to the soberness and had lost all but two leaves. Carefully, she lifted the jar and placed the rug under it. Today, thc atmosphere of the room seemed appropriate for the task she had to face.

Opening the blinds to let in the thin rays of December sunshine, Joni sat in her chair and stared blankly at the folders stacked on her desk. She hardly knew where to begin. The edict was daunting, and the thought of having to fire a friend was horrifying. However, the board's ultimatum of selling the hospital would be devastating to all of them. Slowly, she opened the top folder and pulled out the papers, which contained the carefully documented expenses involved in running the emergency room.

Scanning the long columns, Joni saw where she could cut a little more out of the supply budget and still have enough to provide care. She decided that there were some tests that the staff could order as backups rather than as the first line of defense. However, even whittling these two expenditures to the bare bone, she could not save enough money to make the emergency room do more than break even.

The figures did not lie. Salaries and benefits were the most costly items on the list. The only way to gain the desired bottom-line result was by firing employees. Since the nurses belonged to a union and were protected by a contract that did not expire until late the next year, Joni had no choice but to study the physician staff as the possible source of reduction.

The unpleasant taste of bile rose in her throat as Joni labored over the figures. Her stomach contracted with each adjustment to the bottom line. Her sharp pencil cut away at head count until no one remained who was not essential to the operation of the unit. Joni treated physicians, physician's assistants, orderlies, and specialists equally in her search for the extra dollars she needed. The effort made her head and fingers ache.

Hearing the wail of a siren stop a block away, Joni put down her pencil and walked to the window. She watched as an ambulance pulled into the driveway. Immediately, two orderlies ran out to help the paramedics. If she implemented the new budget, one of them would not work at City General when the new year began.

Pushing the papers into the folders and switching off the light, Joni rushed to the ER. She could do nothing more with the figures that day and might as well make herself useful. "I'll take a chart, if you need me," Joni offered as she surveyed the room. "By the way, are we still on for a movie tonight?"

"Glad to see you. Here's your chart. The ambulance just pulled in. I thought you were working on the budget," Randi replied.

"I was but I'm stuck. I'll work on it later. I need some time to think. How about having pizza for dinner tonight? I'll treat. I don't especially want to eat alone."

"Sounds good to me. After the day we're having, we could use a chance to unwind," Randi agreed.

"Great," Joni said as she quickly scanned the sheet. Her first patient of the afternoon was a middle-aged homeless man.

"We had to bring him here, doc. The cops found him sleeping on a park bench. They thought he was drunk and tried to make him go to a shelter. When he didn't move, they called us," the paramedic apologized as he stuffed a peppermint into his mouth.

"No problem, Pete." Joni replied with a quick wave. City General was located in the oldest and seediest part of town. Although a private hospital, everyone who came through the door was treated.

The strong urge to vomit struck Joni as she entered examining room one. Sally, one of the nurses in attendance, quickly handed her a mask to help filter some of the stench as they cut away the homeless man's filthy clothing. Lice crawled over the man's puss-caked body. Gratefully slipping the mask into place over her nose and mouth and quickly pulling on gloves, Joni took her place at the head of the table.

Sylvia, Pete's partner, added, "The police suspected hypothermia caused by sleeping off a few in last night's cold weather. That's why they wanted us to bring him in and get him checked out."

"Any idea of his name?" Joni asked as she listened to the

man's shallow breathing and checked his pupils. The stench of rotting teeth, stale liquor, and vomit assaulted her.

"No, sorry, we don't know anything about him. He's not one of our usual customers," Pete replied as he rolled the stretcher toward the door. "Come on, Sylvia, let's scrub out that wagon. He's all yours now, doc."

"Thanks!"

Returning her attention to the unconscious man, Joni ordered the usual blood gases and X rays. Palpating the man's abdomen, she discovered that it was rigid. Listening, she did not hear the usual bowel sounds. As she pressed a little more firmly, the man groaned. Immediately an eruption of black, fishy smelling blood spewed from his mouth.

Reacting instinctively, Sally reached for the kidney-shaped basin and turned the man's head to the side. As the vile smelling liquid flowed, Joni ordered, "Let's get an X ray. This looks like a bleeding ulcer. First, let's clean him up a bit. Suction. His respiration is holding steady and so is his heart rate. Okay, get that film."

"I bet he's been bleeding for some time. He probably stayed so drunk that he didn't feel the pain in his stomach," Sally commented as the orderlies adjusted the straps and rolled the man down the hall.

"I think you're right. Sally, let's get housekeeping in here to clean up this mess. I'll have Randi take this room off the schedule until someone can scrub and sanitize it. It's amazing what people will do to themselves," Joni said as she threw her heavily soiled scrub onto the pile of dirty linen in the corner of the room. She made a mental note to ask Randi to track down the missing hamper.

As Joni approached the nurses' station, she found Randi busily spraying disinfectant around the desk. Casting a quick glimpse at the patients in the waiting room, Joni saw that most of them had covered their noses in an attempt to eliminate the smell.

Coughing from the air freshener, Randi said with a wicked

grin, "I have another patient for you, if you're up to it. After that one, this will be a breath of fresh air. Excuse the pun."

"I'm up for anything after that. Call housekeeping please and arrange for them to clean examining room one. It's off limits until they work their magic. Let me know when the man returns from X ray. By the way, what happened to the laundry hamper from that room? Did housekeeping misplace it?" Joni asked with a chuckle at Randi's weak attempt at humor. The air freshener had already helped a bit.

"I think I know where it is. I saw an extra one in room four. I guess it wasn't extra after all. I'll have housekeeping take care of it," Randi assured Joni as she scribbled instructions on the ledger.

Taking the new chart, Joni headed for the open examining room in which a little girl and her grandmother sat. Introducing herself, Joni commented, "The chart says that Marie fell down the steps and hurt her arm. I'm Dr. Forest. I'd like to take a look. Okay, Marie?"

"Okay, but you have to take care of Tabby, too," the perky little five-year-old with twinkling gray eyes responded.

"Who's Tabby?" Joni asked patiently.

"He's my kitten. I was holding him when I fell down the steps. I think he broke something, too," Marie replied, unwrapping the bundle she held in her lap.

A small gray kitten lay inside an old-fashioned rabbit-fur muff. It peeked its head out and meowed softly. Joni touched its little nose lightly and turned to the grandmother and asked, "What seems to be the problem with the kitten? I'm a surgeon not a veterinarian. I'm not trained to work on animals."

Without hesitation the grandmother smiled weakly and replied, "When Marie fell, she must have landed on the kitten's right front leg because Tabby started crying something awful. I was beside myself with worry about Marie and, quite honestly, I didn't give the animal much thought. Marie's mom is out of town on business. Her dad is in the Navy and on a submarine somewhere in the Mediterranean. I was baby-sitting at their house. When she fell, I didn't know what to do except bring both of them here. She wouldn't let me take the kitten away from her. I know this isn't the place for it, but I couldn't help it."

"You did the right thing. I'll do what I can, but you might have to make another stop at the vet's," Joni advised as she turned her attention to the little girl. Marie sat bravely with one arm cradling the muff and the other hanging limply at her side.

At that moment, Trina, the physician's assistant who had performed the preliminary evaluation of Marie's condition, returned to the examining room with the X ray results. She had not noted the presence of the kitten on the chart. "Dr. Forest," Trina said, "the X ray shows that Marie has a green stick fracture of the radius."

"Thanks, Trina. By the way, what did the film show about the kitten's leg?" Joni asked playfully.

"What kitten?" Trina asked with a concerned frown on her face.

"The one hiding inside the muff. Marie fell while carrying it downstairs and may have broken its leg in the process. Do you know anyone who has ever applied a splint to a cat?" Joni queried seriously as she swallowed the desire to chuckle.

"No, but I'll see if I can scrounge up a book that might help you," Trina offered as she rushed away before she could laugh out loud at Joni's predicament.

"All right, Marie, I'll need to put your arm in a cast to keep it still for a few weeks. After a while, it will itch a bit, but you're not to push anything inside the cast to scratch it. Let me take a look at your arm now," Joni said in a calm voice.

As soon as she touched Marie's arm, the little girl began to cry. "My arm hurts. Don't move it," she sobbed.

"I'll work very quickly, and I'll explain everything I'm doing. First, I'll put your arm in this splint. Now, I'll use this gauze to hold the splint in place while I apply the soft cast.

It will make your arm a little heavier, but it's not too bad. You'll get used to it in no time at all. Finally, I'll tie this sling around your neck. Your arm will rest in here so that it doesn't dangle and put too much stress on the fracture. See, I've finished. That didn't take long at all. You were a prefect patient," Joni exclaimed as she adjusted the knot under Marie's soft brown curls.

"What about my kitty?" Marie demanded, pointing to the little ball of fluff resting inside the muff.

"Yes, well, let me take a look," Joni replied as she gingerly examined the swollen little limb.

The kitten meowed loudly as Joni touched it. "You're hurting my kitty!" Marie cried, protectively placing her good hand between Joni and Tabby.

As Joni began to explain to the little girl and her grandmother that she could not do anything for the cat, Trina returned carrying a volume on veterinary medicine. Placing it opened on the table, she said, "It looks as if you can splint it the same way you'd do for a person. I brought these little craft sticks in case you wanted to give it a try."

"Great," Joni replied with a tinge of sarcasm. Working quickly and carefully, she applied the splint and gauze to the animal's right front leg.

"Oh, Tabby, you look just like me!" Marie cooed as she cuddled the kitten.

"I think you should take the kitten to the vet's office as soon as possible for a checkup," Joni offered as she looked from the child to the relieved grandmother.

"As soon as my daughter comes home later tonight, I'll tell her, but I'm sure you did a fine job, doctor," the grandmother said with relief in her voice.

"Tell Marie's mother that she must keep the cast dry and visit an orthopedic surgeon in two weeks. She can bring Marie back here, if she'd rather, but I think she should find someone in private practice to handle the follow-up. I'm sure her pediatrician can suggest someone," Joni instructed as she wrote out the information for the frazzled grandmother, who gratefully accepted the paper.

"Thank you, doctor. You made a very traumatic experience bearable," Marie's grandmother replied. She gratefully stuffed the note into her handbag.

"It was my pleasure," Joni responded as she left the grandmother and Marie trying to coax the kitten back inside the muff.

"Wasn't that little girl adorable?" Randi commented as Joni handed her the completed chart.

"So was the kitten. You didn't tell me about the animal," Joni replied as she chuckled at having set a cat's leg.

"Some things you're better off discovering for yourself," Randi said, laughing. "By the way, you had a phone call. He wouldn't leave his name, only his number. It looks like one of those international numbers."

"Thanks," Joni muttered as she placed the note on top of the stack of charts she needed to review. From the corner of her eye, Joni caught Randi studying her as she read the number. Turning, she smiled at her friend and nodded before heading down the hall. They both knew who had called.

In the quiet of her office, Joni dialed the number and reversed the charges as the caller had instructed. She waited patiently until the voice on the other end answered. "Hello, Joni. Glad you could get back to me so quickly. I understood you were working on a patient when I called. How's everything in the ER?"

"Don, it's good to hear from you again. How's everything in sunny Greece? It's cold and dreary here," Joni replied in a louder voice than usual. The connection was a bit scratchy. Her heart pounded at the sound of his voice. The last time Joni had spoken with Don privately, she had told him that their relationship was finished. He had refused to believe her even when she would not return any of his calls.

"It's beautiful here, Joni. The sea's a shade of blue that words can't describe. The sunsets turn more variations of red and orange than I've ever seen. The people are so incredibly warm and friendly," Don answered.

"Then why the call? You're in paradise. You shouldn't be thinking about us slaving away here in the gloom of Baltimore. Did you call to rub it in?" Joni shouted.

"I've been thinking about coming back home. Don't get me wrong, Greece is heavenly and a wonderful place to live, but I miss the excitement of the hospital. I'm a little too young to be retired," Don replied in a voice that did nothing to mask his loneliness.

"Really? Have you contacted the board or Bob Turner? I suppose that's where you should start. He could probably find you a position on staff," Joni suggested over the buzzing in her ears. The transmission had gone from scratchy to almost inaudible.

"Yeah, I've spoken with Bob, and he's arranged everything. I'll be back in Baltimore in about two weeks," Don answered slowly.

"Don, the transmission is really terrible. Did I hear you say that you'll be home in about two weeks? That's great. You'll be here just in time for the holidays," Joni responded as she shouted into the telephone.

"That's what I said, Joni. I can hardly wait to see everyone . . . especially you," Don said. "I'm resuming my position as ER chief," Don replied. When she did not respond, Don asked, "Joni, are you there? Did you hear me?"

"I heard you just fine, Don. I just don't know what to say. You've been away for six months. A lot has changed here. I've been running the ER my way and very smoothly, I might add. I'm surprised to hear that you plan to return." Joni spoke in a calm voice that belied her anger at his feeling of entitlement.

"I understand that you've done a great job in my absence. That's why I wanted you to hear this from me. We always worked so well together. I didn't want any hard feelings to develop over my return," Don explained.

"Don, I appreciate that you wanted to share the news with me yourself. However, it's only fair to warn you that I'll do everything I possibly can to retain the position of ER chief. I've instituted several programs that I intend to see through to their conclusion. I've developed a good rapport with the staff and a sound reputation in the community. I'm not going to step down from this job without a fight, Don. I've made this emergency room my home. You can't simply waltz back in and take it away from me. It's not done like that. And as for anything else, I told you before you left that our relationship was over. I don't have any plans to resurrect the dead. It just wasn't working. We were both too busy here to make it work," Joni said, knowing that she had drawn the battle lines with her determination to keep what she felt was rightfully hers.

"I know your performance on the job has been stellar. I knew you could do it. However, none of that will keep me from coming home and resuming my former position. Bob is in favor of it and so is the board. They will thank you as is appropriate for someone who has been filling a job on a temporary basis. After that, you will hand the keys over to me. As soon as I tidy up a few things here, I'll be back. I want everything as it was—everything. Whatever was wrong, we can fix," Don insisted. His tone, even over the crackling phone line, was arrogant and self-assured.

"I'm glad you're so confident about the way this scenario will play out, but I'm not. I'm here, and this is where I'm going to stay. Don't expect us to patch things up. Our relationship wasn't on solid ground long before you left. I don't have the time to work on a nonissue. We're history. I admired your professionalism as an administrator and as a boss. No one could get money from the board the way you could. Once, I loved you, but that's over. I'll see you in two weeks. Goodbye, Don," Joni said as she hung up, her hands trembling from the strain of retaining her composure.

Joni sat staring out the window. When Don first left for

Greece, every day she had expected him to call and say that he had changed his mind. After the first two months passed and he officially resigned, she made several tentative changes in emergency room procedures after being appointed to the position. She began to relax and to think of herself as the chief, although she knew that her title was tenuous at best. When she received accolades from Bob Turner and the board and heard that her name had been placed on the short list for consideration for the permanent position, Joni had breathed a sigh of relief knowing that Don was safely out of her way.

Instead of Don's call being a pleasant holiday greeting from an old friend and colleague, it served as a reminder that Joni was not securely in the position that she held so dear. She could lose it to him or anyone else the board decided to promote over her. She was, after all, a young black woman. There were not many of those in the demanding position of emergency room chief.

Pacing the small office with its faded paint, overused furniture, and pathetic little plant, Joni fumed, "The nerve of that man. What makes him think he can simply waltz back into this job and my life? Being a man, that's what. Well, I'll just have to prove to him that he can't."

"Talking to yourself?" Randi asked as she stuck her head into the office to check on her friend.

Stopping in her tracks, Joni replied, "As you guessed, that call was from Don. He's coming home from Greece, and he wants his old job back. He says that Bob has already assured him that it's his for the asking. Furthermore, Don thinks there's a chance for us. The man must be suffering from sunstroke."

"Really? It certainly would have been nice for Bob to tell you, especially considering all the budget hoopla you've had to endure," Randi commented loyally. "Are you okay? Don has a lot of nerve on both counts."

Randi was the only one in the hospital who knew about the relationship between Joni and Don. Not wanting to start people talking about their personal relationship on the job, Joni and Don had done everything they could to be discreet. They met at little cafés far from Baltimore's bustling downtown. They spent their evenings in one of their condos or on little trips to places as far north as Gettysburg and Hershey, Pennsylvania, and as far south as Fredericksburg, Virginia. Don had never escorted her to a play in town for fear that someone would recognize them and report their relationship to the hospital's board of directors. They always drove separate cars to prevent anyone from thinking they were involved. Exposure would not have been good for either of them. It was only a matter of time before a relationship that never should have started ended.

They had parted in silence, too. They had decided over breakfast one morning at a quaint little inn near the Amish country of Pennsylvania that the relationship had to end if Joni would not agree to marry him. She refused. He was as dedicated to the job as she was. She did not want to follow in the footsteps of many of her girlfriends who had thought that their love could change either their man's devotion to the job or theirs.

With great sadness, Don announced that he would take a much-needed vacation and return when he felt rested. Joni had felt conflicting emotions after he left. She wanted to miss him, but she found that she could not. Her days were so busy in the ER that she barely had time to think about Don. She pinned the postcard from him onto the bulletin board beside the others sent by vacationing staff members and went about her responsibilities without further thought of him.

The evenings, however, were difficult. Joni slept little and ate less. Then, finally, one day, Joni decided that she had to get herself together. The relationship was over, Don was out of her life, and she had to go on. From that moment, she was a new woman. She was not even moved when Don decided not to return.

"Yeah, I'm fine, just angry at the nerve of the man. Don

said that for old time's sake, Bob let him be the one to tell me. You know, Randi, that really takes arrogance. First, he goes on vacation and decides while he's away that he doesn't want to return. And now, he says he wants his old job back. Well, he can't have it. It's mine now, and I intend to keep it. Don doesn't know it, but he has just given me two weeks to prove that I can turn this ER into a profit center. It won't be easy, but I'll do it. The timing couldn't be better," Joni replied with a stern set to her jaw that Randi had not seen her friend display in all the years of their friendship.

"What do you plan to do?" Randi asked. "You know that you can count on me to help in any way I can."

"Thanks, Randi. I'll need it. There has to be some way that I can reduce the budget, save jobs, and turn a profit at the same time. I'll think about it this weekend. I have a glimmer of an idea, but I want to nurse it along and make some phone calls first. I might be able to build on some of the things I've already started. The first thing I plan to do is have a little talk with Bob Turner and the board. I'm going to make sure they understand that I will not simply roll over and play dead where Don Rivers is concerned. I won't give up the ER without a fight, and they might as well hear it from me," Joni said as she unlocked the file cabinet and withdrew her purse.

"The board owes you the same consideration it's giving Don. After all, you've done a great job as the acting chief. By the way, aren't they obligated either to make your appointment permanent at the end of six months or rotate you out of the job?" Randi asked as she watched Joni rummage through her purse.

"The agreement we had stated that the board would search for Don's replacement during the time that I served as acting chief. I would, naturally, be among the candidates. At the end of the six months, they would either make the announcement or gain my agreement to an extension of our temporary contract. Don's return adds a different slant, but as far as I'm concerned, it doesn't change anything.

"As I understand the law, any person performing a temporary assignment of higher rank for more than six months can expect either to be promoted to that position or relieved of it. The only other choice is for us to come to a mutually agreeable working arrangement, which I'd be willing to do if the treatment was equitable. Whatever special consideration Don receives, the board should also show me. At any rate, that's what I intend to tell Bob," Joni said as she stuffed money into her pocket and returned her purse to the file cabinet.

"Are you going somewhere?" Randi queried as Joni stepped past her and into the hall.

"Yeah, it's lunchtime and I'm hungry. Let's go," Joni commanded. "I have a lot of work to do this afternoon."

"I'm right behind you," Randi replied as she turned out the light. Looking over her shoulder, she spotted the little vine sitting sadly in the pale sunlight. Something about it reminded her of her friend who stood alone and determined to survivc despite the odds against her.

Joni only picked at her salad. "How many people have left City General since we've worked here?" Joni asked as she pushed a slice of radish through a puddle of dressing. Her mind was busy planning her strategy against the takeover of the ER.

"Not many. Rita in accounting left when her husband's job transferred him. Mike Cummings took a position at North Shore. I can't think of anyone else. Why?" Randi replied as she studied Joni's face.

"I couldn't think of too many either," Joni mused. "Don was definitely an exception. He probably didn't think twice about leaving because he felt confident in his ability to make it away from here thanks to his family's money. You know, he's the only son of a wealthy publisher. His dad is one of the few blacks in the business. He was disappointed when Don decided to pursue medicine rather than take a job in publishing. I guess Don always counted on being able to return without question just as he always tried to be in control of everything else."

Catching her friend's somber mood, Randi replied, "Well, Don was certainly successful at everything he tried. I heard that he took top honors in school and excelled in his internship and residency. Everything just fell into his lap. I heard that City General went looking for him because of his connections."

"Yeah, and after he got here, he really wowed top management. He definitely had the board behind him. But I have to give him credit, he really loved his work and gave it his all. He was a good boss. I enjoyed working for him," Joni stated as she made a hill of the lettuce.

"Everyone did because he didn't demand anything of them. Just think about it. What did he ever do to make the ER function more smoothly? You made all the changes," Randi offered loyally.

"The ER was a good operation under Don. I just needed to tweak it a little," Joni responded with a smile.

"Okay, but not because of him. You did all the administrative stuff for him. Don stood around with a cup of coffee in his hand all day. Why did he leave anyway? He certainly wasn't overworked," Randi retorted.

"Don't be so hard on the man just because you don't like him. Everything wasn't easy for him. He had the usual trash to deal with and prejudices to overcome. Just because his roommate in college was a rich guy from New York with connections, doesn't mean that Don didn't have to work. The relationships he developed in college and medical school helped, but he still had to prove himself. He worked really hard. When he got to Greece, he decided that it looked like a good place for a new beginning. The climate was perfect, and the people were friendly. He opened a practice in Greece and immediately began to gather a large clientele from among the city's social elite."

"You're taking the news of his return more calmly than I thought you would," Randi commented as she studied Joni's face for any sign of regret, anger, or pain.

With a shrug, Joni replied, "What else can I do? Don has made his intentions clear, and there's no way I can stop him."

"Why do you suppose he decided to come back to the States?"

"He could have lived a leisurely life in Europe, but he really enjoys practicing medicine in a hospital setting. I guess that the jet-set life he fell into in Greece didn't agree with him. At least at home, he could be among people who truly share similar interests and are concerned with something other than the color of their tans," Joni replied with a chuckle.

"Well, it looks as if he discovered that the grass isn't greener in Greece either," Randi commented scornfully. "He should have found that out before he left. I guess he'll try to win you back, too."

"Not if he has any sense, he won't. It was over before he left. When I wouldn't agree to marry him, our relationship hit a snag. I certainly don't have time in my day to worry about Don or any other man for that matter. I've gone from college to medical school to the ER without taking more than two weeks off at any one time. All the men I know need more attention than I can give."

"Even if you had free time, good men are mighty hard to find," Randi interjected with a shake of her head.

"See, that's just one of the sad facts of life in the big city. Good men are a vanishing breed, and we're too busy working to kiss that many frogs in the hopes of finding the one or two remaining princes. I intimidate most of them. They see my position as a successful physician as a threat. That's why I fell into the relationship with Don. It was never really satisfactory, but he was the only man I had ever met who could understand the long hours and the toll of loving this job. However, I have no intention of reviving those old memories regardless of whatever Don might have in mind," Joni retorted.

"Why is it we never discussed him? We talk about everything else," Randi asked as they scraped their plates.

"I guess it was because I knew that the relationship would lead to nothing. Although Don and I shared some laughs together, it had no future. We were both too busy with the hospital. He never made my head feel light the way Parker did. Remember him? He was my first real love during our junior year of college. I cried myself to sleep for weeks after we broke up. I guess I've been looking for that feeling ever since," Joni replied as she followed Randi across the room.

Dumping her silverware into the cleaning bin, Randi said, "Yeah, he is definitely not Parker. That was a fine, considerate, sexy man. I understand he's still married to the woman he met while in law school. Did Don say how he disposed of his practice?"

"The static was bad, but I think he said something about having some business to finish. I guess he's in the process of selling it. All I know is that Don will be back in Baltimore in two weeks," Joni said as she stuffed her hands deep inside the pockets of her white coat.

"That doesn't give you much time," Randi said.

"I'd better get busy. Schedule me out if you can. I'm on my way upstairs to see Bob Turner," Joni said as she headed toward her office.

Joni did not care what had motivated Don's return. She only knew that he had the intention of resuming his position as the chief of emergency services. As far as she was concerned, City General's emergency room was hers. She had worked hard these past six months to secure her hold on it and was not about to let it go without a fight.

Yet, Joni could not help but be a little curious about Don. They had parted as friends. In her mind there had always been the thought that maybe one day they could rekindle the flame. However, the longer Don stayed away, the less likely the possibility became until the thought finally vanished. Although he would return as the enemy, Joni wondered if the old feelings would still be there.

He thinks he'll reclaim his office and me. I have other plans for both.

Three

Pushing Don's arrival to the back of her mind, Joni concentrated on the task of trimming the already lean budget. Monday morning she had to present Bob Turner with her revised budget, a cost-reduction strategy, and a list with the names of the employees she would fire in order to achieve the desired bottom line. She knew that whatever plan she devised was critical to the positioning of the emergency room as a profit center. Now it was also necessary as proof of her ability to manage. None of the other programs she had initiated during her almost-six-month tenure mattered. Everything rested on this one.

Tapping her pencil against her knuckles, Joni knew that compiling the list of names was the easiest part of the task. The difficulty would come in telling the employees that, because they had the least seniority in their specialties, they would be unemployed at the beginning of the new year. Quickly, Joni jotted down the names of a physician's assistant, an orderly, and a plastic surgeon. All three were very important to the flow of patients through the emergency room. She would not release any of them if her alternative plan worked. However, if it did not, she would have to do the unthinkable and give them their walking papers.

Joni had already secured a position for the orderly at Baltimore Memorial and one for the physician's assistant at Hagerstown General. Allentown Hospital Center had eagerly jumped at the invitation to contact the plastic surgeon, who was renowned in the field for her research on the benefits of prompt treatment of facial injury. The chief of that specialty had promised to wait until Tuesday to call the plastic surgeon with an offer.

As Randi used her key to let herself into the condo Joni kept her eyes on the figures and said, "I wondered when you'd get here. I'm starving. I've been up since five this morning working on these projections. I'm already into my second pot of coffee."

"What makes you so sure that I'll always bring breakfast? I might have had a hot date last night who decided to sleep over," Randi retorted with a chuckle as she pushed some of Joni's papers out of the way and cleared a place for her heavy tray of croissants, strawberry jam, and freshly squeezed orange juice.

"We didn't get off work early enough last night for you to have anything hot, let alone a date. We were both too tired to eat if I remember correctly. Knowing you as I do, you were probably asleep before I could finish opening Mitzi's cat food. Besides, you always eat breakfast with me on Sunday mornings. I supply the coffee, and you bring everything else," Joni laughed as she put aside her pencil and stretched.

"Well, I guess next week I'll have to vary my routine. Instead of croissants, we'll have biscuits or bagels," Randi said with a smirk as she spread a heaping spoonful of jelly on her warm, flaky croissant. "How's the work coming? Any chance you won't have to fire anyone?"

"Actually, it looks pretty good. Listen to this as a possibility," Joni said slapping her pencil on the palm of her hand for emphasis. "City General already provides senior care and child day care for families who need someone to watch over members incapable of staying alone during the day. Well, I thought we might expand that facility to include nonemergency medical services, sort of like a clinic.

"I just finished cross-referencing the names of the people for whom we provide day care with their emergency room treatment. From what I can see, it looks as if all of them use the hospital instead of a private physician for medical treatment, from something as simple as a sore throat to heart palpitations. I haven't asked anyone, but we're probably the first-choice provider since these people are already with us. The families probably think that going to someone else would be a waste of travel time. I bet that if we ran a clinic, we'd be able to populate it with not only those patients but also with people from the neighborhood."

"What makes you think we'd have enough business to justify the cost of the expansion and the staff?" Randi asked, giving Joni a chance to lick the jelly from her fingers.

"Yesterday, I ran our files for this year to see how many of our patients are repeat customers. We recognize many of them as soon as they walk through the door, but I wondered how many come so seldomly that we don't remember their faces but who still use our services on a fairly regular basis. I discovered that we provide primary care for approximately fifteen percent of the patients we treat annually. Of that number, the vast majority have insurance that covers the cost of our services. For whatever reason, they would rather come to City General than visit a private physician. Anyway, I don't plan to do any major expansion right now. I want to see our patient load first," Joni explained as she reached for a glass of orange juice.

"If you don't plan to build, where are you going to open this clinic?" Randi asked as she reached for another croissant.

"I'm not sure yet, but I have a space in mind. We'll have to do some construction but nothing major. The clinic patients will share the ER's waiting room for the present. They're many of the same patients anyway. They won't mind," Joni replied. Her coffee was getting cold as she talked.

"Do you think it's because we're a teaching-and-research hospital that people return? Maybe they think their treatment will be better with us than with another hospital or in a private practice. I know City General has always maintained an open-door policy even though it is a private hospital. We've always been fortunate in having generous financial backers who encourage us to provide care first and worry about payment later," Randi said as she sipped her strong black coffee.

"That might be part of it. The other element is that almost all of those people live in the neighborhood, actually within a half mile of the hospital. Many of them are elderly and probably on fixed incomes. It's more convenient and less costly to walk to City General than it is to ride the bus or hail a cab to a private physician's office. Just think about our staff. How many of us have private physicians? I know I don't. I use City General for everything. I don't have time to go outside. I guess the neighbors feel the same way," Joni concluded.

Moving the empty tray to the floor, Randi asked, "How much do you think it would cost to broaden our current services to incorporate a clinic? Where do you plan to find the money? With the budget being so tight, I don't see how you can shake loose another penny."

"I plan to appeal to City General's major benefactors for the money. The staffing will take care of itself," Joni replied confidently.

"How? Explain it to me. I'm still not sure I understand exactly how you plan to pull this off," Randi queried as she pulled a chair up to the dining room table and curled up in it.

"I'll make a presentation to the board's special-interest groups, you know, the ones that regularly donate funds for the nonspecific necessities. One year, they supported the emergency repair of the roof. Another year, they contributed to the revitalization of the main courtyard. Two years ago, they helped oncology redecorate the waiting area and examining rooms. Those groups like doing the extra things that the hospital needs but decides not to include in the regular budget. I'm almost positive that they will help with this project. As a matter of fact, I've already informally discussed this with one subcommittee. The chair has invited me to speak with the members over lunch on Tuesday," Joni replied.

"Great. It looks as if you've started putting things in motion without any trouble. How have you thought to address staffing? I have a few nurses who would like to earn a little extra money. They're always asking me for overtime," Randi said as she took a sheet of paper and a pencil from the pile on Joni's desk. Quickly, she made some notes about the new clinic and ways in which she might be able to help.

"Right now, it looks as if I'll have to outplace a physician's assistant, a plastic surgeon, and an orderly. If I can get the funding from these special-interest committees for construction and supplies, I'll build in the cost of their salaries, too. Regardless of what happens, they won't be out of jobs. I've already taken care of them. From what I've seen, the services that we'll provide in the clinic will be similar to those of a regular doctor's office. Since we won't handle any trauma cases or serious illnesses there, a physician's assistant should be enough. If anything comes up, the PA can summon one of us in a hurry. Even if we expand the facility one day, I think the clinic will probably be next door to the emergency room," Joni explained. Talking out her plans with Randi made everything fall into place. Joni was ready to face the board's subcommittee on Tuesday.

"That's a good idea to keep the two units connected for a while. You can hold down the clinic's personnel costs, maintain job security for existing personnel, guard against emergency situations by being close to the ER, and keep your space to a premium. It certainly sounds like a good idea. You might be able to convince a doctor or two to donate a little time in the clinic, too. I've noticed a few who don't mind sticking around after work," Randi suggested. Joni's rapid-fire responses and logical thinking had made her believe in the viability of the clinic.

Depositing the sleeping Mitzi on the sofa, Joni said, "Good idea, Randi. There's enough flexibility in physicians' schedules on most days that I can rotate each one of them through the clinic to serve an hour each shift. We wouldn't be asking anyone to work any extra hours. Instead of spending twelve hours in the ER, they'd give the emergency room eleven and the clinic one. We'd keep the clinic open from six-thirty in the morning until midnight. That way we'd cover everyone's schedule and all possible hours for our patients' less critical needs. Anything that would come up during the hours that the clinic is closed, we would handle in the ER just as we do now."

"You've thought of everything. I can't see how this would not be a success," Randi exclaimed with pride at her friend's thoughtful preparation.

"Maybe not everything. That's what scares me. Talking this over with you has really helped arrange my thoughts. You've been a great help. Your suggestions are wonderful. Let's go for a run. I could use the exercise, and it might clear my head so that I can find any weak spots in the proposal before I embarrass myself on Tuesday," Joni said as she pulled Randi from the chair.

"Fine. I'll be back with my jogging shoes," Randi agreed as she picked up the tray and hurried two doors down to her condo.

The late-morning air was crisp and refreshing as the two women stepped out of their apartment building on Pratt Street. The bare branches of the trees fluttered in the breeze as they jogged toward the harbor. Turning left at Howard, Joni and Randi continued to weave around cars and foot traffic until they reached the restaurants that dotted the piers and attracted diners to Sunday brunch.

One of Baltimore's oldest neighborhoods sprawled just beyond the hospital grounds. Its tall, narrow row houses with their painted steps recalled the days of Babe Ruth and the time when kids rolled barrel hoops down the street for entertainment. Now, they had been remodeled as in-town residences within walking distance of the city's ball field and football stadium. Towering apartment complexes and converted warehouses, which housed fashionable, trendy condos lay scattered among the old city skyline.

Running up the hill, they passed City General. An ambulance waited silently under the awning. Patients strolled up the path that led to the emergency room entrance. Visitors carrying flowers and balloons hurried through the front doors. With a shared chuckle, they jogged past relieved that they had the day to themselves, although they were curious about the goings-on inside.

"What about weekends? How would you staff them?" Randi puffed as they trudged up the final hill.

"The ER runs at full speed twenty-four hours a day. We never reduce the force for holidays or weekends. I would think that the ER staff should be able to handle any clinic patients on Sundays too. I'll take a look at the numbers to see how many patients we treat in the ER now on Sundays who might visit the clinic if we had one. If we open it on Sunday, it might only need reduced hours. I'll see what the figures have to offer," Joni responded as she made a mental note to herself to take one more look at her proposal before submitting her budget on Monday.

"You know," Randi said as she slipped her key into the lock, "the clinic might become so popular that you'll have to expand its capabilities and its hours. The neighbors might have been waiting for this kind of support. This could be a fabulous profit center for the hospital."

"Oh, I know. Wouldn't that be great! The possibilities are mind-boggling, but we'll take it slowly at first. I don't want to rush the process only to find that the initial patient load was misleading. There'll be plenty of time for expansion if the figures prove true," Joni agreed as she waved good-bye.

The next morning, Joni submitted her budget at eight o'clock as required and attached the addendum that explained her plans for a clinic. By nine o'clock, she had confirmed the lunch meeting with the chairman of the building committee, Robert Brown, who expressed a great deal of interest in hearing her proposal. Since Brown was a prominent builder in the area, Joni hoped that he would appreciate her plans for the clinic and the more efficient use of the existing space. She needed his approval for even minor changes such as new walls and doors to separate the emergency room from the clinic. Joni had already sketched a drawing that showed the location of the combined small nurses' station and billing counter, and the three examining rooms.

Pushing up the sleeves of her sweater, Joni quickly dove into the stack of charts that needed her review and ministered to the waiting patients who demanded her attention. By the time Randi had finished checking the medicine closet, Joni had already stitched a little girl's badly lacerated forehead and taped an elderly woman's sprained ankle. Her next patient had hurt his chin.

"Justin," Joni asked, "how did you say you cracked open your chin? The tissue is awfully mangled. Are you sure you didn't fall on gravel?"

Casting a quick glance toward his waiting mother, Justin replied, "No, Dr. Forest. I fell down the steps at school. I didn't see any gravel in the area."

"Excuse me, Dr. Forest, but Mr. Brown has arrived," Randi interrupted as she entered the examining room.

"Thanks, Randi. Tell him I'll be there as soon as I finish with Justin," Joni replied as she turned quickly to the window where Mr. Brown stood watching her. Smiling, she waved a bloody hand and pointed him toward the waiting room. Holding up both hands, Joni indicated that she would only need ten more minutes. Nodding he moved away from the sight of the squirming teenager as Joni returned to her work.

"Hmm. Now what did you say, Justin, about not seeing the gravel?" Joni repeated as she probed the badly crushed and bruised flesh on the boy's stubble-covered chin with tweezers and a cotton swab. "Look at this. A piece of rock . . . and another. Where did you say you were when you fell? We really should send a complaint to the school board about unsafe conditions in our schoolyards. Your chin is a mess."

As Justin's mother stepped closer for a better look, Justin started to squirm again. Joni could tell that he was trying to hide something. Knowing that the anesthetic had completely numbed the chin, she did not feel sympathetic to his discomfort. However, Joni marveled at the boy's ability to remain true to his story in the face of mounting evidence against him.

"I agree with you, doctor. Justin will carry the scar from the school's negligence for life. As an attorney, I think I'll send them a letter stating my dissatisfaction with their maintenance program. That might prevent them from being so haphazard with their repairs in the future. It's terrible that a parent has to take time out from work to drive a child to the hospital because of someone's negligence," Mrs. Skipper replied as her face contorted at the sight of the bloody pulp. She turned a peculiar shade of green when Joni snipped off the especially mangled section over the exposed muscle.

"He certainly is lucky that the wound isn't any deeper. Another fraction of an inch and Justin would have muscle damage. Hopefully his facial hair will hide the scar one day. The more I examine this wound, the more I think I should call in plastic surgery. We have a wonderful specialist on the ER staff. I'll have her finish this job. She might be able to reduce the scarring," Joni offered as she removed her bloody gloves.

"Doctor?" Justin began as Joni turned toward the door.

"Yes, Justin?"

"I didn't fall down the building steps," he admitted, looking away from his mother. "I skipped class and took my skateboard outside. I guess the gravel on the parking lot was a little loose. Anyway, I lost my balance and fell."

"Thanks for telling me, Justin. That saves me quite a bit of paperwork," Joni commented as she watched Mrs. Skipper move closer. She knew that as soon as she left the room, the boy would hear an earful from his angry mother. She felt sorry for him, but there was nothing she could do to save him from his mother's wrath.

Rushing away before she could witness the exchange, Joni cheerfully greeted her visitor. She stopped briefly to ask the plastic surgeon Regina Bell to finish suturing Justin's chin. Shaking Robert Brown's hand she said, "Welcome to the ER, Mr. Brown. I've arranged for us to have a light lunch in the conference room. I have a few slides that I'd like to share with you."

Opening the door to the cozy conference room nestled between the bank of elevators and the physicians' lounge, Joni motioned to the waiting chairs. The dining-room staff had arranged a large platter of fruit and attractive sandwiches on huge croissants on the table. A pot of hot water and assorted instant coffees and teas sat on the credenza.

"Let me say, Dr. Forest, that I was impressed by the orderly flow of patients through the ER. Your staff certainly knows how to minister to the sick in a caring and timely fashion. I understand that the improved efficiency of this unit is a result of a plan you devised. You're to be commended, doctor," Robert Brown said as he threw his topcoat onto an empty chair and accepted the seat next to Joni.

As they helped themselves to the meal, Joni began, "Thank you, Mr. Brown. I'll get right to the point, since I know you have a full schedule also. I appreciate your taking time out of your day to listen to my proposal for an idea that I believe will prove to be a very profitable venture for the hospital.

"As you are aware, all department chiefs had to submit their revised budgets this morning. While undergoing that process and discovering that I needed to lay off three valued employees, I decided to see where we could streamline services in the emergency room and perhaps provide more comprehensive services to our patients. To my surprise, I discovered that a large number of our patients come to us not only for true emergency treatment but for routine medical care, allergic reactions to foods, bruises, lacerated chins, sprains, and other medical concerns that could be handled in a physician's office or clinic. I was even more amazed to discover that many of these people are elderly neighbors of the hospital who walk in for treatment rather than drive to their personal physicians because they don't feel as confident with their driving as they once did. They use the services of City General because we're convenient, open twenty-four hours a day, and accept their medical coverage without question.

"I started thinking that we should try to tap into this source of income and increased community service by opening a clinic. We already have a child- and elder-care facility that provides day care for fifty older people and twenty children. Most of those families use City General as their primary health-care provider because they know and trust us. We treat their earaches, sore throats, infected splinters, and small lacerations just as a primary physician would in her office. They see us almost as extended family and as someone they can count on to be available when they're in need.

"I called other medical facilities to see what they were doing to meet the needs of their neighbors concerning the operation of a clinic. I was astonished to discover that many of them have come to the same realization that we have about the potential profitability of the clinic. However, none has seized the opportunity. Granted, none of the facilities I contacted is as well supported by outside interests as City General. Many are city-operated hospitals on very limited budgets. All of the hospital administrators with whom I spoke responded favorably to the concept of the clinic.

"To that end, I would appreciate your support in approaching the subcommittees of the board for financial contributions to a new City General clinic that we would house adjacent to the ER. We would staff it with the employees I've mentioned as slated for termination as well as with ER physicians who would rotate through the clinic every hour. I also understand that several nurses might be interested in earning extra income by working in the clinic, if funding allows. We'd be able to retain personnel and provide an invaluable service to the neighborhood. Our clinic patients would enjoy a reduced wait time and the same high quality of convenient service."

Joni then showed slides, which detailed how space in the ER could be used to house the clinic.

"With the support of your committee for the reconfiguration of the space, I'll be able to ask the other subcommittees for funding of equipment and salaries. By opening this clinic, we will reach out to the community that already depends on us for medical care as well as save the jobs of several dedicated City General professionals."

Sitting back, Joni allowed a palpable silence to fall between them. She could see that Robert Brown was busily calculating the cost of the clinic. She hoped that the price tag would not be so great that her project would die before it got off the ground. She was afraid to breathe for fear of the sound distracting his concentration.

"Well, Dr. Forest, you've done it again. You've totally bowled me over. I can't say when I've seen a more thorough presentation or a more thoughtful proposal. I'll report to my committee immediately, but I can tell you without a doubt that we will find the funds to make the necessary changes to the storage room. I think a clinic would be a wonderful addition to the services we offer here at City General," Robert Brown responded as he enthusiastically shook Joni's hand.

"Thank you, Mr. Brown. That's wonderful news indeed. I appreciate your support tremendously. I'm sure that having your support will make raising the rest of the money much easier. I'm very grateful," Joni replied as she silently breathed a sigh of relief. She could hardly believe how easy it had been to secure the funding for the first step toward opening the clinic.

Rising from his chair and slipping into his coat, Mr. Brown said, "I don't think you need to concern yourself about the other committees, doctor. They will see this clinic as a very viable solution to staffing concerns and neighborhood outreach. I can assure you that you'll have the funds you need. I'll be in touch later this afternoon with the starting date for the renovation. You might want to have someone start taking the items from the storage room. I'll free a few of my men to begin the work by the end of the week. Good-bye, Dr. Forest."

Joni waited until Robert Brown was out of sight before she started her celebration dance. Spinning around the room, she laughed happily and hugged herself. The first step was completed—and so easily. Grabbing her untouched sandwich and fruit, Joni rushed back to the ER to tell Randi the good news.

"Hey, lunch!" Randi exclaimed as she took half of Joni's fruit, and pastrami sandwich. "Just what I needed. I've been too busy to take a break. I saw Robert Brown leave. How was your meeting?"

"Great! It couldn't have been better. He'll speak with his subcommittee, but he's positive that they'll fund the project. He might have a crew in place by Friday. He said that he doesn't think I'll have any trouble getting the support of the other committee tomorrow. As a matter of fact, he assured me of the complete support of the others."

"Wow! It certainly pays to have friends in high places," Randi said as she wiped the mustard from her fingers.

"It doesn't hurt to have a little extra cash either. It sounds as if he plans to foot the bill for most of the construction costs himself," Joni commented as she nibbled the grapes. She was too intoxicated from her victory to think of eating the sandwich.

"If you're not going to eat that . . ." Randi said as she eyed the other half of the sandwich.

Pushing the plate toward her, Joni looked across the waiting room toward the door. An ambulance had just pulled up and was unloading a stretcher with considerable difficulty. She watched as one of the emergency room's orderlies joined the paramedics in pushing and half-carrying the heavy stretcher.

Rushing forward, Joni met them at the door and pointed in the direction of examining room two. "What do you have here?" Joni asked as she looked into the blue face of a massive man dressed in the largest three-piece blue pinstriped suit she had ever seen.

Wiping the sweat from his forehead, Tommy answered, "He collapsed at lunch in one of the restaurants on the harbor. The maître d' said the man had just eaten two-dozen oysters on the half shell, shrimp cocktail, clam chowder, teriyaki chicken, and pecan pie. After he paid his check, he stood up, put on his topcoat, and started swaying. Before anyone could catch him, he fell backward into the kitchen door. It's lucky no one else was hurt. This guy has to weigh four hundred pounds. My partner and I had one hell of a time getting him into the ambulance."

"On my count, let's move him to the examining table. I'll need someone else on this side to help me. What are his vitals?" Joni asked as she drew up the pull sheet and prepared to lift the large man.

As Tommy called off the man's blood pressure and respiration, the group lifted with a loud collective grunt. Waving good-bye, Tommy said, "He's all yours, doc. See you later."

"Before you leave, Tommy, did you remember to get your flu shot?" Joni asked as she pulled on her gloves.

"No, I forgot. I'll ask Sally to give it to me right now. Thanks for reminding me again," Tommy smiled as he left the room.

Quickly snipping away clothing and checking for any air-passage obstruction, Joni inserted a breathing tube and ordered the necessary tests. Suspecting a stroke because of the man's dangerously high blood pressure level, Joni ordered, "Check his wallet for identification. There might be something on him to tell us if he's on any medication."

Reaching into the man's pocket, Randi extracted a well-stuffed wallet full of business and credit cards. "His driver's license identifies him as Paul Tanzo of Randallstown, Maryland. His business card says he's an epicure and food critic. He's one man who certainly enjoys his job," Randi stated with a smirk. "There's nothing medical among his possessions. I don't see a home phone number or any family pictures. Also, he's not wearing a ring, not that all married men do. I'll call his office and see what I can find out."

As Joni labored to identify the cause of Mr. Tanzo's collapse, the patient began to groan and stir.

"Do you think it's all the food he ate that caused his problem?" Terry, a new medical student, asked.

"The excess weight he's carrying contributed to the elevation in blood pressure, but the food, unless spoiled, didn't cause the collapse. Do we have any lab results yet? I think we should schedule a scan to rule out a stroke. There's some definite weakness on the right side of his face, and he's beginning to drool from that corner of his mouth. Let's get that BP down fast. He looks as if he's stroking now," Joni ordered as she assessed the changes in the patient with alarm.

Suddenly, the patient began to suffer a seizure. Immediately, Joni shouted over the sound of instruments crashing to the floor, "Let's get the restraints on him."

Quickly, they secured Mr. Tanzo's flailing arms and administered an antiseizure medicine as well as a massive dose of medication to reduce his blood pressure. Checking his vitals, Joni saw that the BP had risen even higher. Between the violent seizures and the rising blood pressure, she feared that the man might take a turn for the worse.

"Call neurology and tell them to get someone down here stat. He's not responding to the meds, and we're at maximum dosage," Joni ordered tersely. She hated to lose a patient. Mr. Tanzo's condition greatly concerned her.

As a tense silence fell over the examining room, the seizures began to diminish in intensity. Scanning the indicator, the group watched as all functions fell to elevated but not fatal levels and the seizing stopped. Slowly, Mr. Tanzo's eyes began to flutter and the color started to return to his cheeks.

"Mr. Tanzo, can you hear me? You're in City General Hospital. You collapsed after eating lunch," Joni said in a clear voice.

"Yes, I can hear you. I don't remember anything after I paid the check," he muttered through dry, cracked lips.

"Mr. Tanzo, do you have a history of high blood pressure? Are you taking any medication for it?" Joni asked, leaning over him and checking the responsiveness of his pupils.

"It's high but under control. I'm very careful about my medicine," the patient struggled to respond.

"Did you eat something today to which you might be allergic?" Joni queried as she watched his vital signs continue to stabilize.

"No, I don't think so, but I ate far too much. I had to try the pecan pie. I know I shouldn't have, but it looked too good to resist," Mr. Tanzo replied with difficulty.

"I'm still concerned about some weakness on your right side. Have you ever suffered a stroke?" Joni asked.

"A few months ago. It left me with a slight limp on the right. That's probably what you see, doctor. I'm terribly sorry for squinting, but I'm blind without my glasses," Mr. Tanzo answered as he struggled to focus on her face.

"I'm afraid you didn't come in with them, Mr. Tanzo," Joni commented as she continued to monitor his vital signs.

"No matter. I'm always leaving them somewhere. I'm so nearsighted that I have to take them off to read the menus. I have lots of extra pairs," he replied.

"While you're here, I want to have you checked for any further complications. We have your vitals stabilized, but I feel that with your history a little precaution would be prudent. We'll transfer you up to neurology now. They'll take care of you for a while," Joni explained as she gently patted his hand. She continued to be concerned about the pressure and weakness, but there was nothing she could do for him in the emergency room. He would need observation, which was something her staff could not offer.

"Thank you, doctor. I hope that I didn't hurt anyone when I fainted."

"No, no one was hurt when you fell. Should I notify anyone that you're here?" Joni asked.

"My sister lives in town. Her number is 301-555-5657. I'd appreciate it if you'd give her a call. Thank you again, doctor," Mr. Tanzo replied trying to smile bravely.

Pulling the sheet under his chin, Joni motioned to the orderlies that they could transport Mr. Tanzo now. After he left the room, Randi mused, "I wonder what makes a person eat until he gets to that point. He must have a very unhappy life if he'll risk his health for a piece of pecan pie."

"One slice of pie did not make him a four-hundred-pound man. I'm concerned that the weakness in his right side appeared to be worsening. I hope the EEG shows something positive. Call upstairs please and check on him. He should have responded faster to the medications," Joni said.

"Yes, but he's a big guy. You did all you could for him. He's stable and on his way to neurology where he belongs. If he is having another stroke, they'll treat him up there. At any rate, he won't be alone and sick as soon as I reach his sister," Randi offered as she began to set up the emergency room for the next patient.

"It's sad not having anyone in your life. Do you ever think about that?" Joni asked as she helped Randi smooth out the sheet.

"Sometimes, but I'm still young. Besides, I'm too busy. Nothing serious would last now anyway," Randi answered.

"You're right. Remember the guy I dated a few years ago? I got a note from Ted on Friday. He's getting married on New Year's Eve. He says he's happy and ready to settle down. We had a good time together, but I was too involved with the hospital to think of getting serious. Anyway, I'm content with my life," Joni said as she picked up her stethoscope and linked her arm through Randi's.

"While you're in examining room one with what appears

to be a badly lacerated finger, I'll call neurology and Mr. Tanzo's sister. How about a movie tonight?" Randi asked as she handed Joni another chart.

"Sure, I'm game. Let me know what you find out about Mr. Tanzo," Joni replied as she darted off again for what she hoped would be a fairly routine case.

As Joni tied the last suture, Randi stuck her head into the room. "Excuse me, Dr. Forest, but you wanted me to check on the patient who we transferred to neurology. It seems that he was indeed having another stroke. The EEG confirmed irregular brain waves. Because of your suspicions and quick transfer of the patient, they were able to medicate him early and stop most of the damage. The patient is stable now."

"That's wonderful news. Did you contact his sister?" Joni asked as she rested the finger in a splint to immobilize it.

"Yes, she's upstairs with him. Good work!" Randi offered as she closed the door.

"Okay, Miss Marks, you can go home now. Have that finger checked in a week. The sutures should be ready to come out by then. You should see a doctor if you notice extreme inflammation or discharge from the area, but I don't think you will. Keep it clean and you'll be okay," Joni counseled as she collected the instruments and deposited them in the appropriate containers.

"Thanks, doctor. I can still play with this finger, can't I? My team is headed for the play-offs, and I don't want to miss the big game," Tanya Marks said. Her records showed that she was a high school senior and captain of the varsity volleyball team.

"Normally I'd say no, but since this is your last season, I advise you to be very careful. It's a bad cut, and it could reopen if you bang your finger into anything," Joni replied slowly. She could remember her days on the court and understood Tanya's desire to continue playing.

"Yes, but I'm right-handed. I don't use my left one as much. I'll be careful, doctor. Thanks," Tanya answered as she accepted the reminder to return for follow-up that Joni had scribbled on a note pad and handed to her.

"Enjoy your senior year, Tanya. Where are you applying to college?" Joni asked as she headed toward the door.

"I'd like to stay in town if I can. I've applied early to Johnson Walkers' premed program. I just hope they accept me. I'm off to the library now for some study time," Tanya replied, gathering her heavy backpack.

"Really? That's my medical school alma mater . . . good luck to you," Joni said as she waved good-bye and returned to the desk.

Randi watched as Joni wrote the last of her notes on Tanya's chart. "She seems like a nice girl," Randi commented.

"She has good taste in colleges, too. She's hoping to go to our alma mater," Joni responded with pride.

"Good. She'll like it there; we did," Randi concluded. "Oh, by the way, Robert Brown called. He said the other committee chairs are anxious to hear your proposal. He's so confident of their support that he has scheduled his men to begin work no later than Friday and possibly sooner. I guess you'd better get that storeroom cleaned up."

Scanning the room and finding everyone busy, Joni said with a smile, "I guess that means me. You'll know where to find me."

Watching Joni almost trot to the storage room, Randi chuckled. Her friend was constantly on the go and enjoyed every minute of the chaos and excitement of her life. Joni had wanted to open the clinic and had worked to make her dream a reality. There was no stopping her when she made up her mind to accomplish a task. Randi only hoped that the board recognized what a valuable asset to the hospital Joni was.

Four

Armed with budget figures, income projections, and preliminary floor plans, Joni sat across the table from the gathered members of the board of directors on Tuesday and presented her plans for tightening the emergency room's budget and establishing the new clinic. If she was successful, she would share the good news with the gathered emergency room heads at the conference next week.

"Ladies and gentlemen, thank you for taking time from your schedules to meet with me today," Joni began as she surveyed the attentive faces. "The purpose of our session is for me to acquaint you with my plans for a new clinic adjacent to the ER. The clinic would help City General turn an existing efficient, highly acclaimed emergency medical unit into a profit center by absorbing some of the less critical patient load. The clinic would immediately provide invaluable community relations, goodwill and potentially serve as a source of revenue for City General in the future.

"Knowing that I was charged with reducing the ER budget, I decided to capitalize on City General's reputation for providing quality health care and warm community service. To that end, I have developed a plan for a clinic that will allow me to streamline the ER budget while building up a much-needed community support facility. By implementing the proposal for the clinic, City General will not only retain all members of its talented staff, but it will provide a necessary service to our community. By simply shifting head count to the new facility, City General's emergency medical services division can reach its profitability goal and its community outreach objective.

"After speaking with Robert Brown and receiving his preliminary blueprints and costs, it is clear that the clinic is very much within our grasp. The facility could be fully operational by next week if no unforeseen problems arise. The ER staff has been apprised of the new opportunity for service and is anxious to begin the new enterprise. We simply await your approval.

"If you'll focus your attention on the slides, you'll see the proposed layout of the space. As you can see, the clinic will initially share some strategic facilities with the ER, making its operation smooth for patient flow into and out of the hospital, convenient for physician support as needed, and reasonably economical in terms of construction costs. Should the figures prove that the clinic could become a viable, independent facility, we still have space for further expansion and development.

"Staffing will not be a concern. All emergency room physicians, orderlies, and PAs will rotate through the clinic on a one-hour basis as part of their regular shifts. That way the clinic will always have at least one PA and orderly on duty at all times. The nursing administrator is currently negotiating with the union to enable the nursing staff to participate in this endeavor. Several nurses have already come forward to say that they would appreciate the opportunity to earn extra income by working their days off in the clinic. Everyone on the staff wants to see this exciting new health-care offering become a successful reality."

As the board members studied the slides showing the projected emergency room savings and clinic revenue, Joni watched their faces intently. She could tell that the idea of not only balancing the budget but making money for the hospital greatly appealed to them. They also relished the idea of retaining highly skilled personnel. Seeing them relax and begin to chatter among themselves, she took the opportunity to change to the slide containing the relatively few expenses.

Clearing his throat, Robert Brown interjected, "If I might, I would like to make a comment while you're digesting the information that Dr. Forest has presented. In an impromptu meeting of the members of my subcommittee at my home last evening, we voted unanimously in support of the construction of the clinic if it gains the approval of the full board. As you know, in construction's slow season, it has always been my practice to help my employees find work. To that end, I will provide the manpower, supplies, and tools to erect the walls, install the lighting, lay the flooring, and hang any necessary doors and signs. The expansion of the physical plant will not put any strain on City General's budget."

The applause for his generosity erupted spontaneously as Robert Brown graciously nodded in humble recognition. Immediately, the competitive spirit that motivated the board members in their own companies sprang up. None of them wanted to be outdone by Robert Brown's philanthropic endeavors. Each of them promised to provide individual support as well as that of their committees. Joni decided to continue while she could hear their wallets opening.

Taking a deep breath and concentrating on the task at hand, Joni said, "Now, ladies and gentlemen, if you'll take a moment to look at this last set of figures, you'll see the anticipated one-time costs for construction and furnishing of the clinic. Mr. Brown's generosity has made it unnecessary for us to discuss construction costs. However, the issue of furnishings still exists.

"I have contacted Mercy Hospital and arranged to purchase at a very nice savings two used examining room tables, four supply cabinets, stools, and assorted other equipment such as sterilizers, contingent upon your approval of this plan, of course. As you know, Mercy's ER recently closed due to a change in demographics and an ensuing reduction in patient load. It might be possible for us to buy still more equipment from them if we need it.

"In light of all that you have heard today, I am asking you to approve the proposal for the new City General clinic. Further, I would like to request that you set your subcommittees to the task of allocating the money for the purchases as soon as possible. Does anyone have any questions?"

At first no one spoke and then the barrage of questions began to fly. They wanted clarification on everything from the placement of the nurses' station desk to the use of the emergency room's waiting room. By the time the two-hour session ended, Joni felt as if she had walked on fire and survived to tell about the ordeal. Yet, before they left the conference room, each board member congratulated her on the thorough preparation and the brilliant suggestion for making City General an even more visible member of the community.

Walking on air, Joni returned to the emergency room. Immediately, she rushed up to Randi to tell her the good news. Breathlessly, she shared the happenings with her friend, saying, "You should have seen the board members hop on the idea. Robert Brown definitely helped set the stage for my presentation. At first, they listened attentively to what I proposed. I actually thought some of them might have been dozing, that's just how quiet they were. Then, they pelted me with every possible question. Finally, they divided up the work and decided which subcommittee would foot the bill for which expense. Each group was determined to better Robert Brown's offer to finance the construction.

"In addition to the usual round of parties, one of the committees decided to host a holiday dinner-dance to cover the cost of a brand-new X-ray machine for the clinic. Another will hold a bazaar to cover the expense of the furnishings that I'll buy secondhand from Mercy. Still another will float the cost until Valentine's Day and then give a dance.

"Oh, and the best part is that the board thinks that the clinic will be so successful that we'll need extra staff, not just emergency room rotations. They want to fund another PA and two full-time nurses if the union agrees. Isn't that great? Unlike some of our friends at other hospitals, we didn't even have to request grant money to build our clinic. The board simply decided to chip in from its own resources. I had to caution them against being too optimistic."

"It doesn't hurt to be associated with a hospital that enjoys celebrity status, I guess. They certainly are generous with their time and money when the hospital needs something," Randi commented as she studied her friend's beaming face.

"I forgot to tell you the best part. Bridgett Laser, the daughter of the shipping magnate, rose to Robert Brown's challenge and pledged to cover the cost of salaries herself until the clinic starts showing a profit. She pledged $100,000 to the clinic's fund to cover the operating costs for the first few months. All we need now is the completed construction, and we'll be ready to open," Joni gushed. She had not been this happy about anything since she graduated from medical school with honors.

"Don't worry about that. The men called about a half hour ago to say that they'll start work after lunch. They should be arriving any minute. As a matter of fact, I think I see them now. So much for a quiet afternoon. At least we don't have many patients," Randi concluded. She looked toward the ambulance entrance to see a beige van with the name BROWN AND SONS CONSTRUCTION blazed in bold, red letters. The men noisily began to unload the supplies they would use when they started the construction of the clinic.

"Yes, but in a few minutes, we'll have lots of dust," Joni exclaimed as she darted down the hall to her quiet, little office.

Following her, Randi said, "You're really eating this up. You love working with the board members and solving tough managerial problems."

"Of course I do, but I enjoy the time I spend treating patients even more. I'm just so thankful that in the last six months I've had the opportunity to see both sides of the operation of the emergency room and the hospital, as an administrator and a physician. Too few people are ever that fortunate."

"You're not at all like Don, who mostly stayed in his office and handled the administrative side of the emergency room," Randi commented. "I'm glad to see that you don't close yourself off from the patients. All he wanted to do was live in the world of figures and hobnob with the governing board. You roll up your sleeves every morning and work alongside the rest of us. The staff really notices the difference."

"You know I could never disassociate myself from the patients. I have a hard time giving myself a few minutes each day for paperwork," Joni replied with a grin.

"I've noticed that you seem to enjoy working with chicken pox-covered kids, elderly people braving Alzheimer's, and pimple-faced adolescents worrying about pregnancy or eating disorders as much as you do with surgical patients. That's what I like about you, you're flexible," Randi commented with a chuckle.

"Just think," Joni said, "I could have gone into private practice to satisfy my parents. I could have made a fortune rather than existing on this relatively small emergency room physician's salary. But, no, I decided that I would miss the challenge of constantly heaping abuse on my body by working sixteen-hour shifts. I love standing on my feet all day and feeling my arches fall."

"You know you love working in a teaching hospital. You like knowing all the latest techniques before any of your buddies at the other hospitals or in private practice. I've seen you gloat when you find out that you know something that they don't. You're a natural for this kind of environment," Randi rebutted as she grimaced at the name on the office door.

"What's wrong?" Joni asked. "You stopped singing my praises. Did you run out of good things to say?"

"No, it's just that name on the door. Don't you think City

General could spring for the cost of a little paint?" Randi replied as she wrinkled her nose at the black letters of Don's name.

"The board will have someone change it when they finally appoint the permanent chief. At least, I hope they'll make a decision that will cause them to change it," Joni replied with a smirk.

"Don't worry. You're a shoo-in," Randi added as she vanished down the hall.

Sitting and talking over pizza at one of their favorite restaurants that night, Joni said, "Randi, I think the board was so very supportive because they want City General to remain on the cutting edge. Despite the need to curtail spending and pay more attention to the bottom line, everyone here wants City General to remain one of the best hospitals on the East Coast and the premier health-care provider in Baltimore. Regardless of how much we complain about the tough times and the lack of money, City General is in much healthier condition than our closest competitor."

"You don't have to tell me that. I attended a meeting last week of the head nurses at three different hospitals in the state. Not one of them enjoyed the facilities, the resources, and the financial support that City General's nurses and physicians do. It's not only money either. The neighborhood is behind us. It never fights us about anything we want to do," Randi commented as she picked the anchovies off her pizza. She had been so engaged in conversation with Joni that she had failed to order her half of the pizza without the salty, little fish.

"I don't think I'd say that they never oppose us. Remember two years ago when the hospital wanted to connect two isolated buildings to the main structure by erecting an elevated walkway? The neighbors had a fit about that. I don't blame them either. This neighborhood is in the process of going upscale. The breezeways would have obstructed the view from many houses.

"The board revamped its plans by building office space into the extensions that connect the outbuildings to the main structure. The hospital lost some of the courtyard space it was trying to protect, but the additional offices generate quite a bit of revenue and the new design looks as if it's an integral part of the structure, not simply additions," Joni corrected as she munched garlic bread.

"You're right. I had forgotten all about that. It seems to me that a number of other hospitals imitated the style of the additions and are making money from their physician offices, too. Trust City General to come out of conflict smelling like a rose," Randi added.

"We're not the first ones to build a clinic in the ER, but I bet we'll do it better than anyone else," Joni replied.

"Will that be the topic of your discussion with the other ER doctors . . . the rise of the hospital clinic?" Randi queried as she sipped her beer and waited for Joni to finish her meal before signaling for the check.

"That's right. I'll share the reasons we decided to add a clinic and what we hope to gain from the new service both in terms of revenue and goodwill," Joni responded as they gathered their things and returned to their apartment building.

Standing in the hall, Randi asked, "What will you do when Don returns? What if he really does have the support of the board? I'd hate to see you get hurt in a political battle. You've worked awfully hard these past few months, and you've done so much for the hospital."

"Don and everyone who might support him will have a fight on their hands. He left unceremoniously under the pretext of taking a vacation. When he found what he thought would be greener pastures, he forgot all about us. From where I stand, he's the one who has to worry about me. I've proven myself to be a capable and maybe even a visionary ER chief. I hope that my record will speak for itself. I've certainly put the board on notice that I don't plan to roll over and give up without a fight," Joni replied with confidence tinged with the awareness that life did not always work out as planned.

"Don't forget that the good-old-boy network has a lot to do with a person's success in business. Don's a man. That'll give him a competitive edge you don't have. They'll forget faster that he's black than they will that you're female," Randi advised as she walked toward her condo.

"That sounds like sexism to me. It's bad enough that I've always had to prove that as a black person I'm as qualified as someone white, now I have to make my mark as a woman. That's a double hit on the glass ceiling," Joni stated with a shrug of disgust.

"But you know it's true. Remember that corporate attorney I dated a few years ago? Well, there weren't any black women at his level in the company, but there was one other black man. Just keep your eyes and ears open, that's all I'm saying," Randi concluded.

"I know and I'm ready for the fight, should it come down to that. I just hope it won't. That would be a bad situation for both of us and maybe the ER, too. I'd hate to see my colleagues and friends having to choose between their loyalty to me and theirs to Don. We'll cross that bridge when we get to it, I guess. By the way, do you ever see that guy? What was his name . . . Frank something?"

"No, it didn't work out. He needed someone on his arm for social functions and I was always at work. He didn't understand that I couldn't simply drop my responsibilities at the hospital whenever he needed me to be with him. He developed an attitude about it and started making noises about my place as his woman, so I cut him loose."

"You're better off without him. It's his loss. They get their egos in a knot if we're not at their beck and call. Someday we'll find the right ones," Joni advised with a knowing nod.

"Yeah, but I'm getting awfully tired of turning over those rocks looking for him!" Randi said, laughing.

"I know what you mean. I remember thinking that Don was my prince, and I guess he was for a while. He wasn't a prince, and I wasn't a princess. Maybe we were a good match and I just didn't realize it," Joni commented with a shrug of her shoulders.

"Good night, Randi. I'll see you in the morning," Joni said, chuckling as she eased into her condo and closed the door behind her.

The next day the sound of hammering and sawing greeted Joni as she entered the emergency room at nine o'clock. Robert Brown's men were hard at work and already they were almost a day ahead of schedule. They had taken the liberty of covering the chairs with plastic but sawdust and drywall fragments flew everywhere despite their precautions.

Turning to Randi, Joni remarked, "They must have started before dawn. They certainly are efficient. At the rate they're working, they'll finish the job even earlier than expected. From the amount of dust they're creating, I hope we have a slow day or else we'll be treating people for allergies too."

"Let's hope they finish quickly. We'll need the space when the weekend traffic begins. I know you had planned to work on your presentation, but you might want to take a look at this patient before you get started," Randi commented as she handed Joni the patient file, scanned the morning's charts, and sorted through the day's work.

"Okay, boss!" Joni saluted sharply and donned her white jacket.

When Joni entered examining room three, she found a woman wearing a wild, curly brown wig, bright-orange stretch pants, and an oversize Baltimore Ravens sweatshirt rapidly pacing the floor with her hands at her sides like a soldier on watch. On her feet, she wore inordinately large men's tennis shoes cut to allow the free movement of her toes, which she had enclosed in purple socks. Over her shoulder, she carried a large, sagging, black cloth bag, the kind that most people used for dirty clothes, which doubled as her purse. The woman's chart said that she was forty-seven, but she could just as easily have been sixty considering the number of wrinkles that lined the corners of her eyes and mouth. She was missing a lot of teeth and the ones that remained were discolored due to cigarette smoking and poor oral hygiene.

"Good morning, Miss Hill. I'm Dr. Forest. Your chart says that you were unwilling to disclose the nature of your problem to anyone except a physician. Although I assure you that our nursing staff and PAs are extremely competent, I am a surgeon. May I be of service to you?" Joni offered by way of introduction.

Immediately, the pacing stopped and the woman spun around to face Joni. The pupils of her light-blue eyes were so dilated that Joni marveled at their size from across the room. Although the woman stood perfectly still, her hands would not stop fluttering. She constantly fussed with her hair or adjusted the sleeves and hem of her sweatshirt. Her eyes darted from Joni's face to the open door behind her.

"Close the door," the woman whispered conspiratorially. "I don't want anyone to hear what I have to say."

"We usually leave them open, Miss Hill, in case we need extra medical help in a hurry. I'm sure no one can hear us with all the construction noise in the waiting room," Joni said as she studied the patient's anxious face. Quickly she penned the words *psych consult* on the chart.

"No, they can hear us all right. They can hear every word we say. Closing the door is only the first step. I have to turn on the radio, too, or else they will listen to everything," Miss Hill replied as she reached into the bag up to her elbow and extracted a battered radio. It was the old battery-operated transistor kind in a bright-yellow case. Joni's mother kept one in the kitchen junk drawer in the event the electricity went out during a thunderstorm.

Joni watched as Miss Hill carefully positioned the radio on

the end of the examining room table and tuned in a classical radio station. Adjusting the volume so that it was just a hair below deafening, Miss Hill confided, "I'm really a double agent for the CIA. That's why I dress like this. No one would suspect a woman who looks like me of being a spy, but I am. I've been to Russia, Angola, Bosnia, and Colombia. They know my face in all those countries. It's not safe for me to travel to any of them anymore. I have to stay in the States, where everyone thinks I'm a harmless bag lady. I've even spied on the British. Did you know that we have spies in Parliament and working in Buckingham Palace? I bet you didn't know that, did you, doctor? Well, we do.

"But that's not why I'm here. Someone has found out about me and is trying to poison me. They must work for a very powerful organization because they have connections in high places. They put it in the water. The Health Department says that there are E coli bacteria in the water, but that's not the true story. It's really poison for me, but those other spies are smart. They don't want anyone to think that the poison is aimed at only one person. It would be too easy to trace, so they put this little bacteria in everyone's water to fool the government, but they get the bulk of it into my water supply. They tap into the pipes that service my apartment building.

"You have to believe me, doctor. That's the only way to save everyone. They'll continue to poison the water until they get me. They don't know that I only drink rainwater. When they figure that out, they'll start poisoning the clouds too. They're mean, sneaky people, doctor."

While Miss Hill spoke, Joni had carefully positioned herself so that she could quickly leave the room or summon help if she needed it. Through the window of the closed door, she could see Randi hovering in the hall waiting for her to call. Signaling for her to enter, Joni carefully studied Miss Hill's calm demeanor. If it had not been for her strange attire and her constantly moving hands, the woman might have looked fairly ordinary.

"No, don't call her. She's one of them!" Miss Hill shrieked as she huddled in the corner.

"No, Miss Hill, this is the head nurse and my dearest friend. I've known her for years, and I assure you that she has never been to any of those countries you mentioned," Joni replied, trying to make the frightened woman feel more comfortable.

"That's right, Miss Hill. I've never been farther than New York," Randi added as she looked over Joni's shoulder at the chart on which she had carefully written her observations and the order for Randi to call psych services immediately.

"Even if she's not one of them, she'll disclose my identity. She's a traitor and a counterspy," Miss Hill insisted.

"Miss Hill, my friend is going to bring you medication that will make you feel much better. After you take it, we'll have another little chat," Joni coaxed as the woman emerged from the corner. Warily, Miss Hill watched Randi leave the room.

"What kind of medicine is it? How do I know that you're not one of them? I'm not often wrong about a person's identity, but I might be this time. I don't think I'll take whatever it is. I've told you too much already," Miss Hill replied as she turned off the radio and dropped it into her bag.

"I assure you, Miss Hill, that your intuition has not failed you. I am not a spy. I'm the head of this ER. I've never been anything more threatening than that. When the nurse returns with the medicine, you will take it. It's very powerful and capable of stopping any external poison from having any effect on your body. You'll be safe even if they should poison the rain after just one dose of this medicine," Joni advised as she smiled confidently.

"Are you sure we can trust her?" Miss Hill asked as Randi returned with a hypodermic needle on a tray. "I can't take any chances. I still have work to do."

"I give you my word, Miss Hill. You can trust the nurse completely. Now, let us help you onto the exam table. We'll put your clothes and bag right here on the chair where you can see them. Slip your arms through here. That's right. This gown will help hide you from them. You'll look just like any other patient. Now, lie down. You'll feel much better after this medication takes effect. Very good. Now, just lie here for a while," Joni instructed as she watched Randi carefully inject Miss Hill with the sedative that would calm her down enough so that they could transfer her to psych services.

"It's fast-working stuff, isn't it, doctor? It's almost like the time they gave me truth serum. I could feel it begin to work in a matter of minutes. Fortunately, I was strong enough to keep it from making me talk. I can resist anything, you know. I was trained to withstand any drug or torture known to man," Miss Hill bragged as her hands began to calm and lie gently on the covers.

"I'll stay with her for a few minutes if you'd like. I've taken care of everything," Randi said as she checked the woman's vital signs.

"No, I don't mind staying. The noise out there is too much for me anyway. In here, it's quiet. Besides, she reminds me of my sixth-grade teacher. Her husband was a psychiatrist and had played all kinds of mind games on her. As a result, she suffered from delusions as well as feelings of inadequacy," Joni responded sadly as she watched the new tranquility spread across Miss Hill's face.

"There's no need to check my blood pressure, nurse. I'm always in training, and I'm in great physical shape. All of this is simply a disguise," Miss Hill said as she reached up and removed her wig, under which her head was bald except for a few wisps of hair.

"Are you on chemotherapy, Miss Hill?" Randi asked as she studied the baldness characteristic of either cancer drug therapy or stress.

"No, the baldness is part of my other disguise. I carefully pull out my own hair. I try to remove only the gray, but some of the brown gets caught too. I used to have only a little gray, but the life I lead has turned almost all of my hair gray now, so I pull all of it out. If you'd seen the things I've seen, you'd lose that mane of hair too," Miss Hill advised as her hands rested on top of the wig.

"I'm sure I would," Randi conceded as she nodded to Jeff Powers from psych services who had just entered the room.

"Who is that man?" Miss Hill asked as she prepared to rebel against Jeff's presence.

"Don't worry, Miss Hill. He's Jeff Powers, a doctor friend of mine. I thought he might be interested in hearing your stories. He's a former Navy SEAL and has worked undercover operations himself," Joni explained as she patted Miss Hill on the shoulder.

"All right, doctor, if you think he's okay, I'll talk with him. I have to trust someone, so it might as well be you three. I'm too tired from all the running to leave here anyway. He can ask whatever he'd like," Miss Hill agreed as she stretched and luxuriated on the clean sheets. From the looks of her attire and body, Joni doubted that she had seen a clean bed in months.

As Jeff Powers began his questioning, Joni and Randi excused themselves and left the room. They were confident that Jeff would agree with their recommendation and certify that Miss Hill would benefit from a few nights under the watchful care of psych services.

"Poor woman," Joni said with a shake of her head. "I wonder what set her off."

"According to our files, she has been treated in both the ER and upstairs in psych services three times in the past two months with the most recent visit taking place in November. She lives in the neighborhood and is an embarrassment to her successful businessman son. When I called him to let him know that she was safe and here again, all he could say was that he was glad she'd get the psychiatric care she needs. He never expressed concern for his mother's health. It's hard to believe that she used to be a senator in the Maryland General Assembly," Randi concluded as she looked sadly at the closed door.

"Wow, I never would have guessed it. I certainly hope that Jeff will be able to get to the root of her problem this time," Joni commented.

"I wouldn't keep my fingers crossed if I were you. According to the psych services records, she checks herself out of the hospital every time she comes here. I cross-checked her file and found out that she has been hospitalized at three other hospitals in the city too, and each time she leaves against medical advice. Her son says that she wanders around as long as she can stand being outdoors. When she becomes tired or hungry, she goes into a hospital wherever she is. She leaves before she can make a true recovery. It's almost as if she wants someone to help her get better, but she doesn't know how to let anyone do it," Randi responded.

"Well, maybe this time, someone will get lucky. You remember my aunt with Alzheimer's, the one who died last year? I can empathize with the frustration and hopelessness that Miss Hill's son is experiencing. I'm sure the feeling of futility has made him appear hardened against his mother's condition. Even being in the health-care business, it was very difficult to be the caretaker of someone with that condition. Working with Miss Hill brought back all the old memories."

"Let's hope we can still reach Miss Hill. She's younger than your aunt. Maybe psych services can do something for her," Randi offered as she tried to brighten Joni's mood.

Looking around the waiting room, Joni waved good-bye, saying, "I can just barely hear myself think. If you need me, I'll be in my office."

The first thing Joni saw as she entered her office was the bouquet of red roses sitting on the tiny braided rug. Reading the card, she discovered that they were from Don, undoubtedly a peace offering in the hopes of getting back into her good graces. Joni immediately tossed the card into the trash. A moment later, she pulled it out again and reread the simple message. I'M COMING BACK FOR MORE THAN MY JOB. LOVE, DON.

With a shrug, Joni dropped the card into the trash again

and turned her attention to her work. She had too much to do to think about a relationship that might not be. Besides she could not allow herself to think that a future was possible with Don. They were too different and too much the same. Work would always come first with them. Neither would bend.

Taking up her pen, Joni prepared what she knew would be a moving, heartfelt discussion of the need for clinics in emergency rooms as the first line of defense against myriad illnesses. With so many people relying on hospitals for their primary care, hospitals had to expand their services to meet the patients' needs. A clinic gave the hospital the perfect opportunity to provide the services that were abandoned with the loss of the general practitioner.

Looking at the little dot of color on the window ledge and thinking about Miss Hill, Joni wondered just how many more people they would be able to treat in clinics like the one she proposed for City General. The convenient location of hospitals and the potential for providing state-of-the-art services made them perfect tools in the war against disease and neglect.

Returning the paper and pen to her desk, Joni abandoned her habit of writing a first draft by hand and moved to the computer. Quickly, she produced a final copy. She wanted to capture her passion for the subject the first time rather than taking a chance on editing the emotion out of her presentation. She knew that with carefully selected slides flashing in the background, she would make a powerful pitch for other hospitals to join City General in its outreach program.

"Move over, Don Rivers, Joni Forest is here to stay. City General and its emergency room and clinic are mine," she muttered to herself as her words came to life on the computer screen. Although she had been too busy to give more than passing thought to his return, Joni wondered what changes would occur when he did reappear. She hoped that her newly won board support would be sufficient to send him packing once more.

Regardless of what happened, Joni would not give up the

emergency room easily. She had worked hard in the last six months to make it run like a well-oiled machine. She had no intention of simply allowing him to walk back into his old position without a fight. She had buried the past and with it his control over the emergency room and her.

Five

Standing before an audience of emergency room chiefs from all over the state, Joni immediately knew that her presentation would be a success. The conference attendees lived with the same charge of making their units profit centers for their hospitals. Many of them had begun the process of opening a clinic, others were thinking about it, and some were still wondering how they could make it work in their hospital. All of them believed that clinics associated with emergency rooms provided needed outreach services to the community and revenue for the hospital.

Joni motioned to the conference coordinator at the back of the room that she was ready. Slowly, the lights dimmed and the room darkened slightly. Gradually, the screen to her left filled with images of City General and its daily operation. Scenes of patients and visitors entering the hospital, ambulances arriving at the emergency room entrance, physicians rushing to respond to pages, and nurses taking histories and providing care flowed before their eyes.

As one image faded into the next, the scenario focused on the emergency room itself. The viewers experienced the energy of the professionals who made emergency medicine their lives and the emergency room the first line of treatment for accident and violent crime victims, the elderly and homeless, mothers with small, frightened children, and people of all economic stations of life. All the while the video played, Joni's voice gently narrated the passage of time, the history of City General, and the success story of the emergency room.

Finally, the construction of the new clinic came into view. The conference attendees watched as the storage closet slowly transformed into a medical facility to which patients would be able to turn with confidence. They would receive state-of-the-art treatment from highly trained professionals with their best interests at heart. Their advocates from the emergency room became their medical service providers in the clinic setting.

The assembled conferees watched as the workmen constructed a half wall that formed the entrance and installed the door, window, and the lighting. They saw pale-yellow paint illuminate the dull, gray drywall. They watched as workmen strategically placed the nurses' station so that the nurse on duty would have a clear view of the doorway and the examining rooms in case someone needed an extra pair of hands. They witnessed the unpacking of the medical supplies and the examining room furnishings. And they felt the enthusiasm as the hospital's chief of staff threw the switch that illuminated the discreet sign in blue three-inch letters that read CLINIC. They cheered as Joni cut the tape that officially opened the facility three days ahead of schedule.

The audience rose to its feet in a standing ovation when the video ended. They were so impressed by the skill of the production and the emotions conveyed by the film that many of them had tears in their eyes. All of them cheered as if recognizing the talent of a great diva.

Those who had attended the conference with even the slightest reservations about the feasibility of opening a clinic were completely sold on the concept after viewing the video. They had seen how easily City General had turned nonproductive space into a much-needed facility. They could hardly wait to return to their hospitals and begin construction.

Accepting their praise modestly, Joni gazed toward the back of the auditorium. She was not surprised to see the chairman of the hospital's board and the chief of staff standing under the clock, but she was taken aback at the sight of the other man with them. She had not expected to see him until the next week.

Determined not to let Don Rivers's return detract from her moment, Joni turned her gaze away from him and back to the audience. Signaling her thanks and asking for the audience's attention, she opened the floor to questions. For the next thirty minutes, Joni smoothed concerns, clarified procedures, and encouraged the others to follow the example in hospital care that City General had so carefully laid.

When the last of the conference attendees left for lunch, Joni gathered her things and walked toward the exit. Walking toward her, the three men joined her in the aisle. Shaking her hand vigorously, the chief of staff Bob Turner said, "Wonderful presentation, Dr. Forest. Top-notch production. I don't think I've ever seen anyone use a video backdrop so effectively. Who was your PR firm? I'll have to hire them for my next talk."

"Thank you, Dr. Turner, but I must confess that I scripted the video myself and had the hospital's own PR department compile the film to suit my needs. It cost the ER budget practically nothing for me to participate in this conference . . . only my time and the production of the film, most of which we already had in archives," Joni replied with a broad smile.

"You did this yourself? I'm very impressed. I can see that you're a woman of varied talents. Well, I'll call on you the next time I'm asked to address a conference. Very impressive performance," Dr. Turner continued as he stepped aside.

"Allow me to second Bob's praise. I've seen several of your other production efforts when you've addressed the board, but you've outdone yourself on this one. Excellent job, Dr. Forest. If you're ever interested in leaving medicine, I could use someone like you on my administrative staff," the chairman of the board proclaimed as she patted Joni soundly on the shoulder.

"Thank you for the offer, Mrs. Grant, but I'm afraid that I'll never be able to wash off the smell of the ER and the taste of its excitement. Anything else would pale in comparison. However, I am glad that you enjoyed my presentation," Joni commented as she accepted her praise.

An awkward silence fell over them as the last man stepped up to offer his congratulations on a job well-done. The chairman of the board and the chief of staff watched as Don Rivers extended his hand. They knew about his conversation with her and her reaction to his proposed return. They wondered if this would be the honeymoon period between the two competitors or if the fur would start flying as soon as they spoke.

With a steady gaze that never left his face, Joni clasped Don's hand in hers. Graciously she listened as he said, "I've always known you to have tremendous people skills, Joni, but I've never seen you control an audience to this extent. Your presentation was most impressive. I'm looking forward to joining that tour of the ER and clinic after lunch."

"Thank you, Don, and welcome home. I'm sure there will be plenty of space for a few more if all of you would like to join us. I'll meet you in the private dining room in a few minutes. I need to stop by the ER first. Thank you again for your kind words," Joni replied as she looked from Don's face to the others.

Clutching her script, Joni hurried down the stairs to the emergency room. She had loved the presentation and the warm reception of her work. Even the questions and the attention from upper management had not put her on edge. However, the interaction with Don Rivers had given her a start.

"How did it go?" Randi asked as soon as Joni entered the busy ER. "Is it over?"

"It went beautifully. The video was incredibly well received. They gave me a standing ovation," Joni replied as she scanned the long list of patients. She felt guilty about spending her day in a conference when her staff was so overworked and could desperately use the extra hands.

"Then why the long face? I would have thought you'd be elated, flying high. What more could you want?" Randi demanded.

"I guess you haven't seen him yet. Don Rivers is here. He and the chairman of the board and the chief of staff sat in the back of the auditorium during my presentation," Joni replied as she drank the half a glass of orange juice Randi handed her.

Carefully Randi asked, "How did it feel to see him again?"

Throwing the empty paper cup into the trash can, Joni responded without hesitation, "I don't know. Part of me was glad to see him, but the other part wishes he'd never returned. He's still handsome with an unmistakable sex appeal. I'm not really sure how I feel. My heart didn't flutter and my breathing didn't come to a halt if that's what you mean. I admit that I felt a little tightening of my throat but that's not enough to make me wish for the old days. Don's the kind of man who needs a lot of attention. A relationship with him is high maintenance. I didn't have the time then, and I'm not sure that I do now," Joni replied honestly knowing that Randi would see through her subterfuge if she was less than truthful.

"Then, what's the problem?"

"You're right. I should be walking on air. They heard me handle the question-and-answer session. They saw the conference members congratulate me as we adjourned for lunch. They watched me control the room and prove my ability to work a crowd," Joni replied as she straightened the already neat sheets of paper in her folder before handing it to Randi for filing.

"Okay, so now I'm really confused. If everything went as well as or better than expected and if they saw your success, I don't understand why you're so down. You showed all of them that you have what it takes to be the chief of the ER. If Don has any sense, he'll head back to Greece," Randi stated matter-of-factly.

"I know that I'm overreacting, but there was something in

his voice that bothered me. It wasn't anything that he said. He was actually very polite and cordial as if he had only been away for a few days and not six months. Maybe that's it. He acted as if he had never left City General or me. He had the carriage of a man who was completely at home and comfortable in the presence of his bosses. He didn't seem to feel like an outsider after being away. He was so relaxed and at ease that he made me feel as if he were my boss. I can't believe it. I felt as if I were being evaluated. That's it exactly. It was as if my boss were congratulating me on a job well-done rather than someone who's up for consideration for the same job. It was as if nothing had changed between us at all. His hands were warm and his eyes penetrating. I almost felt as if we had turned back the clock and I should expect to have a quiet little lunch with him later," Joni lamented as she tapped herself on the forehead with her open palm and shook her head at the realization.

Randi studied her friend's wretched expression before asking, "So, what are you going to do? You have to lead a tour of the new clinic in exactly five minutes. You've got to brush this off."

"I know. I have to pull myself together and fast. I can't afford to lapse into the subordinate role whenever I see Don. I'm the ER chief; he isn't. I proposed the clinic; he didn't. I earned the respect and support of the board's subcommittees. This is my show and not his. I won't let him interfere in my work again. I intend to retain my position. This is my ER. He's neither my boss nor my lover anymore," Joni declared as she straightened her shoulders. She was once again ready for battle. The momentary disquiet had faded.

"Good. That's the Joni Forest I know. Go out there and show him who's boss," Randi replied giving her an appreciative pat on the back.

Marching off with a smile, Joni greeted the conference attendees as they approached the newly opened clinic. The facility, although small and stocked with secondhand furnishings, looked ready for the patients who would begin to fill the chairs and examining rooms the next day. Looking at it with a critical eye, Joni could see that the clinic had an aura of being professional yet inviting. Inexpensive prints and little potted plants added color and life to the small quarters.

Escorting the visitors through the examining rooms and explaining the nature of the care she intended to offer in the clinic, Joni hardly noticed the three dark-suited people standing at the back of the group. When she did, she was only vaguely aware of their smiles of approval. Her attention was riveted on the guests who took quick notes as she responded to their questions about funding, construction time, anticipated patient load, and staffing. She answered each question with confidence accompanied by actual and projected figures.

As she escorted Betsy Jones from Mercy Hospital to the door, Joni felt relieved that the conference had finally ended. She had been on the go and the center of attention since nine in the morning. She had talked until her throat felt dry and parched. She had been on her feet in high heels rather than her sensible walking shoes for so long that the muscles in her legs and her toes had cramped. Now Joni was ready to sit with her aching feet resting in a chair for a while.

Closing the door and relishing the absolute silence, Joni slipped into the battered leather chair and put her feet up on the desk. Turning toward the window, she looked across the driveway toward the park. People dashed along the sidewalk oblivious to one another as they protected their ears and noses from the cold December wind. She could tell from the way they walked with their heads down and their collars up that it had not warmed up since she came into the hospital at seven-thirty. Not even the brightness of the sun could offset the feeling of snow in the air.

Closing her eyes, Joni reflected on the success of the day. Despite the return of Don Rivers, the day had been all hers. Her well-publicized plans for the clinic had drawn the participants to the conference. Her presentation had wowed them to the point of speechlessness. And her answers to their questions had inspired them to consider opening clinics in their hospitals.

Joni did not hear the door open behind her until it was too late to ask the intruder to leave. Without turning, she asked, "Yes, what can I do for you? If this isn't urgent, try to find someone else to help you. Pretend you don't even see me."

"I would but it's difficult to ignore the person who has filled my chair so perfectly, especially since she's the same woman who stole my heart," the deep, gentle voice replied from the doorway behind her.

"I returned it to you long before you left. Besides, that ended much more than six months ago. I'd almost forgotten. We promised that we'd never speak of it again," Joni replied without turning from the window.

"I haven't forgotten, and I don't think that you really have either. I asked you to marry me, but you turned me down," the voice continued without coming any farther into the room.

"It never would have worked. We were both too busy and too driven," Joni answered without moving from where she sat.

"Things have changed since then . . . we've changed. At least, I know that I have. Being away from home and you gave me time to think," he said anxiously, hoping that Joni would turn so that he could read her face. He needed to see her eyes.

"I have too. I'm married to my job now. So you see, you left Greece for nothing," Joni responded as she turned toward the door and Don Rivers.

"One thing I've learned, Joni, is that a job, no matter how much you love it, is a poor substitute for having someone special in your life. Don't make the same mistakes I have. I never should have left knowing how I felt about you. I haven't been able to put you out of my mind," Don replied, unwilling to accept her answer.

"We had wonderful times together that I'll never forget, but it ended. Maybe if you'd faced it, you wouldn't have had to go to Greece," Joni replied calmly.

"No, the setting only made it easier for me to think about the things I hadn't done and the wonderful woman I'd left behind. I'm ready to make amends," Don commented as he shifted his weight. He would have liked to have taken the seat beside the desk, but he could not move until Joni invited him into the office. He could already sense that he was disturbing the serenity of her quiet time. He was not sure that he was a welcome visitor.

"How long have you been back?" Joni asked casually. She wanted Don to feel that her interest in him was simply polite, just as it would have been with any other old friend.

"I returned a few days after our conversation. I had planned to travel a bit, but I couldn't focus on anything except coming home and seeing you again," Don answered from where he stood near the door.

"And getting your old job back, don't forget that. Yes, I'm sure you've been thinking of me, Don. I've moved into your office, and I don't intend to move out again. I'm sure I've been on your mind a lot," Joni replied harshly. She wanted Don to understand that he could not sweet-talk her out of the emergency room-chief position.

"Yes, I want my job back, and I have no fear that I'll got it. Most importantly, however, is my determination to have you in my life again. This time I will not accept no for an answer," Don replied as he stepped closer.

Rising to her full height, Joni squared her shoulders and said, "Let's get a few things straight right now, Don. First, six months have passed and things have changed around here. This place runs smoothly because of policies that I've put into place. I've made this ER my own. The new clinic wouldn't even exist if it weren't for me. I won't simply roll over and give up the ER to you without a fight.

"Second, I'm not looking for a relationship with you or anyone else at the moment. This job consumes all of my time.

I don't have anything left at the end of the day. I don't want someone waiting for me at home with the expectation that I'll be able to engage in casual conversation, cook meals, and provide entertainment. Some days I'm so exhausted when I leave here at night that I even forget to feed my cat. I don't doubt that this job wreaked havoc on your home life. I don't intend to give it a chance to do the same thing to mine. For now it *is* my life. You're wasting your time and mine."

"I appreciate your position and your openness. I'm saddened to see that we can't work out something amicable between us. I won't force myself on you, but it's only fair for me to tell you that I won't back away either," Don responded as he turned and left the office.

Watching him leave, Joni slowly unfolded her arms and relaxed. She could feel the stiffness ease from her shoulders and face as the door closed. Although she had not realized it at the time, she had been standing with her teeth tightly clenched and her hands balled into fists tucked into her armpits. She relaxed her back and shifted into a more casual position.

As she gazed out the window again, Joni reflected on the relationship that had ended six months ago. She had missed him at first, but she quickly found that running the emergency room occupied all of her energy. The more hours she spent in the emergency room, the less she thought about Don. Then one day, she didn't think about him at all.

Now Don had returned to reclaim the emergency room with the assumption that she was part of the package. Joni was equally determined not to give him the opportunity to do either. She had worked too hard and given up too much to allow the emergency room and the clinic to slip through her fingers. She did not care how hard her heart pounded against her ribs. Joni would not let her old feelings for Don interfere with her job.

Studying the lovely roses, Joni saw Randi's reflection in the window before she heard her voice. She was not startled when her friend demanded, "Well, tell me everything. What did Don have to say? I saw him leave here looking very dejected."

Selecting her words carefully, Joni replied, "Nothing much. He only wanted to say that he's back in town and hopes that our relationship can pick up where it ended. I told him that I was too busy. I assured him that the ER has become my life and that I don't have time for another lover."

"Well, maybe he'll leave you alone this time. He's such a louse," Randi proclaimed loyally. She had lost all respect for Don when his relationship with Joni ended. Randi thought that he should have tried harder to convince Joni to reconsider.

"No, I don't think that this is the last I'll see of Don Rivers. He wants his job back, and I don't intend to give it up. That should make for considerable conflict between us. We'll see what his next move will be," Joni replied.

With a deep scowl, Randi asked, "Do you think he'll try something, Joni?"

"Of course he will. He wants to be the chief of this ER as much as I do. That's really what brought him back here, not me. For now at least, he has the time to spend plotting, planning, wining, and dining that I don't. There will be another move on his part. This meeting was purely social. The professional encounter has yet to come. When it does, I'll be ready. Anyway, it's too late in the day to worry about him now. Let's go home."

"Fine by me. It's started to snow. Maybe we'll have some decent skiing this year. Last year was a real bust. I hardly even got my skis wet," Randi complained as she pretended to swish down an imaginary mountainside.

Pulling on her coat, Joni said with a laugh, "You'd better be careful before you break something."

"Piece of cake," Randi replied followed by *"ouch!"* as something snapped in her back.

"What was that your mother always told you about a hard head and a soft back?" Joni reminded her buddy.

"Maybe you're right," Randi conceded as she limped out of the darkened office and down the hall.

Looking behind her, Joni could see the rug and its little spot of color reflected against the white of the driveway and the trees in the park. The snow had already fallen thickly enough to cover the grass and stick to the road. She hoped that people would drive carefully on their way home from work. She did not want anyone to call her back to the emergency room that night. She needed time to organize her thoughts. Don had caught her off guard this time. She wanted to be ready for their next encounter when more than old memories would be at stake.

Six

Patients holding numbers, sitting on chairs, and leaning against walls packed the clinic and tested the energy of its staff. The patients overflowed the boundaries of the clinic and filtered into the emergency room's waiting area. They covered every age group, ethnic classification, and economic status. To Joni, it looked as if all of Baltimore had a boil to lance, a strain to bandage, or a cough to medicate.

"Who are all these people? I had no idea that so many of them would come all at once. I certainly hope we can handle the load," Joni exclaimed in disbelief as she stood beside Randi, who had been doing double duty between the emergency room and the clinic since the clinic had opened at seven-thirty.

"Incredible, isn't it. If this keeps up, you'll need to enlarge your space after the first week of operation. None of your figures indicated that this many people would seek the clinic for medical treatment. You've certainly tapped into a gold mine," Randi remarked as she surveyed the masses in need of treatment.

"I wonder how much of this is novelty. We're new and they want to check us out. We'll see what happens in about a month. It might look like a ghost town in here," Joni responded as she dodged the hurrying staff.

"We'll see. I have a feeling that this popularity will last. This kind of turnout is more than curiosity. I'm certainly glad we have the extra PAs and the nurses union behind us. We'll need all the help we can get to keep this load under control," Randi remarked as she scurried away.

By noon, the backlog of patients had dwindled, and Joni and Randi were finally able to take a breather. Looking around the waiting room, Joni remarked to Sally, who stood beside her scribbling notes in her last patient's folder, "This was certainly a successful opening day. At last we can have a minute to get caught up on the paperwork."

Without taking her eyes from the pile of charts at her right, Sally said, "It's about time, too. My handwriting was becoming more illegible with each new patient. I must have seen close to twenty patients myself. Granted, some of them only needed minor care, but I don't think I've ever been so busy."

"I didn't expect this kind of turnout. Thank goodness I scheduled the ER physicians to rotate through the clinic. We would still be swamped without their extra hands," Joni replied as she attacked her pile of files.

"I hope this isn't the lull before the storm. I'd like a nice quiet afternoon with a steady stream of patients but not a downpour of them. Let's hope that this was simply a reaction to the grand-opening sign on the front of the hospital. We won't make it to the evening if the traffic remains as heavy as it was this morning. I'll see you after I grab some lunch," Sally added as she carried her files to the waiting cart.

"Don't rush. You deserve a nice long break," Joni replied as she scanned the empty room. For the moment, all was blissfully quiet. With any luck, she would be able to get caught up on her charts and the emergency room duties that she had neglected all morning.

Joni was so busy with her work that she barely noticed the figure that came to rest beside the nurses' station. Waving her hand, she said absently, "I'll be with you in just a minute. Take a seat if you don't mind."

"Doctor, I'm afraid that I cannot wait. I need help right now," the deep, demanding voice answered.

Looking up, Joni gazed into the expressionless face of a man who did not appear to be in distress. Giving his neat, navy blue suit, white shirt, and striped tie a closer look, Joni asked, "What seems to be the problem, sir?"

Leaning a little closer, the man lowered his voice and replied in a voice tinged with a southern accent, "I am afraid that I have been shot. I would appreciate your assistance as I am feeling quite faint."

As means of proof, the man pulled open his topcoat and jacket to expose the spreading bloodstain on the right side of his shirt. From midchest to above his belt and immediately below his armpit, an expanding deep red stickiness covered the crispness of the white shirt. With a slight wince, he allowed the coat to close.

Speaking through tightly clenched teeth, the man added, "For your own well-being, doctor, I suggest that you act quickly. If I'm not mistaken, my associate has just entered the hospital's front entrance and will be joining me in a matter of minutes. She will not take kindly to finding me standing here in this deplorable condition."

Quickly pushing a wheelchair to the other side of the desk, Joni said, "I'll take you into one of the ER examining rooms immediately."

"No, not the emergency room," the man objected softly. "There are too many security officers lingering there. Right here will be fine."

As the man settled onto the table and accepted Joni's offer of assistance in removing his clothing, a tall, blond woman of about thirty joined them. She also wore a business suit with sensible shoes, dark stockings, and a white blouse. With her briefcase slung securely over her shoulder, she could have been a corporate executive or attorney. However, Joni had the distinct impression that these two were anything but law-abiding citizens.

"How bad is it, doctor?" the woman demanded urgently as she positioned herself between Joni and the door. From where she stood, she had a clear view of the emergency room waiting area, the nurses' station, security guards, and the exit.

"I can't tell until I probe for the slug," Joni replied quickly.

Helping the man lie on his side, Joni quickly draped and cleaned the area. The entry site of the bullet had done considerable damage to the surrounding tissue. Quickly, she injected the area with painkiller and waited momentarily for it to take effect.

"What are you waiting for, doctor?" the woman snarled in a tart Southern drawl that might have been lovely if she had not spat out her words. "We don't have all day."

"I'm probing the site now, miss. There's been quite a bit of tissue damage. I'm afraid that the wound is too deep for my instruments. We'll have to X ray and transfer him to surgery. I can't do anything more for him down here," Joni replied as she turned away from the man's pale, contorted face.

"You'll have to fix him up the best you can. We won't be able to stay here for long. There isn't time for X rays and transferring him to surgery," the woman barked without taking her eyes from the door.

"I won't do anything that would jeopardize his life. I must have an X ray, at the very least. We have a unit here in the clinic. I'm the only one here. No one will see him," Joni responded in a calm, level voice, although her heart pounded viciously in her chest.

Looking at her partner, the woman softened her tone and replied, "Do what you must but do it quickly. We haven't any time to waste."

Swinging the machine into place, Joni snapped pictures to confirm what she already suspected. The bullet had lodged between two of the man's ribs and would require surgical removal. Taking a deep breath, Joni returned to the examining table on which the man lay looking lifeless. The woman stood almost as still by his side.

"There's nothing I can do for your associate. He needs an operation to remove the slug. We're not set up for that in this clinic. I can transfer him to the surgical unit, but, other than that, it's beyond my control," Joni advised slowly and deliberately. She did not want to turn the worry on the woman's face into anger. An instinct told her not to question the contents of the briefcase.

"Your name tag says that you're a surgeon, which means that you are qualified to operate. Right, Dr. Forest? Well, then, operate. Right here and now. You may not transfer him to the surgical unit. We don't have time for an overnight stay," the woman hissed through tightly clenched teeth.

"You don't understand. I don't have the correct tools. My blundering around without the proper instruments might do more damage to the underlying tissue than good. We don't keep the more sophisticated supplies in this clinic. Let me at least transfer him to the ER. We're better equipped to handle this problem there," Joni stated frankly as she tried to reason with the woman.

"No," the man whispered, "we can't risk any further exposure. I need your help, doctor, but we have to do this my way."

"All right, but I warn you that without the proper support, I am in no way responsible for the results," Joni conceded reluctantly as she quickly took stock of the instruments she would need and hurried off.

"Don't tell anyone about us, doctor. I'll be watching you," the woman instructed as she took her position beside the nurses' station. Turning her body slightly, she could watch her associate and the emergency room at the same time.

"I won't share any more than necessary, but you'll have to trust me," Joni replied with authority, although she could feel the stress of working under such hostile conditions.

"Yes, just as you'll have to believe that I'll use this if those officers follow you back here," the woman replied as she brandished her weapon.

"They won't follow me. I'll close this door to keep out any patients," Joni responded as she partially closed the sliding door that separated the clinic from the emergency room waiting area. Walking as calmly as possible, she rapidly crossed the space between the clinic and Randi's nurses' station desk.

"What's up? You look upset," Randi asked as she studied Joni's flushed face.

"I'll have to fill you in on the details later. Could you get me some type O blood while I collect a surgical kit? I have a patient who refuses to allow me to transfer him to the ER and insists on having the procedure done in the clinic. Also, cancel all rotations to the clinic until further notice," Joni instructed as she collected the gauze, sponges, surgical tape, and instruments that she would need to remove the slug from the man's chest.

"Are you in danger? Should I call security?" Randi queried as she quickly stacked two units of blood on the pile of supplies in Joni's arms. She stood so that her back was turned toward the clinic.

"No, don't do anything. I'll be all right as long as I do exactly as they ask. The sight of security will only cause them to react. I'll be just fine," Joni answered as she ran her eyes over her collection to be sure that she had not forgotten anything.

"Do you want me to go with you? You might need some help," Randi offered as she laid her hand lightly on Joni's arm.

"I can't ask you to do that. They're armed. The man appears too weak to do anything, but the woman is definitely on edge," Joni explained as she smiled weakly at her buddy.

"You didn't ask me. I volunteered. Give me some of that stuff. I might as well make myself useful from the beginning," Randi replied as she joined Joni on the walk back to the clinic and the waiting woman.

"I told you not to bring anyone with you," the woman challenged Joni and Randi as soon as they approached.

"Randi's a very capable nurse. I might need her assistance during the operation. Besides, having her with me will help the process move faster. Shall we get started?" Joni replied in a calm voice that belied her nervousness. She refused to let the blond woman see that the gun she held inside her handbag had caused her any worry.

"After you, doctor," the woman replied as she stepped aside.

Hooking up an IV and placing the blood in readiness, Joni and Randi opened the surgical kit, donned their gloves and scrubs, and connected the man to monitors. From his complexion alone, they could tell that the wound and loss of blood had greatly reduced his strength.

As she worked, Joni said, "I don't know what you plan to accomplish by taking your associate away from here when I finish the surgery. He's in no condition to travel and will be very groggy for some time following the procedure. You should let me admit him."

"No, that's out of the question. The police would be all over him before I could reach the sidewalk. He goes with me, and that's final. Give him as little sedative as possible. He has to be able to get into the car. He'll be all right. He's tough," the woman replied with determination in her voice. She would not be swayed from her plans even though her partner's life lay in the balance.

"I'll do as you order, but he'll be very uncomfortable," Joni responded as she made the initial incision through the skin and into the muscle of the man's chest.

The wounded man groaned in his sleep from the pain of the incision and the probing instruments. Fortunately, his vital signs remained steady, although his moans increased in intensity as she cleaned the wound. His bound hands clenched in reaction to every move Joni made with the scalpel.

"See, I told you he could take it. During the Civil War, they only had bottles of booze to dull the pain after the medicines ran out. They survived and so will he. My partner knows that we don't have time for babying ourselves," the woman gloated as she watched him suffer through the probing.

"If I could put him under deeper, he wouldn't feel anything," Joni argued without any result.

"No chance, doctor. I told you that he has to be able to walk out of here. Now, hurry up. You've had long enough to remove one slug. They work faster than that on television," the woman ordered as she gazed nervously at the new patients milling around the emergency room waiting area, confused by the closed sign on the clinic's door. It would not be long before someone came to investigate the gathering and the unexpected closure of the popular medical facility.

"Yes, they work faster on television, but this is real and your partner's life depends on my steady fingers. Now, don't rush me, and everything will turn out all right. How did he get this wound anyway? You two don't look like the bank-robber types," Joni commented as she slowly extracted the slug and dropped it into the pan Randi held for her. Its dull thud echoed in the empty clinic.

"Let's just say that it's an occupational hazard in our line of work. You don't need to know anything more about us than that. As a matter of fact, the less you know, the better off you'll be. You won't be able to help the police track us down," the woman replied as she continued to survey the waiting room.

Quickly, Joni sutured the incision and bandaged the site as the woman's partner began to waken. His eyelids fluttered slowly, and the color started to return to his pale lips. Looking around the room, he smiled slowly at Joni and mouthed a silent "thank you" before slipping into sleep again.

Checking his vital signs, Randi offered, "I think he'll be all right without the transfusion. However, the doctor's right; your partner should stay as quiet as possible."

"Thanks for the advice, ladies, and for the care you've given him. Unfortunately, we have to leave your lovely establishment. My partner will have plenty of time to rest as soon as we're away from here. Help me get him into that wheelchair. You, Randi, will have to come with me to the car. He's too heavy for me to handle alone. The doctor needs to reopen the clinic so that no one will be the wiser," the woman replied as she stepped up to the table and gently shook the patient.

The man immediately woke up and smiled lovingly into the woman's face. Watching them, Joni knew instinctively that they were more than business partners. She could read the affection in their eyes as they looked at each other. The woman, despite her brave exterior and sharp tone, had not taken her eyes from her partner's face for more than a moment during the surgery. She had shown more than collegial concern for his health.

The three women struggled to ease the groggy man into the wheelchair. As Randi pushed it into the now-full waiting room, the woman turned and hissed, "Don't think about reporting us to your security people, doctor. I'll have my gun pointed at Randi the whole time. Until she's back inside the hospital, you keep still. Tend to your patients, but don't you say a thing about us to anyone. Understood?"

"Completely," Joni replied as she looked into Randi's brave face.

"Don't worry," the woman added, "she'll be back in no time. I don't want the complication of hostages. Besides, you did what I asked of you. I owe you one for saving my partner's life. We're even now."

For a few minutes, Joni stood glued to the spot as she watched Randi and the woman roll the wounded man out of the hospital's massive sliding doors. Not wanting to alarm the waiting patients, she said slowly, "Please take numbers. I'm sure you remember who was here ahead of you. I regret any inconvenience the delay might have caused you, but that patient needed extra care. I'll be with you in just one minute."

Quickly, Joni restored examining room one to order with hands that trembled violently. Stopping to catch her breath, she leaned against the wall and covered her face with her cold hands. Her entire body shook from the stress of the operation and from her concern about Randi. She hoped that the woman would keep her word and send Randi back without harming her.

Straightening her shoulders and composing her face, Joni returned to the waiting room to find that the physician's assistant and the nurse had reported for duty as soon as they saw that the clinic had reopened. She knew that they studied her face in hopes of discovering the reason behind the unexpected closing, but she was confident that they saw nothing. Joni watched as they shrugged and handed her a chart while they each took one. Leaving the nurses' station, Joni joined them and rushed into the examining rooms, followed by patients who were anxious to receive their treatment and be on their way.

As Joni worked on the sprained finger of a teenage girl, she constantly checked the door to see if Randi had returned. Without knowing how far away the woman had parked, she could not estimate Randi's return time. She could come back in only a few minutes or even as many as thirty if she had to walk any distance in the crowded streets. Until Randi returned, Joni tried to put her mind on her patients as much as possible.

By the time Joni had extracted a deeply embedded nail from a construction worker's foot and administered the necessary tetanus shot, she was almost beside herself with worry. Forty minutes had passed since Randi had left with the woman and her partner. Joni's mind played out every imaginable scenario to explain the delayed return. As each one ran its course, she became more anxious for her friend's safety.

Scribbling the last notes in the man's chart, Joni could no longer convince herself to wait calmly. With only three patients waiting, she felt that her presence was not absolutely necessary. Turning to the nurse she said, "Trisha, I need to run a quick errand. Vince is on his way to relieve me. I'll check back with you when I return. Everything looks under control for now."

"Sure, Joni, we're fine. We'll see you in a little bit. Is there anything I can do to help?" Trisha replied as she studied Joni's drawn face. She had been watching Joni as she functioned on instinct and practice. She had wondered what had so upset her that her mind was not really on her job.

"No, thanks, I have to handle this alone. I'll be back in a few minutes. If Randi returns, tell her that I went out to look for her," Joni explained quickly as she pulled on her coat and grabbed a sweater for Randi.

Rushing onto the busy sidewalk, Joni headed south in the direction in which she had seen Randi and the woman push the wheelchair. Fearing the worst, she searched each alley as she hurried along. Glancing quickly at each parked car, she looked for any sign of her friend.

Joni stopped when she reached the corner. Standing at the busy intersection, she had no idea in which direction to turn. If she continued in a southward direction, she would reach the busy harbor. She doubted that the woman would have parked in any of those expensive and always crowded lots. Although Joni did not know how the man had been shot, she could not imagine anyone engaged in a crime taking the time to activate the parking ticket machine or pay the attendant on the way out.

Looking to the east, Joni only saw lines of taillights as people made their way out of town toward Route 95 and Washington, D.C. High-rise apartments and hotels covered every block, but she could not see any place where the woman might have parked her car. Unless she lived in one of those buildings, there was no reason for her to turn right at the intersection.

To the north lay Monument Street, Johns Hopkins University, the old baseball stadium, and, eventually, the road out of town. Office buildings, music schools, and museums dotted the path along the downtown section, and stately homes with tall fences lined the posh upscale neighborhood on the outskirts of the real Baltimore. The couples' appearance said that they were not ordinary burglars. They had probably robbed someone who lived in one of those homes. Joni did not think that it was likely that they would return to the area that might be crawling with police.

Deciding on the western path, Joni rounded the corner into the strong winter wind. It stung her eyes and caused tears to cascade down her red cheeks. Brushing them aside with her gloved hand, she bowed her head against the force and trudged onward.

Joni could feel her heart pounding from anxiety for Randi's safety as she continued to search every shadow along the quiet street. She did not know which way they had traveled when they left the front of the hospital, but Joni had hoped that she would find Randi within a few blocks of the building. Now that she had walked almost four blocks past the hospital's perimeter, Joni was really worried.

With the wind pushing at her back, Joni retraced her steps. She turned right and walked along the street directly behind the hospital. It lay almost completely in the shadow of the massive structure. A gale whipped through the wind tunnel created by the hospital and the medical library across the street.

Joni continued to press against the wind as she stared into the recesses of the hospital's back service entrances. Seeing no one lurking in the doorways, she turned her attention to the few cars parked at the meters along the street. On the windshields of several of them fluttered faded parking tickets and tow-away notices. The cars had been parked illegally on the street since the last time the overworked Baltimore police did a sweep of the area.

She was ready to return to the hospital when something unusual about one of the cars caught her attention. Slowly, Joni walked toward the third vehicle for a closer look. Unlike the others that were covered with rain-spotted dirt and dust, the black station wagon looked clean in the afternoon shadows.

Approaching it carefully, Joni ran her finger along the hood.

Looking closely, she saw that little dirt clung to the white wool of her gloves. Although the parking ticket was as faded as those attached to the other cars, the station wagon had not sat in the open for long.

It was not unusual for people to place old tickets on their illegally parked cars. They wanted the police to think that someone had already ticketed the vehicle. They hoped to avoid getting yet another citation.

Joni's skin tingled as she moved slowly down the side of the car. She could feel the hair on the back of her neck stand up with anticipation. Her heart pounded louder with each step along the deserted street. With her breath escaping in quick puffs, Joni slowly looked into the front seat. Finding it empty except for several discarded fast food soda cups and sandwich wrappers, she peeked into the backseat. A paper bag stuffed full of carefully folded newspapers sat on the seat next to a few empty beer cans and a pair of dirty torn tennis shoes.

Joni felt tension gripping at her throat and chest as she walked toward the cargo area. Breathless in the cold air, she peered into the space instinctively knowing that she would find something there. But, she did not want to see it.

As her eyes adjusted to the darkness of the station wagon's storage area, Joni could make out the figure of a person covered by a filthy gray blanket. The person's head was partially visible. The disheveled brown hair covered the face and hid the features.

Gasping, Joni whispered, "Oh, my God, it's Randi!"

Joni pounded frantically on the wagon's window with her knotted fists. "Wake up! Randi, can you hear me? Wake up!" she shouted as she shook the car.

Slowly the figure began to move. As it did, the hair slipped from its face revealing a youthful, bearded man. Blinking, he stared at her and smiled. "What's up, sweetheart?" he asked thickly.

Joni was so stunned that she stood motionless for a few

minutes, staring at the sleepy man. Shaking herself from the trance, she replied through her tight throat, "Sorry, I thought you were someone else. Are you all right in there? I'm a doctor. Do you need help?"

"Everything's cozy in here, doc. You're welcome to join me if you'd like," the man replied with another quick, drunken grin. When she hesitated, he said, "Thanks for asking."

As he gave a shaky thumbs-up and turned over, Joni felt the tears slide down her cheeks. Fear for her friend's safety once again gripped her insides. Randi could be anywhere or even dead.

Pulling her coat more tightly around her shivering body, Joni rushed up the street and around the corner to the front of the hospital. With every step she prayed that Randi would be sitting inside drinking a cup of coffee and waiting to tell her about her treatment at the hands of the woman and her partner.

As she burst into the emergency room, Joni saw that someone had called the hospital's security patrol and Baltimore's police department. Three uniformed officers stood at the nurses' station blocking her view of the nurse on duty. They were heavily engaged in questioning whoever stood on the other side.

With her heart pounding loudly in her ears, Joni advanced on the desk. Not waiting for the officers to notice her, she muscled her way between them. As they slowly parted for her, she burst into the tiny space between their bodies and the desk.

"Randi!" Joni exclaimed as she rushed forward and pulled her friend into her arms. Tears of relief glistened in her eyes as she continued, "Are you all right? I was so worried that I went out searching for you. I brought along this sweater for you."

"I'm fine. They didn't do anything to hurt me. Actually, the woman was very appreciative of the care we gave her partner. From the wild way you look, I'd say I'm in better shape than you are," Randi replied as she wrapped her arms around Joni. The two friends clung to each other so fiercely that it was difficult to tell which one was more relieved at their reunion.

"I just knew that they had hurt you or kidnapped you. I was so worried. I was so afraid that I'd never see you again," Joni said as she held Randi close.

"I must say that the same thoughts ran through my mind, but I'm fine, really. There isn't a scratch on me. But I am glad to be back here. I don't ever want to go through something like that again," Randi commented as she shook herself at the memory.

"Ladies, we'd like to finish our investigation if you don't mind. We might have some success in catching these creeps if we act quickly," Sergeant Hewlett interrupted.

"Sorry," Joni said as she stepped back. "Can I do anything to help you?"

"We'll get to you as soon as Randi finishes telling us her story. Now, Randi, where did you say they left you?" Sergeant Amos asked. Sergeant Amos and his partner were the regular officers who patrolled the neighborhood around the hospital and knew all of them on a first-name basis. He and his partner always attended the emergency room's parties.

"They drove north to Monument Street and left me at the Walter's Art Gallery on the south corner. From what I could tell, they continued over the hill. I couldn't see where they went from there," Randi replied as she handed Joni a tissue.

Joni listened carefully as Randi told of her ordeal with the man and woman. "Neither one of them did anything to hurt me. He wasn't in any condition to do anything, but she didn't even tie my hands. She asked me to sit in the back, and she secured the doors using the car's childproof locks. When she was ready for me to get out, she unlocked them, waited patiently for me to get out, and then drove away. I never really felt threatened at any time, except that I knew she had a weapon in her purse," Randi replied as she blew her nose.

"Can you describe the car, Randi?" Sergeant Amos asked.

"It was a large, black Buick. That's all I know, Mitch. It smelled new. There were no unusual markings on it," Randi replied with a shrug.

Turning to Joni, Sergeant Amos said, "All right, Joni, it's your turn. How did you happen to treat this man in the clinic?"

"I was finishing up a chart when he walked up to the desk. I didn't think much about him until he showed me his bloodstained shirt. I wheeled him to an examining room and by that time his partner, the woman, had joined us. She insisted that I close the clinic and operate on him to remove the bullet myself. Neither of them would say how he got it. She insisted that I work quickly and with a minimum of anesthesia. Other than that, she didn't have much to say," Joni replied with a shudder as she relived the horror of the experience.

"Did either of them give any indication as to which way they planned to go when they left City General?" Sergeant Hewlett asked.

"Not while they were here. Other than their mentioning a car, I know nothing about their escape plans. They were well dressed in conservative business attire, carried briefcases, and spoke in soft, refined Southern accents. Nothing about them stands out as spectacular. Even their suits were nothing special. They weren't designer, but they were of a good-quality wool that flowed with their movements. That's all I know about them," Joni answered without hesitation.

Randi added, "They appeared to be more than merely partners, too. Neither of them slipped up and used a name, but the way they looked at each other showed a deep affection, maybe even love. I had the impression that they were married."

"Did you think that, too, Joni?" Sergeant Amos asked, following the line of questioning.

"I sure did. Neither of them wore a wedding ring, but there was definitely something on the order of devotion between them. They might have been sister and brother, now that I think about it. It might not have been amorous love that we saw on their faces but rather the familial kind. Whatever their relationship, they're very close. The only thing they paid attention to was their briefcases," Joni responded.

"I'm sure the woman never let those cases out of her sight," Sergeant Amos remarked.

"The man wouldn't put his down even as he leaned against the counter in obvious pain. She stood with them beside her feet the entire time she waited for me to operate on him. The cases were made of fairly soft cowhide leather and appeared lightweight, not at all like the old-fashioned heavy cases that weigh a ton when empty. Hers had a wide, padded shoulder strap that she wore across her body. Both were burgundy. His was the usual shape and size with a matching finger-grip handle and brass stud feet. They both had four-digit combination locks. Oh, yes, I could smell the newness of the leather coming from both of them," Joni commented in the hopes that the details might help the investigation.

"He was very pale when they left me on the street. You might want to alert all the hospitals and hotels around here about them. He might need attention during the night. I don't think she would allow him to suffer or die without taking him to a hospital or doctor's office," Randi interjected.

Joni offered, "They both wore their brown hair in conservative styles that showed little if any gray. We have X rays if they'll do you any good, but, unfortunately, we didn't have time to type the blood. The only samples I can give you are on the surgical tools I used. I stashed those under the counter in a plastic bag before I started working on other patients."

"We'll gladly take anything you can offer. Hair samples,

blood, tissue . . . anything. If either of you think of anything more, you know where to find us. That was a good idea to keep those surgical items for us," Sergeant Amos said as he followed Joni to the clinic.

"Do you think you'll be able to catch them? Has anyone reported a robbery?" Joni asked as she handed him the carefully preserved surgical instruments, scrubs, and linens.

"I hope something turns up. So far, no one has reported anything. I doubt that they robbed a bank. Their description doesn't match the profile of the kind of people who would do that. I suspect that they might have hit a private home and been discovered or they shook down a wealthy man who shot at them for their troubles. No one has reported a theft. Whoever it is either doesn't want the exposure for whatever unexplained reason or doesn't feel that whatever the crooks stole is worth the publicity. We'll have to wait and see," Sergeant Hewlett replied.

Sergeant Amos added, "The best chance for apprehending them will come if they visit a doctor in the next few days. If the doctor manages to call the police while they're in the office, we can surround them on the spot. Until something breaks, these things will come in handy. Right now, the most we can do is try to locate the late-model black Buick Randi rode in. Maybe we'll get lucky and find something there, but I doubt it. This couple strikes me as smooth operators.

"We'll check the FBI just in case they might be looking for kidnappers who fit this profile, but that's not likely. Taking Randi along for a ride appeared to have been an afterthought rather than part of the plan," Sergeant Amos said as he carried the evidence back toward the emergency room and the exit.

"Thank you both. We'll let you know when we find them. We'll need you at the lineup," Sergeant Hewlett said as he and Sergeant Amos eased through the busy waiting room to their car parked at the emergency entrance.

Turning toward Randi, Joni asked, "Well, what do you think? Will they ever catch them?"

"I don't know. Unless the man needs help, I wouldn't think it would be too easy to track them. There are an awful lot of black Buick sedans on the road," Randi replied.

"The car was probably rented anyway. Well, let's hope we never see them again. That kind of excitement I don't need in my day," Joni commented as she and Randi headed for the lounge and a cup of steaming-hot coffee.

Settling together on the sofa, Randi said, "I wonder what makes people like that couple become thieves. They were refined and appeared educated. What motivated them?"

"I guess we won't know that until the police catch them. I can't help but think that they're upscale jewel, bond, or art thieves who just happened to get shot by one of their victims. I just don't see them doing the ordinary burglary kind of thing," Joni replied as she sipped her coffee. Just as she had not noticed the police cruiser in the driveway in her concern for Randi, she had not realized that she was chilled from her search of the neighborhood. The cup of hot coffee felt deliciously warm in her hands.

Rushing up to them, Don burst into the conversation and asked, "Are you all right? I heard the news while on the golf course. I came as soon as I could. Has anyone been hurt?"

"We're fine, Don," Randi replied with sarcasm that she reserved only for him. "I was just kidnapped, that's all. Who were you playing, the chief of staff?"

"Don't take my head off. I'm ready to help if you need me," Don countered with a helpless lift of his hands.

"Everything's under control. Thanks for checking on us. Sorry to interrupt your game, but we're really okay. Randi was released without physical injury," Joni replied gently seeing that he really was concerned and not just acting the part of an administrator.

"I wasn't doing too well anyway. I couldn't concentrate. It

seems I have more pressing matters on my mind," Don commented with a handsome smile that he directed toward Joni.

"Oh, yeah. Like what? Taking the ER away from Joni?" Randi cut into the conversation not liking either the expression on his face or her friend's reaction to it.

Bracing to do battle, Don replied, "Not that it's any of your business, Randi, but I didn't come back here only for the job. I need Joni in my life and won't take no for an answer this time."

"You'll win her back and then leave again. I thought she said she was over you," Randi bristled. She did not try to hide her loathing.

"That's enough, you two. Randi, you know that I'm the one who broke off the relationship. Don, I appreciate your attention, but I think you should leave us now. We're okay and you're upsetting Randi, who's already had a rough day," Joni interjected as she tried to make peace.

"I'm going. I'll call you tonight," Don replied, leaving before Randi could jab at him again.

"Call you? He calls you?" Randi inquired incredulously. "What happened to wanting him permanently out of your life?"

"Leave it alone, Randi. I've told you before that I'm too busy for a romance, old or new. Don's lonely and I'm a good listener. Besides, I still enjoy his conversation," Joni instructed as she returned her attention to the cup of coffee.

They drank their coffee in silence until Trisha stuck her head into the room. "I hate to bother you two after all you've been through, but I need a surgeon in examining room two for a woman who lacerated the palm of her hand while slicing a bagel. Randi, there's a call for you at the desk. It seems as if a reporter from the *Sun* wants to interview you about your kidnapping. News travels fast in this little city," Trisha said, looking very apologetically at Joni's and Randi's tired faces.

"No problem, we're on our way," Joni replied as she returned her empty cup to the pile on the table.

Walking together, the two friends left the quiet of the lounge for the turmoil of the emergency room. Each one hoped that the rest of the day would pass without incident. Joni could not remember a time when she had been so frightened for the safety of someone she loved.

Seven

The next day, the news of the clinic's involvement with the alleged robbers captured front page in all the local papers. Every television screen flashed Joni's and Randi's pictures. When the pair arrived at the hospital, the waiting room already overflowed with people who hoped to see the celebrities. Some of the patients were genuinely ill, but many only wanted to show their support of the brave duo. Even members of the administrative staff lined up to give them a rousing cheer.

Although Joni was not surprised by his visit, she did not welcome Don Rivers warmly when he stopped by her office to add his support. Setting a cup of coffee in front of her, Don eased into the chair beside her desk and waited until she finished balancing the emergency room budget for the week. It was obvious from the way in which he slowly sipped his coffee that Don was in no rush.

When Joni laid down her pencil, Don said, "Congratulations on making the papers first for the opening of the clinic and now for your bravery in the face of danger. It's not often that an emergency room doctor gains that level of celebrity."

Smiling graciously, Joni replied, "This isn't what I had in mind as publicity for the clinic. Still, I'll take what I can get. The notoriety certainly hasn't hurt our business. It's amazing how many people feel more comfortable with our services now that the press has singled us out for recognition."

Don studied Joni's face for any lingering signs of their old friendship. Finding nothing but professional regard, he said, "We need to talk. Can you spare me a few minutes?"

"I'm really very busy, what with the press and the patients, Don, but I guess I can give you ten minutes before my meeting with the board. By the way, thanks for the coffee. It's much better than what we normally have here. What's on your mind?" Joni replied as she tasted the steaming brew. He had ordered her favorite: hazelnut blend with light cream and two sugars.

Six months ago, Joni would have been impressed by Don's early morning visit. When he was her boss, Don always scheduled his day to begin at ten. He was not an early riser and hated mornings. By the time he reported to work, she had already scheduled the staff and treated several patients. He would bring her a cup of coffee and wander around the emergency room greeting people. He hardly ever pitched in to help lighten the caseload. He preferred to spend his time on the fourth floor making friends with the administration or sipping coffee with his connections on the board.

It was flattering that he still remembered the way she liked her coffee. However, this morning, Joni found the delicate taste almost overpowering because of its link to their past relationship. Sipping it carefully so as not to get burned, Joni waited patiently for him to speak. She was suspicious of his intentions. After all, she thought that she had made herself perfectly clear when he first returned. Considering that his gaze never left hers, she felt her reactions were justified. And Joni felt her own body betray her determination to remain aloof.

"We have to talk about us," Don replied as he placed his cup on the desk that had previously been his. He exuded confidence and self-assurance.

"What's there to talk about? It's over. It ended before you left both the hospital and me. We've made separate lives for ourselves that don't require the other for fulfillment. I'm sorry that yours did not turn out as you had planned, but sometimes that happens. I'm running the ER now and doing a great job of it. I don't see where we have anything to discuss," Joni stated calmly and without emotion as she returned his gaze. She hoped, as her heart pounded loudly, that her face remained as expressionless as her voice.

"You know that I didn't have a choice. You made that perfectly clear," Don answered. His voice sounded a bit strained as if he were keeping his irritation at being rebuffed at bay. He was not a man who was used to people resisting him. Where women were concerned, Don always had his way.

"This sounds like a personal problem to me. Geography isn't my strong suit, but even I know that Greece is pretty far away. I fail to see what this has to do with me," Joni commented with thinly disguised sarcasm.

"I was hoping that we could begin again. We've had time apart to grow, and I still love you. We could patch things up, Joni. It's not too late," Don replied. His knitted brow was the only sign of his turmoil.

"No, Don, it is too late. I thought I explained that already. I have new priorities in my life. I have the ER and the clinic. I don't need a relationship with you or anyone else right now to muddy the waters. I'm perfectly happy where I am in my life. I have my work. That's enough for now. I refuse to repeat the same mistake. An office relationship just won't work," Joni responded as she carefully placed her half-empty cup on the desk. She refused to fall prey to his charms again.

"I won't believe that I mean nothing to you," Don answered as his confidence began to slip in the face of her resistance.

"Don, I want to believe you, but I can't afford the pain," Joni stated calmly. She would not allow anger to fill her voice. Don would win if he managed to arouse any emotional response. She remained cool and detached as if watching someone else in conversation with a former lover.

The cups of steaming coffee sat cooling between them in the little gray room. Joni and Don sat looking at each other with neither one saying a word. Joni remembered the mutual need that bonded them during the days of their relationship. For his part in the deception, Don felt the sting of her words and struggled desperately to find the proper response. Her aloofness undercut his belief in his ability to win her again.

Don was the first to speak as he pleaded gently, "Give me another chance. I know I screwed up, but I'll make it up to you."

Joni replied firmly, "We can't go back to where we were. That's not realistic. We're not the same people we were then. The ER is my companion. It consumes every minute of my day, and I don't regret my decision. With the new clinic in operation, I'm doubly busy. I can't—no, I won't go back to our old life. I'd have to risk too much. I won't do it."

"We could try. I still love you. I wouldn't have sold my practice and returned to the States if I didn't want you in my life," Don said from where he sat, unable to penetrate the steel of her gaze. He was afraid to move toward her. The rigidity of Joni's body told him that she did not want him in her space, at least not yet.

"You came back to take control of the ER away from me. You didn't come back here to be with me. You told me that you called the hospital and made all of your arrangements before you even phoned to tell me of your return. You thought of yourself and your career before you thought of me. That wasn't exactly the way to win my heart. You've done a rather pathetic job of proving that you love me. Going behind my back and trying to remove me from this office did not exactly endear you to me," Joni spat with anger shining in her eyes as she allowed her temper to flare. Don needed to know exactly how she felt about his underhanded dealings.

"Joni, I had to have a job before I sold my practice," Don replied as he tried to justify his actions. "Besides, I wasn't sure that you'd even speak to me if I called. And I couldn't tell you about the change in the management of the ER until

I had worked out all of the details. I hadn't counted on the success of the clinic making it difficult for me to return to the position that I had vacated. The hospital would have given me back the ER position if you hadn't opened that operation and ingratiated yourself with them. I had underestimated your impact.

"Don't forget that you're only the acting chief while the board looks for my replacement. In a way, my return removes that burden from their shoulders. They have been very understanding of my situation. I'm the prodigal son returned." Don's customary arrogance had replaced his assumed humility. He had grown impatient with Joni's cool treatment of him. He had expected her to crumble after an initial show of righteous anger. He had not counted on her remaining aloof and unbending.

"Well, you certainly are the master of flattery and sweet talk, aren't you?" Joni said sarcastically. "It's no use, Don. You are a scheming, conniving person who doesn't care on whose feelings you trod. You didn't tell me that you planned to return to the ER because you knew that I'd fight you every step of the way if you tried to take this job away from me. You underestimated your opponent. You didn't know that I had made the board recognize my abilities by tightening the reins on spending while maintaining a happy employee base. You're right when you say that you misjudged me. That's a technical error that you shouldn't have made.

"You can forget it, Don. I want nothing from you other than to maintain a pleasant working relationship. I hope that you will respect my wishes and leave me alone," Joni stated as she stood with her hands on her hips and her feet placed firmly in her office.

"No, I won't take that as the final word. I'll find some way to win you back. I'll make it work between us. Remember, I always get what I want," Don responded emphatically.

"It's your call, but this is one time your charm and charisma won't work. You must really like lost causes. This will go down as the only setback you've suffered in your otherwise illustrious career," Joni retorted with a chuckle.

Rising to leave, Don said, "Don't forget that the board hasn't finalized its decision yet. They don't want to alienate you because of all the fine work you've done on behalf of the hospital. Yet they can't afford to let an experienced and highly skilled ER chief like me slip through their fingers. We'll see what they decide soon enough.

"As long as I'm here, I will continue to press my case with you. I won't give up that easily. Yes, I know I should have communicated with you when I first decided to return, but I didn't think that the reception would be too warm. From the stand you're taking now, I can see that I was correct. I don't apologize for going around you to the board. I did what I had to do. I would do it again. So would you if the tables were turned."

"No, I wouldn't, Don. I'm not that kind of person. I believe in being honest with people. Have you finished?" Joni asked. She did not wait for his response but returned to the pile of work on her desk.

"No, I feel a need to make this last thing perfectly clear," Don replied with renewed determination at her continued resistance. "Although I would do anything within my power to win you back, I will not abandon my quest for this office. This ER is all that I have left of the life I used to live.

"Because of what you've accomplished in the ER and the clinic, I've asked the board to expand the budget to allow the clinic to stand on its own. You've proven yourself to be a highly capable administrator. There's plenty of room for both of us here at City General. The members are considering that possibility right now. If the clinic were a separate profit center, I could run the ER and you could head that operation. You would be able to enlarge its staff and facility as well as secure an appropriate position for yourself. I think the members will approve my recommendation during the first session of next year."

Sputtering with fury, Joni replied, "How dare you think that you can waltz in here and make changes that don't need to be made? We've managed very well without you these six months. I've turned the ER into one of the best-managed profit centers in this hospital despite our high overhead and unpredictable expenses. I've trimmed the budget and anticipated our expenses on a monthly basis with almost precise detail. I've motivated the staff to work efficiently and collegially. All of these things you couldn't or wouldn't do. You were too busy kissing up to your wealthy friends to take the time to manage the ER properly. There's nothing I haven't taken into consideration in making this the best run ER in the state.

"Don, the clinic is an offshoot of my efforts and the icing on a very rich cake. There's no reason to separate the ER from the clinic. They work well together. The figures don't justify the cost. The timing isn't right. Separation this early in the game might spell failure for the clinic. It needs the protection of the established ER until we work out all the procedural bugs. We need to see what our patient load will be before the clinic can stand on its own feet. City General cannot afford to separate the two units until the clinic is profitable.

"Let me make something perfectly clear, Don. If you want a fight, you'll have one. I will not back down on this for old times' sake or for the good of any new working relationship. Now get out and don't come back. We have nothing more to say to each other. You've interrupted my work long enough."

Silently, Don walked toward the door. As he opened it, he turned and gave Joni one last, long look. Then he said, "I had hoped that we could move forward. I want us to work together amicably. We could be this hospital's one-two punch. My ER and your clinic could really put this hospital on the map if we could settle this animosity that lies between us.

"You've changed while I've been away. You've become tough and driven. I guess that I'll have to adjust to the new you. You want to do battle for this turf? Fine, I'll go the distance with you. Look out, Joni, I'm back and I'm here to stay whether you like it or not."

Leaving her staring angrily at the closed door, Don walked quickly down the hall toward the elevators. He knew that Joni would waste no time in drawing up a plan to remove him from City General and he had to be ready. He had hoped for a gentler reunion, but he would have to settle for what she offered him. As much as he hated to admit it, he was on her turf now. Don would have to tread carefully until he could assess her weaknesses. So far, he only saw strength that he did not know she possessed.

Joni stood at her desk clenching her fists in her rage. She could taste the blood in her mouth from where she had bitten the inside of her mouth in her anger. Her entire body shook with the force of her fury. Not since she had been in medical school and tried to prove that she had what it took to be a good doctor had she felt such ire. It had been a long time since someone had tried to make her feel small while holding out an olive branch.

"Ridiculous," Joni muttered angrily. "Does he really think that he can do this? What makes him think that he can just push me around like that?"

Suddenly the door opened and Randi entered. "I thought I saw Don leave. What did he have to say?" she asked. Seeing Joni's pinched expression, Randi did not doubt that it had not been a positive meeting.

"He only wanted to tell me that he still loves me. And, oh, yes, he's going to do everything in his power to take the ER away from me. I'm having trouble believing the nerve of that guy. First, he leaves when the pressure becomes too real, and now he wants to return as if nothing has happened between us. Unreal," Joni replied as she closed the budget ledger with a loud bang.

"I hope you told him that he had burned that bridge," Randi remarked acidly.

"I certainly did and in no uncertain terms, but that didn't stop him. He told me about a proposal he made to the board regarding the separation of the clinic from the ER and the creation of two separate profit centers under different chiefs. He made the assumption that the board would return the ER to his control and that the management of the clinic would remain my responsibility. He did all of this without consulting with me. He thought that I'd be hostile to his suggestions. Me, hostile. What do you think gave him that idea!" Joni responded as she slammed her chair angrily against the metal rim of the desk.

"I'm sure it had nothing to do with the icy way you've treated him since his return or the fact that you've made it perfectly clear that you don't need him in your life or your ER," Randi commented sarcastically.

"Why should he expect me to be anything other than cold? His expectation of simply picking up the pieces without preamble is ridiculous. The most insulting part of all this is that Don never considered that the ER would thrive with me at the helm. He thought that the ER and I would waste away during his absence. He honestly expected to return to find things as they were or even worse. He didn't give me any credit for being able to run this department," Joni fumed as she righted the toppled coffee cup and wiped up the spilled coffee.

"Well, what's your next move?" Randi asked dropping the sopping paper towels into the trash can.

"I'm going to see the board this morning. I'll make my pitch then. I just hope that they listen to my side of this scenario with as much enthusiasm as he said they did to his. I have to convince them that separating the ER and the clinic at this time would be a gross waste of money and personnel as well as a risk to patient care. The shakedown period isn't over yet. This would be a big mistake. We need more time to assess the figures," Joni replied as she scribbled some notes on a pad of paper.

"I'll leave you alone now. Let me know how the meeting turns out," Randi said as she left.

A few minutes later, Joni sat in the conference room with the assembled board members around her. She had planned to bring them up-to-date on the success of the new clinic and the further improvements she had made in the operations of the emergency room. In light of Don's return and her declaration of war, she now wanted to learn their reactions to her programs and his proposals.

After presenting her figures and plans for the continued operation of the combined emergency room and clinic, Joni leaned back in her chair. Her eyes scanned their smiling faces as she tried to read the unspoken messages. She knew that they were weighing her words against Don's, and she wondered who would come out the victor.

Clearing her throat seriously, Mrs. Grant, the chairman of the board stated, "Dr. Forest, the board is greatly impressed with the changes you've made in the ER. It clearly functions as a profit center under your direction. The clinic has already proven itself to be a brilliant addition to the community and City General's reputation.

"As you know, we had planned to announce the new chief of the ER at the Christmas party. There was little doubt in our minds that your outstanding performance in that position has earned you the right to the job on a permanent basis. However, with Dr. Rivers's return, we find ourselves divided in our decision knowing that he served the hospital loyally in the past.

"Dr. Rivers has proposed a solution to our dilemma, which we are currently studying. In the meantime, we hope that you two will be able to work out a congenial division of responsibilities during our deliberations."

Feeling neither relieved nor alarmed, Joni stated, "I am familiar with Dr. Rivers's plan to separate the clinic from the ER. I would like to state for the record that I am opposed to any such action at this time. The clinic operates smoothly now because of its proximity to the ER. We can transfer patients between the facilities without undue paperwork. Staff is able to float between the two units without first cutting through the red tape. We contain costs by operating with one chief of staff rather than two and rotating physicians between the facilities. Separating the functions would mean enlarged staffs and considerable new expense for which the clinic has not proven that there is justification. I do not believe that this proposal would be in the best interests of City General at a time of maximum cost containment."

"We appreciate your candor, Dr. Forest, and, as always, we respect your judgment," Robert Brown, head of the facilities subcommittee, commented. "However, Dr. Rivers's proposal bears merit, and, therefore, we must examine it also. The increased patient flow to the clinic might speak for itself in this matter and necessitate the action he has recommended."

"It might, Mr. Brown, but I would caution the board not to take this step prematurely. Right now, the clinic is new and the novelty of having it within easy access is drawing people to our doors. When they become more accustomed to us in a few months, they might begin to take us for granted. If that happens, we will not need to increase our staff. We will find that we have anticipated our staffing and facility needs perfectly. I hope that the board will wait to make any decision concerning the separation of the ER and the clinic until we have experienced the initial shakedown period."

"Very well, doctor, we will take your concerns into consideration. You have made many valid points. We don't want to act too hastily. In the meantime, I trust that you and Dr. Rivers will find a way to work together amicably as cochairs of the department while we continue our deliberations. We will make both of you aware of our decision as soon as possible," Mrs. Grant commented as she adjourned the meeting.

"Excuse me, but I'm not content with this arrangement," Joni began firmly and without hesitation. "I've given my all to City General these past six months. I've taken the risk of transforming it into a thriving profit center. I don't want to take anything away from Dr. Rivers's contributions to the ER, but the changes that you see now were neither initiated by him nor suggested by the board. They all came from me. I can understand the position in which Dr. Rivers's return has placed all of you, but you must understand how it makes me feel to have all of my efforts shelved until further notice because of him."

The board members stood in stunned silence as they listened to Joni's accurate summation of their actions. They were unaccustomed to being challenged by department heads, who normally presented their proposals and resolutely received the board's verdict on the implementation of them. Usually the sheer number of somber faces across the expanse of conference room table made the department heads feel humble and intimidated. They were relieved to be dismissed and scurried away.

But Joni was different. She had worked too hard to accept their pronouncement without a fight. Squaring her shoulders, she continued, "I spoke with Dr. Rivers prior to this meeting and expressed my belief that his desire to split off the two portions of the ER functions is self-serving at best. He resigned from City General and now wishes to return, to use his term, as the prodigal son. During his absence, I have functioned as the acting chief of the ER in such a manner as to cause you to consider me the likely candidate to fill the position on a permanent basis. As you say, if he had not returned, you would not be experiencing second thoughts about me. While I appreciate your loyalty to a former member of the staff and hope that you will extend the same courtesy to me should the need arise, I am not content with being asked to serve in a joint capacity with him until you make a final decision.

"In my opinion, the decision is quite clear. I have served City General loyally while Dr. Rivers served his own personal interests elsewhere. With all due respect, I feel that my performance, the ER's strong financial standing, and the overwhelming success of the clinic state my case clearly. I deserve a response by the end of the year as stated in the contract I signed when I initially assumed the position of acting chief of the ER."

Joni sat confidently, waiting for Mrs. Grant's response. Externally, she looked cool, collected, and self-assured. She indeed had the terms of the contract that bound her to City General in her favor. She had been promised a decision by December thirty-first. Considering her performance and the fact that the board had not been able to find any candidates with her stellar qualifications, Joni felt within her rights to demand satisfaction.

Internally, Joni shook from head to toe. She was afraid to speak again for fear everyone in the room would hear the chattering of her teeth. Her hands felt like ice where they rested on the folder in front of her. The blood pounded in the veins in her neck and temples. Her knees knocked violently under the table making her wonder if she would be able to walk to the door when she had to leave the room. Her armpits were wet and sticky. Sweat ran between her breasts and down the center of her back. Waves of heat and cold flowed over her body.

As all eyes remained focused on her face, Joni could feel her confidence start to flag. She had taken the chance and spoken up for herself and her rights. Now Joni was not sure that she had done the right thing. Perhaps she should have been more of a team player. She wondered what a man would have done in her position. Then, she thought of Don and his cocky belief that the emergency room was his for the taking.

Her resolve stiffened as did her back. Joni knew that she had played the hand she had been dealt perfectly.

Unlike Don Rivers, who had only been concerned with his welfare in both his leaving of City General and in his proposal to split the emergency room's operations, Joni had the hospital's best interests in mind. He had not questioned the correctness of his behavior except in his personal relationship with her. He had not wondered at the impact on the hospital of either action. Joni did not act unless she knew that the hospital would benefit from whatever she proposed. She would not question her decision now.

"Very well, Dr. Forest. You're absolutely correct about our promise to you. We are grateful for what you've done here at City General. There's no disputing the fact that you have implemented many valuable changes and initiated a clinical service that will place our facility among the best in the state and perhaps the nation. You have brought considerable positive publicity to our door. Your request is quite appropriate. As originally stated in your contract, we will make the announcement of the permanent chief of the ER on or before December thirty-first. If we find that we are unable to comply with the terms of your contract, we will consult with you and gain your concurrence on an alternative date. Thank you, doctor, for reminding us of our legal responsibility to you," Mrs. Grant replied with a brief inclination of her head. She looked at Joni with renewed respect.

"You look terrible. How did it go? You were up there a long time," Randi demanded. She had been anxiously watching the elevator and staircase doors for the last half hour.

"I won a few points and I lost a few. Regardless of the outcome, I couldn't have played it any other way," Joni responded as she shoved the file in the drawer and pulled on her white coat and stethoscope.

"What does that mean?" Randi asked, trying to understand Joni's vague response.

"The board wanted to postpone naming the permanent head of the ER until after it could evaluate Don's proposal to split the ER and the clinic. I'm opposed to doing it and presented contradictory evidence. I'm so glad that I'm a pack rat when it comes to figures. I had already worked out a cash-flow analysis of the feasibility of maintaining separate functions. The cost is definitely prohibitive at this stage. Perhaps in the future after the clinic proves itself we can split the two functions but not now when the novelty factor is very much in effect," Joni replied shaking her head slowly. She had a splitting headache that stabbed behind her ears with every movement.

Handing her two aspirins from the bottle in her pocket, Randi asked, "How did they respond? Are they going to back you or Don for the job?"

"That's the part I can't tell. Mrs. Grant agreed that I have a legal right as stipulated in my contract to know the identity of the permanent chief by the end of this month. I don't know which of us they will select. As you know, there are no other candidates. They admitted that if Don had not returned the job would belong to me. However, they're torn between their loyalty to the old guard and to me, the newcomer and innovator. I can understand that, but I didn't want to acquiesce and live with that uncertainty. I don't feel that the board has a right to renege on its contract to me. I have to think of my own future. The board promised an appointment by December thirty-first, and I insisted that they honor it," Joni replied as she swallowed the pills and washed them down with a big gulp of water.

"Good for you! What will you do if they decide to give the job to Don?" Randi queried as they walked back to the nurses' station.

"I've had headhunters call me since the clinic opened. I've been stalling them by saying that the announcement is due out at the end of this month. They've all said that they'll call back. To be on the safe side, I guess I should give them a call. I'm not really worried. I'll be able to find a job somewhere in the Baltimore-Washington corridor," Joni replied as she scanned the white board and checked the status of their morning patients.

"Let's hope they come to their senses. You don't want to leave City General. You love it here," Randi commented. She would hate for her best friend to leave the hospital.

"I know I would miss it. This is my home. However, I can't work under Don again. Regardless of what might happen with the relationship, that's a given. I've invested too much of my energy in making the necessary changes around here to do that. Still, I don't want to head the clinic yet. The figures show that the clinic is not ready to stand on its own merit at this time. I don't want to get caught in the position of perhaps being dismissed because my department was not capable of turning a profit. We'll see what happens at Christmastime," Joni responded with a confidence she did not really feel. She knew that as a woman, she was up against serious obstacles.

"You certainly took a chance this morning. It was a big gamble either way. I'm really proud of you for sticking to your convictions," Randi beamed as she hugged Joni.

"Thanks. It's great having a friend who understands that there are just some things in life that I have to do. I know I've taken a risky stand. It would have been so much easier to roll over and let Don push me out of my position. I just couldn't do it. I have to fight. I've worked too hard to give up now," Joni responded with a smile. She knew the realities of life in a big hospital.

"If you're feeling up to it, I have a patient with an infected pierced belly button for you to see," Randi said as she handed Joni the chart.

"You certainly know how to make me return to the reality of the here and now. Thanks. A pus-filled belly button is just what I need to make me feel humble," Joni replied with a chuckle.

Randi watched Joni as she walked away. She hoped the board would not overlook her friend's contributions to City General. The glass ceiling could not be that low and the board could not be that unappreciative of hard work and dedication.

Eight

By the next morning, everyone on the staff knew about the conflict between Joni and Don Rivers over the management of the ER, although they knew nothing about the personal side of their conversation. Many of them had committed themselves to remain neutral, having enjoyed working with both of them. Equally as many had clearly taken sides. As one of the players in the drama, all Joni wanted to do was get on with her duties at City General and her life.

"Did you see the paper this morning? They've found the robbers who took me prisoner," Randi said as she thrust the folded newspaper into Joni's hands.

"Really? Where did the police find them?" Joni asked, not wanting to dim Randi's excitement at telling the story by reading the article for herself.

"According to the article," Randi replied, "the man developed a high fever, and the woman took him to a hospital in D.C. He's in stable condition and expected to pull through without any problem. She's in jail for armed robbery. It seems that they have a long string of thefts under their belts.

"They specialize in winning the confidence of rich elderly gentlemen who, in their loneliness, spill the beans about their finances and investments. The robbers learn where the men store extra cash, jewelry, portable art, and negotiable bonds. Armed with this information, they wait until the gentlemen leave their houses, and then they burglarize them.

"This time, the gentleman they intended to rob did not take the vacation he had intended. However, they did not know that he was in the house when they broke in. After disabling the security system, they entered the library. Drawing from the police report, the journalist wrote that the gentleman heard a noise, got his handgun, and went to investigate. Discovering the library door open, he shot into the darkness and wounded the intruder. The victim said that he didn't stick around to find out who it was. He rushed down the hall to the nearest phone.

"While he was away, the thieves ran from the house. The article makes it look as if the robbers thought they had gotten away until the man in the duo started losing too much blood. That's when she brought him to the hospital for us to treat."

Joni asked, "Did they mention the hospital in the article?"

"Oh, yes, City General is named in the first paragraph. One of our patients showed it to me. We're celebrities," Randi said, laughing.

"Let's not let it go to our heads. We have work to do. Look at all those people waiting for us. I think we should get to work. Besides, a tiara just doesn't go with these shoes," Joni replied, chuckling and shaking her head.

Pulling on her white coat, Joni headed to examining room three where a woman with a strange-looking bite on her arm waited for treatment. "Hello, I'm Dr. Forest. Let me take a look at that bite."

"Dr. Forest, it's lovely to meet ya. You're the physician who treated the robber. It's so excitin' to have a celebrity doctor workin' on me. I'm sure my little bite ain't nothin' special to ya," Mrs. Wilson gushed.

"All my patients are special, Mrs. Wilson. Let me look at this wound. What bit you?" Joni asked again as she reached for the woman's meaty arm with its red, swollen area.

"My dog bit me. Can ya do somethin' for the swellin'?" Mrs. Wilson queried nervously.

"This doesn't look like an animal bite to me. Who bit you?" Joni searched the woman's puffy face for an answer.

"Doctor, I told ya that my dog bit me," Mrs. Wilson repeated with so much irritation that Joni had doubted her response.

"Mrs. Wilson," Joni replied with the stern voice she reserved for difficult situations, "I've seen many dog and human bites in my career as an ER physician, and I know the difference. This was definitely done by a human. Did someone attack you?"

Reluctantly Mrs. Wilson answered, "I wouldn't say that I was exactly attacked. My husband bit me, that's all."

Joni studied the woman's pinched face and watery blue eyes. She reeked of stale liquor. Her clothing was soiled and rumpled. Her hands were dirty and her nails broken and yellowed by tobacco. A large bruise visible under layers of makeup decorated the side of the woman's face. It told Joni that Mrs. Wilson was an abuse case.

"I'll have a physician's assistant treat the bite in just a minute. I'd like to have you speak with a counselor from social services. I think he might be able to help you," Joni offered.

"There's nothin' anyone can do. Anyway, I've talked with them before. They want me to file charges against my husband. They don't understand that he'll kill me if I do. Just have someone fix me up so I can go home," Mrs. Wilson replied sullenly.

"He might kill you if you don't. That bruise is too close to your temple for comfort. One of these days, he'll use something other than his teeth or fists," Joni cautioned as she examined Mrs. Wilson's battered face.

"Don't worry about me, doc. I can take care of myself. Most of the time, he's so liquored up that he don't even remember to be a son of a bitch. I just forgot to duck this time, and he hit me. Last night, we was just horsin' around and got carried away, that's all. Both of us had too much to drink. This is nothin'," Mrs. Wilson replied.

"Fine, Mrs. Wilson, have it your way. If you don't want to get help, I can't force you. I'll get that physician's assistant now. I strongly suggest that you reconsider your decision," Joni responded with a shrug and a lift of her brows. She hated to see women allow their abusive spouses to continue to batter them when they could get help from social services organizations, but she saw the futility of trying to change Mrs. Wilson's mind.

"Thanks for tryin', Dr. Forest, but I'll take my chances on things the way they are right now," Mrs. Wilson called as Joni left the room.

Breathing a sigh of relief and sadness, Joni handed the chart to the first PA she could find. As she was about to retire to her office, she heard screaming from the examining room at the end of the hallway. Rushing toward the sound, she pushed past empty wheelchairs, boxes of supplies, overflowing trash cans, and baskets of dirty laundry.

As she passed the nurses' station, Joni called, "Randi, have someone from housekeeping come down here immediately. We have a safety and fire hazard in this hall. Get someone to move this stuff."

"I already called. Someone should be here in about ten minutes," Randi shouted back over the racket from the examining room. "What's going on down there?"

"I'm on my way to find out right now," Joni replied as she pushed her way through the door.

"Doctor, you've got to do something to help my husband," a woman shouted as she grabbed at Joni's coat.

"I'll do what I can. I'm on my way now. Please wait in the lounge. Someone will come to speak with you as soon as we finish examining him," Joni replied as she pried open the woman's fingers and gently patted her hand.

Wide-eyed medical students filled the examining room. To Joni, it looked as if the entire medical school had decided to visit the emergency room on the same day. The students wore varying shades of pale, green expressions. Squeezing past them with their gaping mouths, she advanced on the attending physician, who was trying desperately to staunch the flow of blood from a man's badly mangled left leg.

Placing her hand on Tom Sullivan's shoulder, Joni said, "Looks like they all remembered that they needed this rotation to finish out their semester."

"You're right. I just wish they had picked another room. I have my hands full and don't have time to explain what I'm doing," Tom replied. He had been a medic in the Army for ten years before deciding to enter medical school. He was usually very calm, but today the amount of blood flowing from the patient's leg and the number of helpless students in the room threatened to drive him to the edge of his tolerance and patience.

"I'll take the students off your hands," Joni replied as she slipped on her rubber gloves and positioned herself between Tom and the staring audience.

Quickly assessing the needs of the students and those of the physician, Joni began to explain the steps that Tom had taken to stop the bleeding and save the exposed muscle and tissue. As she spoke, she noticed that a number of the kids looked a little green. Thinking about the other students who had flocked through the emergency room in September, she doubted that many of them had seen this quantity of blood in their other rotations. The emergency room was unique in the experiences it offered its staff and students.

Speaking to the students, Joni lectured in a slow steady voice, "This isn't the kind of wound we see often in the late fall and early winter, but we get a number of cases like this in the spring and summer. From the grass stains on his shirt and the bruises on his face, I'd say that Mr. Martin probably flew over the steering wheel of the mower when it hit a rock or tree limb. It looks as if he landed first on his face and shoulders. He might even have thought to roll away from the blades. At any rate, we know that whatever he did, it was not enough. His mower crunched up the tissue and muscle of his left leg pretty badly. He'll be lucky if he doesn't lose it."

"Ooh!" groaned one of the young men in the crowd as he leaned heavily against the nearest table and promptly fainted.

Looking at his ashen face, one of the female students threw up on the floor at her feet. Joni looked from one to the other as many of the students searched the room for trash cans and the familiar kidney-shaped pan. Their attention was definitely not on the patient.

Joni and Tom exchanged glances. With a slight smile, Joni said, "You'll get used to the smell and the sight. Your reaction happens to everyone at some time in their careers."

"This is so embarrassing. I didn't expect to faint. I've never fainted before in my life," the young man replied. He slowly rose to his feet with the help of the only medical student in the room who did not look ready to bolt for the door. His complexion still contained a tinge of green.

"Focus your attention on the leg as an abstract item unrelated to the person. If you see it in a detached setting, you'll experience less stomach discomfort," Joni advised as she remembered her first experience with blood.

As the students regrouped, Joni returned to the discussion of the procedures that Tom had followed to save the man's leg. Slowly, she explained each step that he took.

"Dr. Sullivan is trying to isolate the source of the bleeding. He's tying off the severed artery. The purpose is not to repair the leg down here in the ER but to stabilize the patient until the surgeon can take the appropriate action. If you'll look at the monitor, you'll see that the patient's condition is improving. His blood pressure is returning to normal. Are you ready to transfer him to surgery, doctor?" Joni asked.

"One last quick suture and then I'm ready. Done!" Tom replied as he made the last stitch. "I'll speak with his wife on my way out." The orderlies rapidly pushed the gurney to the waiting elevator.

Turning toward the students, Joni saw that they had regained their composure. All but one of them looked hail enough to progress to their own assignments under the guidance of an emergency room physician. When their rotation through the emergency room ended, they would have forgotten the humiliation of their introduction.

Slipping her arm around the shoulders of one of the female students, Joni escorted her to the physicians' lounge. Handing her a soda, she watched as the young woman accepted the can with a shy, crooked smile. Her hands shook as she drank.

"I think I'm feeling a little better now. I left this rotation 'til last hoping that I would build up a tolerance to the sight of pain, suffering, and blood, but I don't think I have. I had a rough time in obstetrics and in pediatrics, but this was worse. I've never seen so much blood," the pale young woman groaned.

"Heaving was a very natural reaction. Right now you're probably more embarrassed than ill. You did fine once you refocused your attention. I wouldn't worry if I were you," Joni counseled gently. She had watched the young woman's interest in the procedure increase as her nausea decreased.

"What if I do that every time I see blood? I'll have to pick a specialty like psychiatry, which doesn't interest me in the least. I want to specialize in pediatric medicine. I can't throw up every time a patient comes to see me with a cut," the young woman lamented.

"You won't. That's part of the learning process. We all have to adjust to the sights and sounds of medicine. You're Jackie Weaver, aren't you? Isn't your father the chief of the ICU at Holly Field?" Joni asked in an effort to make the young woman relax.

"Yes, I am. Just think of the footsteps I have to fill. That puts even more pressure on me to perform," Jackie replied with a sad smile.

"Does he exert this pressure or are you the one with the unrelenting expectations?" Joni asked softly. She remembered feeling that she had to be the best at everything she tried in order to make her hard-working parents proud of her. She wanted to be number one to please them; they were happy with her as she was.

Looking first at the floor and then slowly at Joni, Jackie confided, "You're right. I put the pressure on myself. My father is just happy that I followed him into medicine. One of my brothers decided to go into architecture and the other practices law. My father was afraid that no one would take up his profession. He almost burst his buttons when I told him that I was going to medical school."

"If that's the case, shouldn't you cut yourself a little slack once in a while?" Joni asked as a knowing smile played at the corners of her lips. "I remember that I put much more pressure on myself than my father ever did in my effort to follow in his footsteps rather than make my own. He has always been proud of my accomplishments, not my emulation of his."

"I'll remember that. I know that I don't have to be so hard on myself. It's just that I want so desperately to do well and to make him proud of me. Thanks, Dr. Forest. I appreciate the talk. I'm feeling much better now. I'd better go. I'm supposed to work with Dr. Sullivan for the next two weeks. He's already seen my weakness. It's about time I showed him my strength," Jackie said as she tossed her can into the recycling bin.

"That's at least one advantage to puking in front of the physician with whom you'll spend this rotation. You can only go up from here," Joni laughed as she escorted Jackie back to the busy emergency room.

Tom Sullivan stood with a patient file in one hand and a cup of coffee in the other. "Good, you're back. I could use your help behind curtain number three. No, it's not a new car. It's a man with glass shards in his hand from ramming it through a plate-glass window. Ready?" Tom joked as he motioned in the direction of the examining room.

"Sure, I'm ready for anything, doctor," Jackie replied as she gave Joni the thumbs-up sign.

Easing toward her, Randi observed, "You gave her your 'don't be so tough on yourself' talk, I see. It always works. You should tape it and play it back when each new group of medical students rotates through the ER."

"I would do just that except that I'd miss out on sharing the memories with them. It does me good to see their enthusiasm and their innocence. It reminds me of the time when I was like them. They care about the patient first and then the illness or the injury. We've come to treat the problem and then think about the person. Somehow, I think I like their way better," Joni responded as she took a chart from the organizer.

"We'd burn out if we stayed like them. We don't have any choice but to harden ourselves against the suffering. We wouldn't be effective if we didn't," Randi offered. She saw how tired Joni looked from her encounters with the students and the board.

"I know that you're right, but on days like this, I still long for the lost innocence. Working with them puts me in touch with the idealist inside me. After I finish this chart, schedule me out for a few hours, please. I have work to do in my office," Joni said with a smile. Carefully, she wove her way through the crowd to see one more patient before getting down to the task that lay ahcad. She had to design a plan that would not only keep the emergency room and clinic intact as a unit but also preserve her position as its chief.

While Joni worked on revised budget figures, the nurses and physicians in both units were busy with more than patient care. Finding the box of Christmas decorations, they adorned every door, window, and counter in the emergency room and clinic in festive garlands, ribbons, ornaments, and tinsels rather than putting up the faded, torn old Thanksgiving turkey and dried corn.

From her office, Joni could hear the sound of caroling over the usual hubbub of the emergency room. After she finished her last column of figures, Joni pulled open her door to see what was happening in her absence. Seeing the light reflecting off the twirling balls, she laughed to herself and joined in the infectious holiday spirit.

"Hey, what's going on in here? Who's responsible for this? I go to my office for a few minutes and Christmas breaks out," Joni complained with a laugh.

"Well, everything looked so dull around here. It was time we got in the Christmas spirit. I even bought some punch, eggnog, and cookies. They're in the lounge. Hurry in and get some before they're all gone," Randi called from the top of the tree where she was placing the star.

"Looks great!" Joni shouted as she rushed to get a cup of holiday spirit. Even though the eggnog would be alcohol-free, it would help to put her in the right frame of mind. She needed something to boost her spirits considering the load she carried on her shoulders.

Munching a cookie and sipping the thick, creamy mixture, Joni joined in the animated conversation. Philip, one of the residents, had just become a father. He glowed as he shared the photographs of his new daughter. One of the nurses showed pictures of her first grandson. Everyone chatted happily about what they would do over the holidays. They all planned to spend some portion of the week with their families. Even those who had to work on the holiday had plans for Christmas Eve. Those who did not celebrate religious holidays were looking forward to New Year's parties and resolutions.

Suddenly a scream and a crash disturbed their conversation. Rushing into the hall, they saw Randi gripping the overhead water pipe. Her feet dangled several feet from the floor.

"Somebody help me! The ladder fell over. This pipe doesn't feel strong enough to hold me for long. Hurry!" Randi called as Joni and the others ran toward her.

Gus, a six-foot-five orderly, reached up and grabbed Randi around the upper thighs. "Let go and slide down my body," he ordered.

"I'm scared. What if you drop me?" Randi asked clinging to the pipe.

"What choice do you have, Randi? Either grab Gus or take a chance that the pipe will break and dump you on the floor," Joni reminded her friend firmly.

Gus interjected kindly, "Trust me. I won't let you fall."

Looking at all the upturned faces, Randi shouted, "Here goes!"

With Gus's strong muscles straining under her weight, Randi pressed her body against his and slid to the floor. Her hands gripped his shoulders tightly. Her straight, white uniform skirt eased up her trim body to expose white pantyhose and lacy undies.

"Thanks, Gus. What a way to start the holiday," Randi commented as she adjusted her skirt and tried to regain her composure and dignity.

"Think nothing of it, Randi. I rather enjoyed being a human rope," Gus grinned.

"You rascal!" Randi replied as she slapped at his arm.

Now that Randi was safe, the entire emergency room erupted into gales of laughter. Looking over her shoulder and feigning annoyance, Randi said, "Enough already. Don't you people have anything better to do?"

Holding her sides, Joni replied, "Nothing that compares to what we just saw."

Casting her friend a "drop dead" look, Randi tossed her ponytail over her shoulder and walked away. She left the sounds of laughter behind her.

"What are you doing this holiday, Joni?" Jackie asked as she joined Joni on the sidelines. Jackie no longer looked ashen from the fainting episode, but she continued to be a little embarrassed by the spectacle she felt she'd made of herself.

"I'm working on Christmas Day. As chief of the ER, I scheduled myself for the holiday. After my shift, I'll go to my parents' house in Columbia. They hold dinner until I arrive.

My sister and her two kids will be there. It's always a nice, quiet time. What will you do?"

"I'm spending the holiday with my dad. My folks divorced when I was eighteen, and my mom moved to California. Last year, I flew out to see her. I missed the snow and cold, so this year, I'm spending the time where I know there will be a white Christmas. I grew up in Upstate New York and have a hard time not waking up to snow on Christmas morning so Dad's taking me there. When I finish medical school, I'm moving back home. I can't live in a town that doesn't have at least a foot of snow for the holidays," Jackie replied with a big smile.

Jackie looked so much like a child that Joni had to resist the urge to chuckle. Instead she said, "I love a white Christmas, too. I guess we all romanticize about it. However, this is home. I've hardly ever had one and love this area. I guess I'll just have to dream about waking up to it."

Suddenly, Randi burst into the room. "Joni, I hate to interrupt, but you're needed in the ER stat," she announced with an urgent wave of her hand.

"No problem. I'm on my way," Joni replied as she drained the last of the eggnog from her cup. Tossing it into the nearest trash can, she followed Randi down the hall.

"What is it?" Joni asked as she and Randi walked to the nurses' station desk.

"A kid with a gash on his forehead. Seems he fell in his day-care center and bumped his head against a metal storage shelf. The cut looks pretty deep. I thought you might want to handle it. I tried getting someone from pediatric plastic surgery, but everyone was booked," Randi explained as she handed Joni the chart.

"Fine. This will give me a chance to practice some of my technique. By the way, I hope you're not angry about the teasing a while ago. You did make a very funny sight," Joni replied as she accepted the chart.

"Not at all. I'm glad I could provide a little levity. Your day will come," Randi replied with a wicked smile.

Laughing, Joni hurried to the examining room. Although she loved the pace of the emergency room and would not leave it for any other service, Joni occasionally missed the experience of doing delicate surgical work and of seeing treatment through to its completion. In the emergency room, she performed mostly quick-fix procedures before sending the patients to other departments for care. Even the clinic did not give her more than the usual physician's office experience. Knowing her need to perfect her technique if possible, Randi tried to give Joni patients that required total emergency medical care whenever she had the chance.

Slipping on her gown and rubber gloves, Joni introduced herself to the softly crying four-year-old and his worried mother. "I'll take good care of your son, Mrs. Peterson. It looks as if he'll need quite a number of stitches. Jason cut the forehead muscle in his fall. I have to suture not only the skin and tissue but the muscle as well. It's going to take me a while. When was the last time he had anything to eat?" Joni asked as she examined the gaping wound.

"About two hours ago, I think. The kids usually have an afternoon snack around two," Mrs. Peterson replied as she cradled her son on her lap.

"Unfortunately, I won't be able to give him any anesthesia. I'll have to rely on only a localized painkiller. He won't really feel anything, but he'll hear everything that I do. For a child that sound can be quite frightening. We usually recommend putting the patient in a straitjacket as a restraint. I know it sounds cruel, but it's a great benefit in this kind of surgery. It'll keep Jason from thrashing around too much while I'm working," Joni explained to the horrified mother whose eyes grew wide with fright.

"A straitjacket? Is that really necessary?" Mrs. Peterson asked.

"We can start the procedure without it if you'd like, but if he wiggles a lot, I'll have to insist on restraints. I've found that despite the sound of it it's less traumatic for the child to be restrained from the beginning than to have me stop and secure the straitjacket after I start the procedure. However, it's up to you. You know your son far better than I. Do you think Jason will lie still for the half hour to an hour that it will take me to close the wound if he is not restrained?" Joni asked as she studied Mrs. Peterson's worried face.

"Maybe not, but we could try if you wouldn't mind, doctor. I just don't like the thought of my child being in a straitjacket," Mrs. Peterson replied as she cradled her son to her chest.

"I can understand. I'll get my supplies ready, and then we'll begin. Would you lay him down on the bed, please?" Joni responded as she pulled out the suture kit and straitjacket. She wanted it to be easily accessible if she needed it. From the way the child squirmed on his mother's lap, she knew it would come in handy.

Mrs. Peterson tried to shift her son to the bed, but he only clung to her more tightly and screamed. Looking at Joni with a helpless expression, she asked, "He's very frightened. Do you think you could stitch him up while I hold him on my lap?"

"I could try, but we'll have to be very careful. Slip this cap over your hair and put on this cover. We need to try for a sterile environment in order to prevent infection. All right, Jason, I'm going to spray this cool liquid on your forehead. It won't hurt, but it will make your face feel a little numb," Joni said softly as she approached the child.

The little boy watched as she brought the bottle toward him. Just as Joni was about to press the plunger, Jason turned away and buried his face in his mother's bosom. "Jason, you have to let the doctor help you. Turn around, honey," Mrs. Peterson coaxed gently.

"No!" the child shouted. He was not crying now, but he was determined that Joni would not treat his wound.

"Jason, this medicine won't hurt. Let me spray some on your hand. See, it's only a little cold," Joni said softly as she waited for the child to turn his face toward her.

"No, go away. I won't let you spray that stuff on my face," Jason replied into this mother's body.

"I'll spray it on a cotton ball first and then put it on your cut," Joni countered as she moistened the tuft in her hand.

"No!" Jason bellowed.

Joni realized that there was little point in continuing the discussion with the child. Jason was undoubtedly frightened, but he was also quite willful. She knew that he would never stay still for the procedure even if she did manage to numb the area.

Turning to the mother, Joni said, "Mrs. Peterson, Jason isn't cooperating at this initial stage. I have no reason to believe that he will change considering the array of instruments on this tray. As I see it, we have two choices. I can close the wound with butterfly strips and hope for the best, or you can help me put Jason in the straitjacket. If I do not suture the wound, it is very likely that he will have reduced muscle control on that side of his face. His frown will probably be crooked. He could experience difficulty lifting that eyebrow. I would like to suggest that we not delay any further. The wound really needs the sutures."

"I hate the idea of the straitjacket, but I don't want his face disfigured. All right, doctor, let's put it on him," Mrs. Peterson responded reluctantly.

Immediately, Jason released his hold on his mother and hopped off her lap. He laughed gleefully as he ran around the room. In his new liberty, he upset the table holding the suture kit, threw the pillow off the bed, and knocked over a trash can. As they watched in shock, he bolted out the door.

Joni beat Mrs. Peterson to the door as they dashed after the escaping child. "Grab that boy!" Joni shouted to Frank as he stacked boxes of newly arrived supplies in the hall.

Turning quickly, Frank made a grab but missed the light-footed child. Unfortunately, Frank's foot hit the pile of boxes and caused them to tumble to the floor. Cursing under his breath, Frank bent and began picking up the mess that now covered the hall. The child only laughed as he darted around the corner.

"Jason baby, come back!" Mrs. Peterson coaxed as she followed Joni down the hall.

Joni dodged parked wheelchairs and gurneys as she ran toward the row of elevators. If Jason managed to board one of them, he could become lost in the hospital's maze of halls for hours. There was no telling how much mischief and havoc he could wreak in that time.

"Randi, call security. We have a runaway child. Head him off at the elevators if you can," Joni instructed as she darted past the nurses' station.

"Got you covered," Randi replied as she quickly picked up the telephone before joining the chase.

Rounding the corner, Randi approached Jason from the left with Joni running from the right. Jason darted in an effort to evade Randi's steady approach. Just as he was about to jump between the closing elevator doors, Joni grabbed the hood of his sweatshirt and slipped her arm around his waist at the same time.

The force of his struggling arms and legs threw Joni off balance. With her arms still tightly wrapped around the boy's body, she fell into the boxes of new forms that had just arrived. Her feet flew from under her as she landed in an unprofessional tangle of legs and cardboard.

"Now, I've got you!" Joni hissed into the child's ear.

"Oh, doctor, I'm so sorry," Mrs. Peterson apologized as she grabbed Jason by the waistband of his sweats with one hand and helped Joni from the floor with the other.

"No problem, Mrs. Peterson. However, I think we should use that straitjacket, don't you?" Joni replied as she straightened her clothing.

"Is everyone all right?" Randi asked as she surveyed the heap of boxes and Joni's lost shoe.

Slipping her foot into the shoe, Joni responded sarcastically, "We're fine. Just a bit of an afternoon workout to liven up the day. Nothing like a little jog to get the blood pumping."

"I'd say we're even now, wouldn't you?" Randi commented softly.

Glaring at her, Joni snarled, "Good thing we're friends."

Immediately Randi turned away to hide her smile as Joni and Mrs. Peterson led the errant boy back to the examining room. If Joni's face had not been such a thundercloud of embarrassment and anger, she might have laughed at the sight. As it was, Randi would not allow her face to move at all. Joni was not in the mood to consider the spectacle of herself in the least humorous.

Perspiration dripped from the faces of the two women by the time they finished strapping the boy into the straitjacket and attaching the ties to the bed restraints. Quickly, Joni numbed his forehead and began to suture the wound. Although he could feel nothing, Jason angrily screamed, cried, and howled. His mother stood by nervously wringing her hands.

"You might want to leave the room, Mrs. Peterson. This has got to be tough on your nerves. Go get a cup of coffee or take a walk outside. He's not in any pain. As a matter of fact, Jason might quiet down a bit if you leave the room," Joni shouted over the boy's racket.

"I think you're right, doctor. I'm not doing anything to help out anyway. I'll be back in twenty minutes," Mrs. Peterson agreed. Relief was written all over her face at being excused from the sight.

"Make it thirty. The damage is even more extensive than I originally thought," Joni advised as she turned back to the boy. The head and body restraints at least gave her a chance to work, but the noise was deafening.

"Whatever you say, doctor. Although my heart aches for Jason, his screaming is tearing me apart. I've seen him throw some fierce tantrums, but this one is the worst one yet. I'll be in the waiting room if you need me," Mrs. Peterson replied as she hurried away.

Working rapidly, Joni first stitched the muscle on the slope of the boy's forehead, then the tissue, and finally the skin. Commenting as she worked, Joni said, "He certainly did a number on his face. Good thing the cut was straight. With luck and growth, the scar should fade into Jason's hairline."

"He's quiet," Randi added.

"You're right. I thought it was my imagination, but his mouth seemed to have opened less often after I inserted the ear plugs. He thrashed his legs less viciously, too. I guess when he realized that I couldn't hear him, Jason stopped screaming and kicking. Now that I've finished, it looks as if he might be asleep. He probably wore himself out. He's lying completely still. I'll have to wake him to get him out of this straitjacket."

Counting the instruments, Randi replied, "I'll help you. For all his noise, he was just a frightened little boy."

When Mrs. Peterson returned, Jason was sitting on Joni's lap contentedly sucking on a cherry lollipop. He rested against her chest and chatted calmly about all the things he expected Santa to bring him. As she listened, Joni found herself being drawn by the child's magnetic personality. Now that he was not screaming, she could see that he was a beautiful hazel-eyed darling with sandy hair. She could easily understand how he had wrapped his mother around his little finger.

"Jason came through the procedure with flying colors, Mrs. Peterson. Here are the postsurgery care instructions. You shouldn't have any trouble. If he needs medical attention, take him either to your private physician or to our clinic. We'll be open every day including Christmas," Joni instructed gently.

"Thank you, doctor, for all you've done. I'm sure it wasn't easy. I hope you didn't hurt yourself when you took that fall," Mrs. Peterson replied as she hugged her son.

With a chuckle Joni showed her the earplugs and said, "It

wasn't bad at all once Randi gave me these. Have a Merry Christmas both of you."

" 'Bye, doctor!" Jason waved as he scampered along beside his mother. Her grip never loosened on his hand.

Watching Joni write the last notes in Jason's file, Randi commented, "I don't know about you, but I'm ready to call it a day. Let's join the others at Tobias's for drinks. By the way, you handled that fall with grace. It must have been those ice-skating lessons from your childhood that prepared you for it."

"No, it was watching you swing from the pipe that did it. I was determined not to follow your example. Tobias's sounds good to me. Just give me long enough to get my coat," Joni replied as she handed Randi the file and hurried to her office.

Pushing open the door, Joni was impressed with the silence of the room. After working with the nervous medical students and Jason, she was ready to go home. Slipping out of her white jacket and low-heeled shoes, she changed into a sporty red-and-brown tweed jacket and pumps. Giving her hair a quick brush to remove the dust from the fall into the boxes, Joni closed her closet door, clicked out the light, and left the office.

Tobias's Bar was a trendy, upscale hangout for the young professionals of the area. That night it was packed with not only medical staff from the hospital but with young attorneys in scuffed shoes carrying new briefcases, newly graduated M.B.A.'s with scrubbed faces, and seasoned veterans like Joni and Randi.

Seeing them enter, the rest of the emergency room staff waved them over to their table. As they squeezed through the happy crowd, Joni scanned the room for other friendly faces. Although she and Randi usually hung out with their City General friends, they had been frequenting the bar for the last few years and knew almost all of the regulars.

They stopped to chat along the way with friends from a

very prestigious law firm. Beaming, Virginia called, "Congratulate me. I made partner!"

"Hey, that's great! When did you find out?" Joni asked as she hugged her friend.

"They threw a party for me about an hour ago. I'm walking on air, girlfriend," Virginia replied as she beamed happily while she sat at a table with other black women professionals.

"Aren't you one of only two black attorneys in the firm? I'd say you earned your stripes and then some," Randi commented with a broad smile.

"Yeah! It's a big firm with nearly forty associates and partners and there are only two of us not counting the clerical support, but I'm the best! You know what they say, 'The blacker the berry, the sweeter the juice,' " Virginia gushed as her beautiful brown skin glowed with happiness. Her friends laughed warmly and patted her on the back.

"It's great news! You deserve it. You really worked your butt off. Now, maybe you'll be able to take a vacation this year. You haven't taken any time off in the last two years," Joni added as she playfully scolded her.

"Now isn't that the pot calling the kettle black. You practically live in the hospital. We're both due for a rest," Virginia shouted as she motioned to a seat beside her.

"One of these days, I'll take a vacation but not yet. I still have plans to finalize and a budget to balance. I'll catch up with you some other time. I have friends waiting for me. I'll see you later. Congratulations again," Joni replied as she pointed to the waiting group.

"See, neither of us will ever get away. We're workaholics and proud of it," Virginia responded as she returned to her friends.

Joining their hospital friends, Joni and Randi sipped their beers and munched on the delicious pizza. Everyone was looking forward to the holidays. The little impromptu party in the emergency room and the decorations hanging from the rafters in Tobias's made them feel even more festive.

"What's going to happen with the chief's job?" Melanie asked the question that lingered on all their tongues. She was a resident in emergency room medicine and had been Joni's medical student. They had become good friends in the process.

"I'm sure that the board will give each of us a fair hearing," Joni replied with confidence.

"But it seems so unfair that Don could just waltz back in here and try to take over. After all, he resigned," Thad commented. He was one of the nurses who now worked in the clinic and loved every minute of it.

"True, but Joni's young and female. They might hold that against her. It's been known to happen," Karen, a CPA in a local firm, stated bluntly as she pushed wisps of red hair from her eyes.

Joseph countered loyally, "It won't happen this time. No one can be that blind. Joni's the right *person* for the job; the rest of the stuff doesn't matter."

With wisdom beyond her years, Joni commented softly, "It shouldn't matter, but sometimes it does. I'm prepared for a hard fight."

"You're the best administrator this ER has ever had. The board couldn't possibly overlook that fact," Randi stated firmly.

Everyone at the table nodded in agreement and support. They were all rooting for Joni to become the permanent chief of the emergency room. They had worked for Don Rivers and preferred Joni's relaxed, leisurely approach to administration. She was always available to speak with them and included them in her decisions as appropriate. They enjoyed knowing that she was one of them.

"I can understand the board's perspective. Don served City General loyally while he was here. He implemented a few very beneficial cost-cutting measures. However, I'm inclined to believe that I'm the best person for the job because I feel that I've done more in these six months than he did in all of his years at City General. But, it's not for me to question, at least not now. I just want to relax with friends," Joni replied, looking from one face to the next.

Stubbornly, Melanie argued, "Well, I know that if the board passes you over in favor of him they will have made a big mistake."

Giving her friend's shoulders a hug, Joni said, "Thanks Melanie and all of you for your support. Everything will work out. Just wait and see."

The rest of the evening passed with small talk about the holidays. They danced on the tiny floor at the other end of the bar. As tired as Joni was after a long day and her experience with Jason, she accepted every invitation to dance and offered a few of her own. She loved spending the evening with her friends and was grateful that her position as their chief had not shaken the foundation of their relationships. She wondered, however, what would happen if she ever had to dismiss one of them. Joni hoped that she would never find out.

Nine

Preparations for the holidays did not stop the traffic through the emergency room. In fact, the variety of the traumas changed from the old, familiar ones to those that reflected the hurried feel of the season. Everyone was so preoccupied with shopping, baking, and seeing the old year out that they forgot to take the usual precautions. Lacerations, bruises, sprains, and breaks often resulted from their frenetic pace. People who usually did not put themselves at risk rose to new heights of vulnerability in the spirit of the season.

"Bring him in here," Randi instructed as she led the way to examining room three. "I'll get a suture kit and Dr. Forest."

The paramedics followed Randi's instruction as they wheeled the gurney through the emergency room door. The patient lay perfectly still as they navigated the path he had walked so many times in the past. His embarrassment increased with each squeak of the turning wheel.

"Let me get started cleaning that cut for you," Randi cooed as she examined the cut. "Yes, you'll definitely need stitches. Dr. Forest will be with you in just a minute. Can I do anything to make you more comfortable? It's not easy being on this side of the table, is it? Don't worry, she's very good at her job. You won't feel a thing."

Before the patient could answer, one of the paramedics

chimed in saying, "Yeah, I cut my hand slicing a bagel once. She stitched it up so that the scar hardly shows. She'll have that flap of skin reattached in no time."

Leaving the room, Randi handed Joni the patient's file. With a wink she said, "He's all yours. Let me know if you need any help. He looks pretty subdued to me, but physicians often make the worst patients."

"Thanks, I'll call you if I need any help," Joni replied as she pushed open the door.

"Hello, Dr. Forest," the patient greeted her sheepishly.

"Good afternoon, Dr. Rivers. I see you wanted to check out the efficiency of the ER from the other side of the gurney. You really didn't need to go to such extremes," Joni replied with a chuckle. "I would have given you the twenty-five-cent tour personally."

"Believe me when I say that this was not planned. I was helping a neighbor hang some lights around the eves of his house. The ladder started tilting. As I reached to prevent what could have been a nasty fall, I cut my hand on the gutter. When it didn't stop bleeding, his wife panicked and called an ambulance. I don't think it's all that bad," Don answered uneasily under Joni's steady gaze.

"Let me be the judge of that, doctor," Joni replied as she examined the laceration. It was not nearly as severe as the tension in the room.

"Well, what do you think? I'm in a bit of a hurry to get out of here. I have an important dinner meeting. Obviously, I'm not exactly dressed for it," Don said as Joni squirted saline solution into the wound to wash out the leaf and rust particles.

"You were right. It's not that bad. You'll need a few stitches and a tetanus shot," Joni said as response. "I'll send in one of the nurses as soon as I finish. Lie still. You won't feel a thing."

Applying a topic anesthetic to the area, Joni concentrated

on closing the wound. With each stitch, Don winced a bit in reaction to the movement of the needle.

"You can skip the shot. I had one before going to Greece," Don commented as he watched Joni make several neat even stitches in the underlying tissue before reattaching the flap of skin.

"You'll have to sign the usual waiver. All done. I'll send someone in with the form and a shot of antibiotic as a precaution. You know the drill . . . keep it clean and change the bandaging regularly. If you see any sign of infection, visit your doctor," Joni instructed from the door.

"Thanks. By the way, do you think we'll be able to sit down to a cup of coffee together any time soon?" Don asked as he swung his long legs to the side of the bed.

"What do we have to talk about? Any discussion of either the ER or the clinic would be premature until after the first of the year. I can't think of anything else that we'd want to discuss," Joni replied as she hesitated impatiently. She had paperwork to do. Talking with him was not getting her work done.

"Us," Don answered.

"I've told you before that there's nothing to discuss on that score. We can plan our professional interaction once the board makes its final decision on the chief position. On the personal front, there's nothing between us," Joni responded with a clipped, businesslike tone.

"There used to be quite a lot between us, if I remember correctly. I don't see why there can't be again," Don said as he buttoned the cuff of his red-and-green flannel shirt.

"I would appreciate it if you'd respect my wishes and not bring up this subject again. If we're to work together amicably, we must put this part of our past behind us," Joni replied tersely although she could feel her resolve weakening.

"We could make it right between us again if you wanted to try," Don persisted as he swung his jacket over his shoulders with his good hand.

"I think we covered every aspect of the topic already. No, I meant what I said in my office the other day. We'll interact as much as we must on a purely professional basis. There's no need for anything more. Now, if you'll excuse me, doctor, I have work to do," Joni responded as she left the room.

Approaching the nurses' station, Joni called, "Randi, would you send someone in with a shot of penicillin for Dr. Rivers and a disclosure statement, please? I've noted on his chart that he declined the tetanus shot, but I want the form on file. Thanks."

"Christy will take care of it. May I speak with you in your office for a minute?" Randi asked in a very serious voice.

"Sure, what's on your mind?" Joni inquired as she studied the expression of concern on her friend's face.

Walking together, Randi confided, "Don Rivers, that's what's on my mind. What's happening between you two? Every time I turn around he's here."

Closing the office door, Joni replied, "Nothing's happening. I won't let it. He wants things as they were before he left, and I want them to stay as they are now. That's all."

Shaking her head, Randi stated, "I would think that he'd get the hint. You've been telling him the same thing ever since he returned."

"Well, at least he's determined. I remember when we first started dating, Don did all the right things. He sent me flowers and cute little cards. After a while, he forgot and our relationship became routine. I guess that's when it started to cool. At least now he's paying attention," Joni commented from the window where she fingered the newest bouquet of roses from Don.

Randi replied curiously as she perched on the corner of Joni's desk, "What will you do if he continues this pursuit?"

Gazing out the window, Joni responded, "I'm not sure yet. Don has a long way to go before I believe that he has turned over a new leaf. There's plenty of time for him to revert to type. We'll see."

"By the way, how's Don's hand?" Randi asked with a slightly raised brow.

"It'll be just fine in a few days. It's a good thing he didn't cut it any more deeply. Another millimeter and he would have severed the nerve. Fortunately, he's not a surgeon," Joni commented as she spread out her papers.

"I'll go check on him . . . show him that the ER gives all of its patients top-drawer treatment, even the obnoxious ones," Randi replied with a chuckle as she closed the door behind her.

After Randi left, Joni worked diligently on the numbers she would need to justify any future expansion of the clinic. She was confident that, if the number of patients increased as predicted, the clinic would grow beyond the confines of its small, cramped quarters. However, she was equally sure that a reduction in caseload would mean that the existing space would serve the hospital perfectly. She did not want to miscalculate and propose the wrong move.

Joni had been in contact with the other hospitals with clinics and had found that in the early days of their operations their administrators had experienced the same concerns. All of them had labored over the subject before deciding to let the matter rest for a year. Eventually they had expanded the space after weighing the ebb and flow of patient traffic.

Joni had hoped prior to Don's return that she would have the luxury of allowing the figures to settle before making any further plans. Now that he had proposed the separation of the emergency room and the clinic into two distinct work groups, Joni knew that the time for leisurely reflection had passed. If she was successful in swaying the board to her way of thinking, she would have at best a short grace period to continue the reevaluation of the figures. However, no matter what happened, she would have only a few months, not a year, in which to make the recommendation. Fortunately, City General's clinic showed no signs of losing popularity, but Joni had to be prepared.

Reluctantly immersing herself in the budget figures, Joni concentrated her attention on the task at hand. Happily, she still had not found any numbers that would substantiate Don Rivers's claim that City General should immediately separate the emergency room and clinic into two units. To the contrary, all the facts substantiated her belief that the split would be premature until the patient load stabilized and the novelty wore off.

That night Joni sat in the living room wrapping presents and watching the late news. Letting herself in, Randi joined her on the floor and quickly slipped her finger out of the knot as Joni pulled it tight. Looking over her glasses, she said, "Maybe it's the holidays, but I was just thinking that we really don't tell our friends how we feel about them and how much they mean to us. I suppose we just assume that our friends know that we love them."

"Well, just in case you've forgotten, let me tell you right now that I love you, Randi. You're my best friend. My life would be awfully dull without you," Joni declared with a little quiver in her voice.

"I love you, too, Joni. We've been friends for so long that I can't remember when we weren't," Randi responded as she smiled happily.

"Merry Christmas, Randi," Joni pronounced as she hugged her close.

Raising her can of soda, Randi toasted, "To us, to Christmas, to happiness!"

"And to friendships that survive the test of time!"

The paper sparkled its promise of a happy holiday season as the two friends continued to chat and wrap presents. Their lives were so closely woven that neither of them could imagine facing a day without the other. They had held hands through broken love affairs, dried each other's tears at shattered dreams, and lifted glasses together in celebration of victory. It was not by chance that they had found apartments in the same building and on the same floor. Joni and Randi knew that a strong relationship between two female friends was harder to nurture than one with a man. They valued each other's opinions and trusted each other's silences.

Ten

The holiday season infiltrated the emergency room as it did the shops and street corners around town. A Salvation Army volunteer cheerfully rang her bell outside the hospital entrance while festive music played on the battered ER radio someone had set on the nurses' station. Physicians and nurses baked cookies, sang carols, hung more decorations, and greeted each other with extra cheer. Even the patients seemed less cross despite their ailments. Everyone found the excitement of the season hard to avoid.

"A little more to the left," Randi instructed motioning energetically with her outstretched hand.

"More? It looks like the Leaning Tower now. That's why I'm up here. I couldn't stand it any longer," Joni objected as she tilted the star at the top of the tree.

"That's it. Perfect!" Randi pronounced as she held the ladder steady while Joni climbed down.

"Finally! And I didn't fall like you did," Joni exclaimed as she straightened her jacket.

"You're becoming quite a grouch in your old age. You should do something about that," Randi teased in the relative silence of the emergency room.

"If I'm in less than perfect temper, it's because I'm out here correcting your mess when I should be in my office working. We don't get these quiet days often. I have paperwork to catch up on," Joni rebutted with feigned anger.

"It's good public relations for the staff to see that the head of the ER also has a soft side. You're always so busy that people have a tendency to forget that you're human too," Randi replied as she returned to the nurses' station.

"Well, they've certainly seen it today. You've had me hanging garland and ornaments all morning. I hope you're satisfied. Now, I'll have to work at home tonight just to keep up," Joni complained with a smile.

"Do you have something else to do tonight? I wasn't aware that you had any pressing social commitments on your calendar. Are you holding out on me?" Randi snipped with a chuckle.

"I had planned, if you must know, nurse nosey, to get my hair cut after work and to turn in early for a change. Now I'll have to cancel the appointment and stay up late again," Joni replied as she returned the empty ornament box to the shelf under the desk.

"Change the appointment to Saturday so we can go together. You don't need sleep. Your body wouldn't know what to do with it anyway. We haven't slept more than six hours a night since we started working here," Randi chuckled as she turned up the volume on the dispatch radio.

Listening closely, Joni asked, "Did you hear something? It's hard to believe that we haven't had a call all day."

"I thought I did, but no one's on the channel now. I'll call you if I need you. You're free to return to your office now, doctor," Randi responded as she shooed Joni away.

"Well, thank you, nurse. I'm sure you will not hesitate to interrupt my solitary existence if patients start arriving," Joni countered as she waved good-bye and hurried away.

Much to her relief, Joni was able to work for an hour without being disturbed. She managed to put the finishing touches on the report due to the board at the end of the month. She worked as hard on ignoring the gold-wrapped box on her desk as she did the report. She had refused to open it and would return it to Don as soon as she saw him. She would not allow him to distract her from her last effort to prove that the emergency room and the clinic should remain as one unit until she could do a more in-depth assessment of the feasibility of separating them. If the board chose to ignore her recommendation, she thought that the split would take place by the end of January at the latest.

Joni ignored the sound of increased activity in the hall until Randi finally stuck her head into the office. "Sorry to disturb you, but we could use an extra pair of hands," Randi said with a crooked smile.

"No problem. I finished the report. I'll be with you as soon as I run it upstairs," Joni replied as she sealed the envelope containing the ten copies of her document.

"Don't take too long. An ambulance should arrive in about ten minutes. There was a shooting at a fast-food restaurant downtown. We're getting the more serious victims," Randi responded as she held the door open for her.

Following her, Joni rushed upstairs taking them two at a time with the report in her hands. It only took a few minutes for her to deliver the finished document to the office of City General's chief administrator. However, by the time she returned to the emergency room, patients and anxious families occupied every chair. Joni was appalled by the number of children she saw lying on gurneys along the walls.

Returning to the nurses' station, Joni asked Randi, "Another ambulance? We haven't finished working these patients out of here yet."

"So much for a quiet evening," Randi replied as she picked up the microphone.

Entering examining room three, Joni encountered a group of bubbling preteen girls. They were so impressed by the handsome medical students that they had almost forgotten their trauma in the restaurant. The one with the badly lacerated right hand hardly looked in Joni's direction as she examined the cut.

"Penny, I'll have to put a few stitches in your cut to close it. It'll only take a few minutes," Joni said to the back of the girl's head.

Turning slowly and with obvious irritation at being distracted, Penny replied, "Do whatever you think is best, doctor. And you don't have to rush. I'm in no hurry to leave here."

Looking across the room, Joni saw Patrick Carter standing with the other medical students and decided to have a little fun. Calling to him she said, "Mr. Carter, I could use an extra pair of hands over here, if you would."

"Certainly, Dr. Forest," the young man of about twenty-two replied as he hurried to Joni's side.

All three of the girls immediately stopped giggling and became mute. They cast their eyes on an imaginary spot on the floor and did not look up as Joni gave the introductions. The girl with the lacerated hand turned bright red as Joni said, "Mr. Carter, I'd like for you to irrigate the wound with saline before I begin suturing it. That's right. Hold her hand over the basin and slowly wash the area. Allow the solution to flow through the wound, completely washing away any trapped dirt or glass particles."

"I hope I'm not hurting you too much, Penny. This is my first time," Patrick muttered in his soft baritone voice.

Penny only shook her head in response.

Looking quickly at Penny, Joni saw that the girl's face had deepened into a bright shade of red. Her friends had grown bold and were now staring openmouthed at Patrick Carter as if he were a marvel of creation. They watched as Patrick cradled Penny's hand in his and very professionally irrigated the cut. From the rapt expressions on their faces, Joni could tell that each one of them would have gladly endured the pain of a lacerated finger to change places with Penny.

Penny, whose lips trembled with teenage sexuality, never looked up. Nor did she utter a single word of protest or pain as Joni quickly and expertly stitched the nasty cut. As long as Patrick Carter stood watch over Joni's shoulder, Penny felt nothing except the power of his presence.

As Joni sutured Penny's hand, she noticed that Penny's pulse had slowly returned to a normal pace. It no longer raced under Patrick's presence. Remembering her own teenage crushes on older men, Joni controlled the urge to laugh. She knew that Penny would have been mortified if anyone so much as snickered at her obvious infatuation with Patrick Carter.

Penny was no longer shy. She gazed directly into Patrick's serious face as he watched Joni clip the ragged skin and create a neat line of sutures. Her expression had changed from that of shy childlike bliss to womanly rapture.

"All done, Penny," Joni said interrupting the teen's preoccupation with Patrick.

"So soon? Don't I need a tetanus shot or something?" Penny asked without taking her eyes from Patrick's face.

"A nurse will administer one in just a few minutes. She'll give you instructions for the care of the wound, too, but it should be okay. If it gives you any discomfort, see your doctor," Joni replied as she tossed the rubber gloves into the trash can.

"You mean, I can go now? I've suffered a terrible trauma. Don't I need to speak with someone in psychiatry?" Penny inquired with genuine distress written across her pretty blond features.

With a chuckle Joni replied, "You watch too much television. You're fine. As a matter of fact, you might not need a tetanus shot. When did you have your most recent one?"

"Last year when my horse threw me. A nail went into my arm. The doctor at the hospital gave me a shot then," Penny responded with disappointment.

"Well, then, you're free to go. Stop by the nurses' station for the care instructions on your way out," Joni instructed as she motioned to Patrick Carter to follow her. She did not want to leave him alone under the scrutiny of the young girls.

As Joni and Patrick left the room, she could feel the eyes of the young girls following them. Turning to Patrick, Joni said, "You did a nice job on the irrigation. Nice bedside manner, too. You certainly appeal to the younger crowd."

"Yeah, it was kind of embarrassing," Patrick replied staring at the toe of his shoe.

Chuckling Joni said, "I won't keep you any longer. You're free to rejoin your group."

"Thank you, Dr. Forest. I'll do that," Patrick replied. He was relieved to receive her compliment and to be released from the young girls' attention.

Joni watched him hurry away as Randi joined her. "Patrick has a lovely manner that would take him far if he could overcome his shyness," Randi confided. "I've watched him take the history of several older patients. They warmed up to him very easily. I'm sure he'll do just fine as he gains a bit more confidence."

"It's a shame that we don't offer a course in surviving teenage girls. They were very impressed by him. It must be hard being that handsome, young, and in the company of adoring females. He did a good job irrigating the wound even with their eyes boring a hole in his face," Joni replied with a laugh.

Randi handed Joni a cup of coffee as she said, "I know, I was watching through the window. I was impressed by his ability to keep his cool under fire. Between your watchful instructive gaze and their teenage crushes, he had quite a bit to overcome."

Don Rivers appeared around the corner and joined their conversation. With a big smile, he said, "Hello, ladies, it's nice seeing both of you together. I hope you're having an enjoyable holiday season."

Smiling through her teeth Randi replied, "Merry Christmas, Don. Excuse me. I've some work to do."

Leaving her alone to deal with Don, Randi scurried off. Turning her attention to him, Joni commented, "It's a lovely time of year. You picked a great time to return."

"I stopped by your office looking for you. I see you haven't opened my present yet," Don stated as they walked toward Joni's office.

"Actually, I wanted to talk with you. I can't accept a Christmas present. If I did, I'd give you the wrong message," Joni replied as she stood beside her desk.

"Think of it as simply a token of my enduring devotion and friendship," Don responded as he perched on the edge of the desk within arm's reach of Joni.

"I know you better than that. Whatever is in that box is not a simple token. I can't accept it," Joni insisted without moving from her spot. She refused to let Don think that she was intimidated by his closeness.

"I'm not going to turn this into another bone of contention between us. If you don't want to open it, don't," Don replied with a mixture of anger and disappointment on his face.

"Look, Don, I don't want to hurt your feelings. It's just that I'm still hesitant about reestablishing a relationship between us," Joni added trying to soothe his feelings.

"Still don't trust me?"

"I can't say that I do. You didn't exactly do anything to make me feel comfortable or to make me believe in you. Putting the job before our relationship wasn't exactly the way to prove your affection. Running off to Greece really put the skids to us. Right now isn't the best timing. The ER is keeping me pretty busy," Joni replied, holding her ground despite the intensity of Don's gaze.

"Somehow, I think you're doing the same thing now. You're refusing me because of the job, too, if I remember correctly," Don rebutted as he eased his hand a bit closer to Joni's on the desk.

"My situation is not the same at all," Joni responded bristling slightly at his new closeness and his accusation.

"Isn't it? I'm only asking that you give me another chance, Joni. I'm not the same guy. I've met my demons and conquered them," Don countered as he placed his hand gently on Joni's shoulder.

With a sigh, Joni asked, "What exactly do you want from me, Don?"

Smiling Don replied as he handed her the gaily wrapped package, "First, I want you to open this. Next, I want you to go to dinner with me one evening in the near future. We won't have to hide this time. I don't care who sees us. I want you in my life and I don't care about the gossip."

Tearing the paper with a reluctant smile, Joni replied, "I'll take this one step. I won't commit to anything more."

Don watched as Joni opened the box and removed the smaller one inside. Giving him a suspicious glance, she lifted the black velvet lid and peered inside. Lying on a bed of white satin was a magnificent diamond ring.

"I didn't come back just to get my old job back. I love you. Will you marry me, Joni?" Don asked as he studied her face for any signs of softening in her resolve.

Lowering the top slowly and wording her response with care, Joni replied, "I respect your medical and managerial skills, Don, but I cannot accept this ring or commit to a relationship with you. What we had was wonderful and difficult and nourishing and devastating. I'm not ready yet to return to it. Thank you for caring, but I'm not ready for a committed relationship and certainly not marriage."

Taking the box from her outstretched hands, Don said, "I'm going to do everything I can to make you change your mind. Good-bye, Joni, and Merry Christmas."

Joni waited as Don closed the door and the sound of his footsteps disappeared down the hall. Tension, stress, and raw emotion proved too much for her as she sank into the chair. Shaking, she buried her face in her hands and cried for the old memories and old love, the days lost and the ones never to be found, and joyous, laughter-filled holidays and the lonely ones. She remembered the days of love and wondered if she could ever have that kind of relationship with Don again.

Drying her tears, Joni packed her briefcase and headed toward the hall. She would wait until they arrived home to tell

Randi about her meeting with Don. Over a glass of wine, she would share the thoughts that kept her from reaching out to him.

As they passed the tree, Joni and Randi stopped and looked at the merrily twinkling crooked little star on top. For a moment, neither of them spoke as they tilted their heads slightly to the side. Then, they burst into simultaneous laughter and left the emergency room.

The few patients looked after them quizzically. "Too much eggnog, I guess," the man with the infected splinter in his thumb speculated.

"You're probably right," agreed the young mother with the feverish baby on her lap.

"I could use some about now myself," the man added wistfully.

"Me, too."

They watched as Joni and Randi braced against the cold. They had no way of knowing that it was not eggnog that made them so merry. It was the enjoyment of the small things of life after a long day of treating its misery that made them almost run down the street like happy children freed from the classroom.

Eleven

Baltimore was recovering from one of the heaviest snows on record; high drifts made walking a chore. People had already broken their New Year's resolutions as the cold and hardship made them forget about being good. Returning to work after their vacations, they struggled to walk along the slippery sidewalks. City General was once again bustling as a full complement of staff returned to their units and offices.

"Have you heard anything?" Randi asked as soon as she had finished making out the schedule for the week.

"No, not yet. It's still early," Joni replied trying to sound nonchalant although her insides were already in a tight knot.

"Is the board meeting still in session? They promised you an announcement last week, but they didn't deliver. They claimed they couldn't reach a unanimous decision with so many of them on vacation. They said they didn't want to decide something as important as your career without a clear understanding of the hospital's direction. You graciously allowed them to break their contract with you. The least they should do is give you an answer today. It's already past the first of the year. They need to make up their minds," Randi stated angrily.

"As far as I know, it's still in session. I was the fourth division head to give the year-end report and the projection for the new year. Vince Potter of pediatrics and Holly Piper of obstetrics were waiting their turn when I left. They'll probably break for lunch before taking up the issue of splitting the ER."

"Joni, how can you be so calm? The future of the ER lies in the balance," Randi demanded irritably.

"I know that, but there's nothing I can do about it now," Joni replied slowly. "I made my pitch, showed them the figures, and explained my objections to making the change at this stage. There's nothing I can do now but wait."

"Have you seen Don?"

"He followed me into the board meeting."

"Did he say anything to make you think that the board had already decided in his favor?"

"Don't get paranoid, Randi. All he said was good morning. I don't think I can make anything earthshaking out of that."

The piercing cry of a baby broke into their discussion. A girl of about sixteen ran into the emergency room carrying the red-faced infant in her arms. "Help me, please," the girl cried as she thrust the baby toward Randi.

"What's wrong with your baby?" Randi asked as she took one step backward into the safety of the nurses' station. She had learned from experience never to take a child from its mother or caretaker until she had all the information. The one time she had, Randi discovered that the child had been the victim of a kidnapping. The kidnapper had deposited the baby in her arms and run away.

"She's not my baby. I'm only the sitter. Take her. Stop her from crying, please," the girl demanded.

"Not until you tell me exactly what happened. I'll need the telephone number for the child's parents, too. What's your name?" Randi responded sternly.

"My name is Susan. I don't know what happened exactly. I laid the baby on the bed while I answered the phone. When I looked around, she was on the floor. I guess she rolled off or something," the girl answered with a nervous glance from Randi to Joni.

"Did you call the mother?" Randi demanded.

"No, I just grabbed the baby and ran over here," the girl answered as she twisted her hands.

"Did the child stop breathing at any time?" Joni asked. She had been watching the drama unfold and did not believe the girl's story.

Susan was of average height and build with wild, frizzy, blond hair that curled around her head and face like a large yellow cotton ball. Her eyes were bloodshot and blue. Her nails were well manicured, but her fingers were stained yellow from cigarettes. Her lipstick was of the red-black shade that all the girls seemed to prefer. She looked about sixteen although she might have been younger under all that makeup.

While Randi was busy trying to conduct the initial interview and uncover the possible problem with the child, Joni studied Susan's stark-white face. The most striking thing about her was the shifting of her eyes. Susan looked constantly from Randi to Joni and then to the door as if she were searching for a way out. Seeing one of City General's security police chatting with an orderly near the entrance, Joni caught his attention. With a slight nod, she let him know to be on his guard.

"I don't know. I was too scared to check. I just knew I had to get her to the hospital," the girl answered as she again thrust the baby at Randi.

"No, you hold her while I telephone the mother. What's her work number?" Randi responded as she turned to the telephone.

Looking furtively from one face to the other, the girl suddenly placed the baby on the counter. Pushing past the other patients in the waiting room, Susan bolted for the door. Her poncho flew out behind her as she ran.

"Stop her!" Joni shouted to the alert officer.

Before Susan could step on the pad that controlled the automatic door opener, the officer had thrown both arms around her. She wrestled against his massive body in a futile effort to break free. Her wild mane of hair tossed in the air as she struggled.

"Let me go!" Susan shouted as she struggled. "Let me go! You have no right to stop me."

"We'll see about that, miss," Roger Steinman, the emergency room's security officer, replied.

"Thanks, Roger. Bring her into the examining room, please. I'd appreciate it if you'd stay with us until we can find out what's wrong with the baby," Joni instructed as she led the way to examining room four. She carried the wailing infant in her arms.

"Now," Joni demanded, "give us the mother's phone number."

Rolling her eyes in anger, Susan spat out the digits. No longer was she nervous about the call. She had changed into a spitting cat as soon as she realized that she was trapped.

"What did you do to the baby?" Joni demanded as she examined the child's head.

"Nothing," Susan spat through the narrow red-black slit of her mouth.

"Then, why did you bring her here? Did she fall off the bed as you originally said? Did you drop her? What happened? You'd make my job much easier if you'd tell me the truth," Joni prodded. Her anger and suspicion grew with equal strength.

Susan stood stone-faced and silent. She did not make any attempt to open her mouth to say anything. Joni knew that the girl would not be of much help in uncovering the problem with the crying infant.

Slowly unwrapping the layers of blankets that swaddled the baby, Joni at first saw nothing wrong with the child. The head and face showed no signs of bruising. The baby had at least not fallen from the bed or been beaten about the head. Except for the redness from the constant crying, the child's skin looked healthy. She was clean and plump.

However, when Joni removed the little footed pajamas, she

discovered the truth. Festering red burns and angry welts covered the infant's legs. Turning the child over, she saw that the little back bore the same marks and additional scratches. As she pulled down the diaper, Joni found that bite marks disfigured the baby's buttocks.

Looking at Susan with tears of anger brimming in her eyes, Joni demanded, "Who did this? Did you?"

"No, no, I didn't do it. I tried to stop him, but I couldn't," Susan cried. She had changed once again. This time she was a sobbing, frightened teenager.

"Stop who? Who abused this baby?" Joni spat as she signaled to Roger to tighten his grip on the girl's arm.

Susan only hung her head and sobbed. Her shoulders shook with the force of the tears that ripped through her body. Her fuzzy curls fell over her face hiding the contorted features.

Joni covered the baby's tormented flesh and cradled her tightly. The infant no longer cried but slept fitfully. She had sobbed herself to sleep. Her tiny face had finally relaxed from its pain.

"Who did this horrible thing?" Joni demanded in a soft, choked voice.

"My boyfriend," Susan whispered.

"Why?"

"He's jealous, I guess. He wanted me to go out with him, but I couldn't. He said that if he hurt the baby bad enough, she'd fall asleep. Then we could leave her alone in the house. I tried to stop him, but he only pushed me away and laughed," Susan replied as she wiped her eyes on the sleeve of her sweater.

"Why didn't you call the police?" Roger demanded gruffly. His expression said that he doubted her honesty.

"He said that he'd hurt me, too. Besides, he's my boyfriend. I couldn't rat him out," Susan replied, looking up for the first time since her tears began. Her gaze was direct as she looked from Roger to Joni. Joni thought she saw contempt and arrogance beginning to replace the fleeting moments of regret.

"Where is he now? He certainly cares a lot about you, doesn't he? He's letting you take the heat for his actions," Roger said with more than a hint of sarcasm in his voice.

"I don't know where he is. He left when the baby wouldn't stop crying," Susan responded as she struggled to free herself from Roger's strong grip.

"So, you stood by as he tortured this helpless baby. You're as disgusting as he is," Joni commented as she turned her back to Susan.

"What was your part in all of this? Are you sure you didn't help him a little bit?" Roger pressed. He was a retired Baltimore police officer and had seen too many of these cases.

"I already told you that he did this. I only brought the baby here. Leave me alone. You don't have any right to question me. You're not even a real cop," Susan snarled.

At that moment Randi entered. "I've called the police, social services, and pediatrics. They'll all be here in a few minutes. The baby's mother just arrived. I'll bring her back, okay?"

"Thanks, Randi. Have you prepared the mother for what she'll see?" Joni asked as she turned toward Randi.

"Yes, she knows that we suspect that someone abused her baby. I'll go get her now," Randi replied as she vanished into the crowded hall.

Joni looked at Susan who stood defiantly with her eyes fixed on the open door. Roger held her arm tightly in case she decided to bolt. The girl for all her arrogance was really only a terribly frightened and troubled child. She needed the comfort of her mother's arms as much as the infant did.

In a moment, Randi returned with the baby's mother. The woman looked both distraught and relieved. She had read the newspaper articles about the child abuse cases that resulted in the death of abused infants. Regardless of what the sitter and her boyfriend had done to her child, at least the baby was still alive for her to love.

Rushing toward Joni, the mother cried, "Dr. Forest, please give me my baby. What have they done to her?"

Joni watched as Mrs. Morton buried her face in the sleeping child's warm neck. Her heart-wrenching sobs filled the examining room. Her shoulders shook violently as she pressed the infant to her bosom. Slowly, Mrs. Morton unwrapped the child and examined her scarred body.

Turning her streaming eyes to Joni, Mrs. Morton asked, "Two kids did all this to my baby? Will she be all right? Will she be permanently scarred?"

Resting her hand on Mrs. Morton's arm, Joni replied gently, "As soon as the police finish their investigation, we'll transfer your baby to pediatrics. Until then, I can only say that the wounds, with the exception of the bites and burns, do not look too severe on initial examination. However, the doctors in pediatrics are much more skilled at assessing injuries to infants than I am. For the moment, I will postpone any prognosis until after they have examined her."

"How could anyone do this to a helpless baby?" Mrs. Morton demanded impotently as she looked from Joni to Roger and Randi. Turning to Susan she said, "If you didn't want to take care of her, you should have phoned me at work. I could have made arrangements for my mother to keep her until we found someone else. You didn't have to hurt my baby. She couldn't even defend herself."

When Susan did not reply but only stared at Mrs. Morton arrogantly, Joni interjected, "Susan says that her boyfriend is the one who inflicted the injuries on your child. She claims that she did not stop him out of fear for her own safety."

"You must be one miserably unhappy young woman to have a boyfriend like that. A monster who would do this to a baby will kill you without thinking twice about it. If I were you, I'd find someone else. What will your mother say when she finds out about this? She'll be so disappointed," Mrs. Morton replied.

Susan looked away without the slightest sign of remorse or

regret. Joni was beginning to wonder if Roger was correct. Perhaps Susan was as guilty as her absentee boyfriend for the abuse of the baby. Maybe there never was a boyfriend; Susan might have fabricated his existence to remove the guilt from her own shoulders.

"I'd appreciate it if you would give us her mother's telephone number and name. Susan hasn't been very cooperative along those lines," Joni commented as she looked at Susan's straight back.

"Gladly. Her mother is my best friend. I've known her mother since before Susan was born. She's from a wonderful, loving family. You never know how kids will turn out. Her parents have given her every advantage. Now just look at her. I hope my baby turns out better than Susan has. She has been baby-sitting for me while my regular woman took a holiday break. Susan volunteered to take care of my baby this week. She's my weekend sitter. She has always been so good and gentle with the baby. I don't understand what went wrong," Mrs. Morton replied unhappily.

"Let's hope it's not too late to help Susan. Social services will do what's best for her," Joni commented confidently.

Within minutes, the police and the representative from social services arrived. The police officers immediately read Susan her rights and began taking photographs of the abused child. The baby wailed and kicked at the new indignation and the glare of the flashbulbs. Susan stood by stoically and watched as the police snapped pictures of the angry welts and bites on the infant's body.

After a few minutes alone with Margery Smith of social services, Susan finally seemed to understand that any cooperation on her part would help her case. She had stopped rolling her eyes and pursing her lips in teenage arrogance. She even told the police where they could find her boyfriend. She sat at Margery's side with a fearful expression on her downcast face and handcuffs confining her delicate wrists.

As soon as the police finished taking the required photos,

Joni stepped forward and began cleaning the infant's wounds with saline. With Jack Kelly of pediatrics at her side, she carefully applied antibacterial ointment to the burns and welts. After careful examination and consultation with Jack, Joni decided to use butterfly strips to close the bite marks. They were the deepest wounds and most likely to become infected because of the amount of bacteria residing in the human mouth.

Turning to Mrs. Morton, Joni instructed, "You can take her home now. I'd like to suggest that you take her to the pediatrician's office as soon as possible. I didn't give her a tetanus shot after we telephoned your doctor for the baby's vaccination record. However, the doctor might decide that one is necessary if the wounds appear red in the next twenty-four hours."

"Thank you, doctor," Mrs. Morton replied. "What's going to happen to Susan?"

"The police will take her down to the station and hold her until her mother arrives. I don't know about anything else. You'll have to check with them if you want more specifics," Joni replied as she marveled at Mrs. Morton's capacity for sympathy toward the wayward teenager.

Wrapping the blanket around her child against the cold, Mrs. Morton said, "I'll accompany Susan and wait with her until her mother comes. She's a very troubled child. I can't leave her alone without someone to look after her."

Joni watched as Mrs. Morton followed the police officer and Susan into the late afternoon sunshine. "I wonder if I'd be strong enough to do the same thing for someone who had just abused my child."

Randi commented, "Probably, but I hope you never find out."

Walking to the nurses' station together, Joni asked, "Any news from the board meeting?"

"Nothing, not a word. I haven't seen anyone or heard anything. It's getting late, too. Maybe they haven't come to a conclusion yet," Randi replied.

"If they haven't, this will be the first time in recent history that the board has not come to a speedy agreement on an issue. I hope they decide something soon. This waiting is hard on the nerves," Joni retorted as she scribbled the last of her notes in the baby's folder.

"I know how you feel, but don't worry. They'll come to a decision soon. They can't keep you waiting much longer. By the way, Don stopped by while you were busy. He left you a note. I put it in your mailbox in the physicians' lounge," Randi said as she turned her attention to the schedule for the next day.

"Did you read it? What did it say?" Joni asked as she finished her last chart.

"No, I didn't read it. The note was addressed to you. Besides, it was sealed too tightly. I'm a snoop, but I don't open other people's mail," Randi replied with a chuckle.

Laughing on her way to the lounge Joni said, "Randi, you know that I'll share it with you anyway. You could have opened it."

"What does it say?" Randi asked as soon as Joni returned with the note and two cups of cocoa.

"Be patient. I'll read it to you. You waited this long, you can wait another second or two. Let's see, it says: 'Dear Joni, I hope that there are no hard feelings between us. After the board makes its decision today, we will find ourselves working together again. I know I'm being foolish, but I'm still hoping for more than a professional relationship. Here's to happy times and a renewed friendship. Don,' " Joni read between sips of her hot chocolate.

"Well! He certainly won't take no for an answer."

"No, he won't. Maybe he knows more than I do. Anyway, he probably only wants to make nice with the person he assumes will be his new subordinate," Joni commented as she crumpled the note and tossed it into the trash can.

Exchanging the cup for a chart, Randi said, "I don't think that'll happen, but, if it does, he'll be in for a shock. You're not the same woman you were when he left here last summer.

You've come into your own. You're not pining away for him. You have a very successful professional life. He'll figure that out after a week of watching you work around here. You hardly have time to drink a cup of cocoa for all the work."

"Excuse me, but who is it that keeps piling on the charts? I was ready for a little break, but you've just given me more work to do," Joni rebutted with a hearty laugh.

"We're shorthanded and you're here. Next time, read your mail in your office," Randi quipped cheerfully.

"Some thanks I get for being generous and sharing it with my best friend," Joni retorted as she eased her way toward examining room four.

"Joni, thanks for sharing!" Randi called after her with a wave and a big smile.

"Anytime. Glad I could please," Joni responded as she grabbed a pair of latex gloves from the box at the door.

"I'll get you immediately if a call comes from the board," Randi assured Joni as she glanced over her shoulder at her friend's retreating back. With a wave of her hand, Joni thanked Randi as she introduced herself to the next patient, Tammy.

A few minutes later, Randi stuck her head into the examining room and said, "Helen called. You're to appear before the board in thirty minutes."

"Did she say why?"

"No, I asked, but she was pretty closemouthed about it."

"Well, I guess I'd better get cleaned up a bit," Joni replied as she rushed to her office.

Splashing cold water on her tired face and running a brush over her hair, Joni tidied up as best she could. Although she was anxious about being summoned to appear before the board, she was too tired to do more than a quick repair. Working with Tammy had drained her of her energy. She felt frustration, pain, anger, worry, and fear for the young woman who had gotten herself into an untenable situation.

Emerging from the office in high heels, lipstick, and the muted tone multifunctional tweed jacket she kept on hand for emergencies, Joni stopped by the nurses' station and said, "I'm off. Wish me luck. I'll fill you in on everything as soon as I return."

"Good luck, but you won't need it. Everyone at City General knows that you're the most qualified for the job," Randi replied loyally.

"Let's hope you're right," Joni responded as she vanished behind the closing doors of the elevator.

Upstairs, the board members milled around waiting for Joni to appear. They understood that a busy physician could not drop a case and rush to answer their call. Still, it was getting late. They were ready to adjourn and go home after having taken only Christmas Day off from their grueling pace. They seemed to have forgotten that they were the ones who demanded the delay, not Joni.

"Dr. Forest, thank you for joining us. I know how difficult it is for you to get away during your busy day," Bob Turner welcomed her warmly.

"I'm sorry to have kept you waiting," Joni replied as she shook hands and gazed at the smiling faces around the room. To her surprise, Don Rivers was among them. "I don't understand the reason behind this meeting. I had thought that when you finally decided to name the permanent chief of the ER, you would inform each of us in private, so I find myself at a disadvantage. Helen's message was cryptic. Should I have brought the December figures with me?"

"Oh, no, not at all necessary. We'll be brief and very informal in our discussion today," Bob Turner responded as he pointed to the empty chair.

Taking her place among the others, Joni sat and waited. The members of the board appeared poised and relaxed although tired. They certainly did not search one another's faces for answers to unspoken questions as if waiting to see who would be the one to break the news.

Bob Turner crossed his hands calmly on the mahogany table and said, "The board has granted me the honor of being the one to present its solution to the matter of the ER chief's position to you. Having worked closely with both Dr. Forest and Dr. Rivers, I can state that both have exhibited the highest level of professionalism in dealing with City General's patients, employees, and senior administration.

"These past months have been most difficult for all of us. We have undergone many changes. A tireless physician resigned for private practice, leaving us with heavy hearts. When he found it not to his liking, he returned, and we welcomed Dr. Rivers home with open arms.

"Fortunately for City General, in his absence, Dr. Forest proved herself to be a highly capable administrator, who initiated programs that brought the ER into the foreground and positioned the hospital as a trendsetting institution. Most impressive among her accomplishments has been the new clinic, which has been in operation only a few short weeks and has already proven itself invaluable to the community."

Bob Turner paused as a spontaneous round of applause burst from the assembled board of directors. Everyone rose to give the two physicians a well-earned show of appreciation. Joni and Don accepted the praise graciously with slight inclinations of their heads.

Continuing, Bob Turner said with a chuckle designed to dissolve the tension in the room, "We find ourselves in an unusual predicament. Never in my tenure as the chief of staff of this hospital have we enjoyed the dedication of two eminently qualified individuals both of whom are vying for the privilege of spending backbreaking hours in the service of City General. They want to be considered for a position that will put a strain on their personal relationships and their bodies. When you find two such dedicated gluttons for punishment, I say use them."

The board members responded as Bob Turner had anticipated. The slow chuckle spread through the assembled members until it became a rousing laugh. Even Joni and Don found themselves sucked into the current of the wave.

Allowing the silence to return, Bob Turner spoke once again, saying, "Unfortunately, there is only one position available for the chief of the emergency room. Both of the candidates have presented overwhelming and convincing evidence as to their qualifications. Their individual reports have addressed the prosperity of the ER and the new clinic. Each has rebutted the other as to the viability of the clinic as a standalone entity. The reasoning has been flawless from both camps. Both predict continued success of the facilities, although one favors postponing the inevitable splitting off of the clinic until the initial figures can be validated. We have promised both parties a speedy resolution. Unfortunately, we have not been able to keep our promise in the past and do not see a way in which to satisfy it in the present. However, City General cannot afford to lose such dedicated and talented staff. The board is, therefore, left in a quandary for which I believe I have a temporary solution.

"Recognizing our desire to maintain our relationship with Dr. Rivers while we analyze the figures as presented in Dr. Forest's sound financial document, I am hereby appointing Don Rivers as acting chief of staff during my three-month sabbatical. As you are aware, he has held that position on many occasions during the last five years. Being free from the responsibilities of a managerial unit, he is the logical candidate and has graciously agreed to step into my shoes during my absence. I leave my proxy vote in the hands of the board should it need to call a special meeting to decide the outcome of this issue prior to my return. I know that we can count on their continued devotion to City General until the board can make the final decision."

"I guess we'll be working together again, Don," Joni said as she offered her hand to the acting chief of staff of City General.

"Just like old times, isn't it?" Don replied with a smile as he gave her hand a familiar squeeze.

"Is it? I don't think so. Remember, this is only a temporary arrangement," Joni replied as she moved toward Bob Turner to offer her best wishes for a restful sabbatical. Seeing no purpose in lingering in the conference room, Joni rushed back to her office.

Randi cornered her as soon as Joni returned to the quiet emergency room. "Well? What was the decision?" she demanded without giving Joni a chance to catch her breath.

"There wasn't one. The board took the easy way out. Actually, when I think about it, I feel that I received a vote of confidence today. They decided to wait until after the clinic has been in operation for a while before making the final ER appointment. In the meantime, Don will be the acting chief of staff during Bob Turner's absence," Joni replied as they walked toward her office.

"Are you content with that? Isn't this simply a postponement?" Randi asked, taking her usual spot on the edge of Joni's desk.

"You're right. The fact is that the board decided not to decide. Maybe they're hoping that the problem will solve itself. I could take another position. I've certainly received enough calls in the last few weeks. They know about the headhunters who have been after me," Joni answered, as she filed away the emergency room and clinic figures

"Or they might think that Don will get tired of waiting and see this acting position as a bone. His ego might force him to leave. He'll get quite a bit of exposure from it and some job offers, too," Randi added. She twirled a pencil between her fingers like a baton as she spoke.

"I guess we'll just have to wait and see what happens. I'm too busy and too tired to worry about it very much. I love City General, but the bottom line is that I'd have a job somewhere in the area no matter what the board decides. That's a good feeling. I'm not too sure that Don can say that at the moment after being away for a while. I feel sorry for him," Joni said as she tidied up her desk. She was exhausted and ready to go home.

"Why? This is the same guy who nearly broke your heart!" Randi responded in disbelief.

"I know. I guess I'm softening in my old age," Joni replied. "Besides, Don's return to City General did not exactly work out the way he had envisioned. When he phoned me to say that he was coming home, he knew that the board would receive him as the returning prodigal son and he counted on me to welcome him with open arms. He hoped that I'd feel the same way about him. He hadn't anticipated that I would change. He looked a little less than completely confident today."

"I wouldn't worry about him. He's a man and he's arrogant. The 'good old boy' network will take care of him. He'll land on his feet. For all you know, he might have already positioned himself within easy reach of the gold ring. Bob Turner isn't exactly young. He might decide to retire rather than return from sabbatical. Sailing, lounging, reading, and lecturing might prove to be too enjoyable to leave. Don might have landed a real plum of a job," Randi commented scornfully.

"You could be right. Still, I wouldn't want to be in Don's shoes. He looked lonely and quite unhappy," Joni replied, as she slipped out of her heels and into her tennis shoes for the walk home.

"That's just the romantic in you talking. He's in a great position. I'd watch my back if I were you. It's for sure that no one on the board will. They've already made you wait far longer than they should have, and now they're delaying even longer," Randi commented.

"I've thought about all of that, but I think the board is dealing honestly with me. After all, Don hasn't been appointed the ER chief. His future is on hold, too," Joni countered.

"Well, I don't want you to forget that women don't have the same safety net as men. The glass ceiling is very much alive and well for us. The people who allow women to have these jobs always remember our gender. Besides, you've got another strike against you in that you're black. Black women have it even harder than white ones. Don's black, but he's male. That male-bonding football- and golf-playing thing gives him a real advantage over you. No matter what kind of mess men create, they always find a way to come out on top. That all-male professional club won't allow anything else. They can steal from the firm, cheat on their wives, and kill their partners, but they always come out on top. They cover up for one another all the time," Randi advised from her perch on the desktop.

Chuckling, Joni retorted, "Hey, I thought I was supposed to be the cynic. You're the one who always looks for the silver lining, remember?"

"I guess I've just seen this happen too many times to watch them do this to you. You deserve the appointment. They're jerking your chain. Don't forget that the glass ceiling is lower for black women. The board might be trying to find an easy way to show you your place," Randi argued with unaccustomed determination in the face of Joni's willingness to forgive the board's mistreatment of her.

"You could be right, but I'll reserve judgment until I know for sure. This has not been an easy decision for them. I still have confidence that the board will do what's right," Joni replied as she collected her things and switched off the light.

"You're not softening on him, are you?" Randi demanded.

"Maybe a little, but not enough to accept that ring and his proposal. Don still has to prove to me that he has changed," Joni answered as she locked the door.

Don's name on the door glowed in the dim light of the hall as a constant reminder that the board had not yet named her the chief of the emergency room. Joni hoped that soon she would see her name shining radiantly as the sign of the board's recognition of her contributions to City General and her ability to lead the ER and clinic. She would hate to exercise her other option and accept one of the numerous offers from interested hospitals that flowed across her desk.

Twelve

The emergency room kept Joni so busy that she hardly had any time to think about the long-awaited appointment. As an early warm spell brought trees into leaf and people into the streets, the ER and clinic were busier than usual. Everyone seemed to be in a hurry to enjoy the weather before it turned cold again. In their haste to seize the day, they inflicted unusual injuries on themselves.

"What do you mean? How did he get a fishhook in his back? It's the middle of February. It's not fishing season," Joni asked in disbelief as she accepted the chart. Scanning it, she read the note penned in Randi's neat handwriting.

"It's just as I said. The man has a fishhook embedded in his back. He said that he went fishing yesterday in this unseasonably warm weather and hooked himself. I know it sounds strange, but I've seen it. It's sticking out of his back. It makes my flesh crawl just thinking about it. I've seen many horrible things in this ER, but this is really disgusting. The sight of blood and guts doesn't bother me, but this fishhook is too much," Randi said shaking her head and reaching for another sip of cool water. Little beads of perspiration dotted her top lip.

Looking closely at her friend, Joni commented, "I've never seen you like this. Should I get someone to stay with you? You look faint."

"I'm okay as long as I keep my mind off that patient. Just

get him out of here as quickly as you can," Randi replied looking a strange shade of grayish green.

Rushing to examining room four, Joni entered to find Josh Redman lying facedown on the bed. His trousers covered his lower body, but his back was exposed. His friend sat in the chair next to him holding his torn shirt.

"Hi, doctor. I'm Neal Cushing, Josh's friend. Is it all right with you if I stay? I'd like to see how you go about removing that hook in case we have this kind of accident again. We're avid fishermen under all kinds of conditions. This kind of thing was bound to happen sooner or later. I guess we've been pretty lucky so far," the man in the wading boots, angler's vest, and cap explained.

"No, I don't have any objections if it's okay with Mr. Redman. Let me take a look at that wound. You certainly did hook yourself good. I hope this happened at the end of your trip. This looks like the kind of thing that could really spoil a day off," Joni commented as she examined the hook embedded in the fleshy portion of the man's right shoulder blade.

With a slight smile, Josh Redman replied, "It's not so bad unless I flex that shoulder. Then it hurts a bit. Actually, it happened as soon as we reached the lake. I hadn't cast my line out far enough and wanted to try for a better location. When I sent it out again, it snagged me. If I had been wearing my shirt, I would have been okay, but I had taken it off to get a little sun. I wasn't about to turn around after a two-hour drive early in the morning, so I fished all day with the hook in my back. Neal put a bandage on it to keep bugs from landing on the sore. Look, I took a day off so that I could go fishing and the weather was perfect. I don't regret a minute of it."

"I hope you caught something other than yourself," Joni commented with a slight smile in her voice.

Mr. Redman looked out of the corner of his eye. For a minute his expression was serious. Then he broke into a big laugh. "Don't make me do that. It hurts. Damn right I caught something. Biggest fish I've ever caught. Twenty-pound trout. It's in the trunk on ice. I can hardly wait to dig into it tonight for dinner."

Turning to Neal Cushing, Joni asked with a chuckle, "Is it really that big? I've heard plenty of fish stories in my time. I don't know if I should believe this guy."

Laughing, Neal responded, "Oh, no, doctor, Josh is telling the truth about that fish. We've never caught anything close to a twenty-pound fish before today. Most of our catches have been nothing to brag about. He was a real fighter, too. I had to help because of Josh's shoulder. He could have done it alone if that hook hadn't gotten in his way. Josh is very strong for a corporate attorney. I guess all those hours in the gym paid off."

Smiling at his enthusiastic response, Joni carefully probed the wound. She could not see the barb of the hook. It was embedded much too deeply for her to ease it out of the flesh. Besides, Neal's head almost blocked her light. He was so intent on learning the removal process that he had encroached on her area.

"Mr. Cushing, I'm going to have to ask you to step back just a little bit. You're in my light, and I can't see the area."

"Oops, sorry. I got carried away."

"No problem. As you've seen, the barb isn't within view. If it had been close to the surface, I would have just pushed it slightly forward, cleared the barb, and extracted it. Mr. Redman would have experienced a little discomfort but not much. Some peroxide to the area and a little bandaging would have been enough, assuming his tetanus shot is up to date."

"What'll you do about this one?" Neal asked, "I've seen fishermen pull out the simple kind before. They didn't appear to be a problem, but I've never seen anyone remove one that's this deeply embedded."

Nodding Joni replied, "You're right. This hook will be more difficult to extract. I'll try to do it without administering any topical anesthesia since the shots can be rather painful themselves. However, if Mr. Redman feels too much discomfort, I'll have to stop and numb the area. My advice to you if you ever need to extract a hook is to examine the wound for depth of penetration and to assess the patient's tolerance to pain. There's no point in inflicting unnecessary agony on anyone. And, never, ever try to remove a fishhook embedded in the eye."

"Don't worry. I won't," Mr. Cushing responded with a visible shudder. "I'm not too sure that I'd want to extract a hook that's this far under the skin."

"This process isn't as bad as it looks. Watch carefully," Joni advised as she looped a piece of strong surgical thread through the bend of the hook. "Now, using my left hand, I'll push the hook forward slightly. Mr. Redman, you'll feel a little pressure and maybe some pain. Try not to tighten your muscles. That's it. Stay as loose as possible.

"By pushing the hook a little deeper, I free the barb from the skin a bit. As you can see, I have to continue to hold it in place as I grip the thread in my right hand. Now with a quick jerk, I should be able to pop out the hook. Sometimes it takes two or more tries. I hope this time that I'll be successful on the first attempt."

"You're not the only one who's rooting for a successful first try. This smarts a bit," Mr. Redman replied as he turned his face away from Joni and Neal.

"Don't worry, Josh, she'll have you free in a minute," Neal said trying to make his friend feel better.

"Let's see what happens," Joni said as she gave the thread a quick jerk at the same moment that she released the hook.

"Ouch!" Josh Redman shouted. "That hurt! The first time didn't work. Now what?"

"The hook's even more embedded than I thought. I'll have to push it all the way through and cut off the barb. Do you want me to deaden the area or can you stand the pain?" Joni asked as she tilted the hook upward. Blood bubbled around the hook and formed a puddle in the wound opening.

"I'm dead either way. I'm afraid of needles. I have trouble going to the dentist. Will it hurt a lot?" Josh Redman asked as he looked from Joni's face to Neal's.

"The barb is almost through the skin now. Pushing it the rest of the way won't hurt too much. That's really the most unpleasant part. You might find it a little uncomfortable when I pull the stem of the hook back out. However, the anesthesia will hurt almost as much or so I've been told," Joni replied as she watched Neal return to his chair. He had taken on the same grayish-green coloring Joni had seen on Randi.

"Forget the shot. Just push it through," Josh replied. He clamped his teeth tightly closed in anticipation of the pain.

Quickly, Joni pushed the hook through the skin. Using the wire cutters that Randi had placed on the tray of supplies at his bedside, she handily snipped off the barb and discarded it.

"Gee, that hurts!" Josh Redman groaned. "How much longer, doctor?"

"Almost done. Just one more little tug," Joni answered as she gripped the tail end of the hook and pulled.

"Aaah, you're tearing a hole in my back!" Josh Redman screamed.

"All done. You'll have a little bruising and maybe some discomfort, but it should heal in a few days. If it doesn't, you should see your physician or visit our clinic. Lie still while I clean the wound. When did you have your last tetanus shot, Mr. Redman?" Joni asked as she washed the area in saline and applied a clean gauze dressing.

"Last year," Josh gulped as he struggled to calm his breathing. "That hurt more than a little bit."

"Sorry, I've never experienced it myself. I'm not a fisherman. One woman said that it was nothing compared to giving birth," Joni replied with a slight smile of apology.

"What did she deliver . . . an elephant?" Josh quipped as he sat up and slipped into the shirt Joni handed him.

"How does your back feel now?" Joni asked as she felt his pulse.

Wiggling his back and shoulder slightly, Josh replied, "Not bad actually. Wow, look at Neal!"

As Joni turned, she saw that Neal Cushing sat slumped over with his head between his knees. In his hands, he held a kidney-shaped pan. His complexion had drained of all color. When Joni touched him, she found that his skin felt clammy and cold.

"Mr. Cushing, are you all right?" Joni asked as the man groaned softly.

"I'll be fine in just a minute," Neal muttered softly. "The sound of skin tearing, the sight of blood, and that awful scream just about knocked me to my knees. I'm feeling much better now."

"Sit up very slowly," Joni instructed. "I'll have the nurse bring you some juice."

"No, that's fine. I'm okay now. I thought I was going to be sick for a minute. I don't know how you get used to all this. You must really love being a doctor to work with pain and suffering every day," Neal replied as he handed Joni the pan and rose carefully on wobbly legs.

"I do love it. Let me help you," Joni responded as she took Neal's right arm and Josh grabbed the left. Together, they propelled him toward the waiting room where he sat while Josh received the last instructions on taking care of his wound.

"Thanks, doctor," Josh called as he helped Neal walk from the hospital. Watching them, no one would have known that Josh was the one who had just had a fishhook removed from his shoulder and that Neal had tried to lend his support.

As Joni and Randi stood at the nurses' station, Randi commented, "I told you that fishhook was a unique experience. Which one of those men had it in his back? I thought it was the taller one, but now I can't tell."

"It was," Joni laughed. "His friend wanted to watch me extract it just in case one of them managed to get a fishhook embedded in his flesh again. He almost fainted when the patient screamed."

"I heard him all the way out here. I don't think the lady who delivered in the wheelchair made that much noise. I hope we don't get another patient with a fishhook again," Randi said as she filed the case folder.

"You're getting soft in your old age," Joni teased as she started toward her office.

"You know better than that. There was just something nauseating about that fishhook penetrating his shoulder. I don't like the sight of fish on hooks in the first place. Seeing a man impaled by one of them was just too much for me," Randi replied with a shudder.

"I still say it's old age," Joni retorted as she ducked the flying ball of paper that just missed her head.

Laughing, Joni retreated to her office. The fishhook was the most exciting thing that had happened in the almost six weeks that had passed since the board had named Don Rivers the acting chief of staff during Bob Turner's sabbatical. Despite Joni's misgivings about working under Don again, life in the emergency room had progressed along its usual chaotic yet comfortable lines. He seldom visited and never made any unrealistic demands on the staff. If it had not been for the weekly meetings, none of them would have known he was in the hospital. Joni saw less of him now than she had when he was lobbying for the job of emergency room chief. Don was a highly capable administrator who was trying to prove himself in more ways than one.

In fact, life was so relaxed that, for the first time since taking on the responsibility of the emergency room, Joni had invited a few people to her home for an evening of cards, food, and company. As she gathered her purse and jacket, she thought about all the sacrifices she had made in her personal life since becoming the acting emergency room chief and opening the clinic. Now, with the clinic proving itself capable of being a separate profit center and the emergency room functioning at maximum efficiency, Joni could afford to take a breath and give herself a little leisure time.

Joni sang as she mixed the ingredients for the salad. She had not felt this relaxed in ages. She had cleaned the condo, polished the furniture, set the tables for cards, and arranged the plates and utensils in the dining room. The next step was to shower.

Placing the bowl of salad in the refrigerator, Joni turned to the all-news station. The springlike weather would last through the weekend before turning cold again. No one should have any difficulty making it to her card party.

As the water pelted her skin, Joni reflected on her life. She was a successful administrator at a thriving hospital. She owned a lovely condo. Her finances were in great shape. She had wonderful friends and a very supportive family. Although she was in her thirties, Joni did not hear her biological clock ticking. She was perfectly happy with life the way it was.

Toweling off, she heard someone singing in the dining room. "Randi, I hope that's you," Joni called as she stuck her head into the hall.

"It sure is. The salad tastes delicious. I brought a pineapple cheesecake and a loaf of French bread. I see you've already decanted the wine. Everything looks ready," Randi responded as she eased the bread onto the cutting board.

"They should start arriving in a few minutes. You're not wearing anything dressy, are you?"

"Hey, you said casual. I'm in sweats. How much more casual could I get?"

"Good. I'll go halfway. I'll wear a sweatshirt and jeans. That bread smells wonderful, Randi. It's making me hungry."

"We can always start without them."

"That would be tacky. Just wait. They'll be here shortly," Joni replied as she joined Randi in the living room.

"I'm starving. What if they're late? I haven't eaten since I had that slice of cake at three."

"You're always hungry. I don't know how you keep your weight under control the way you eat."

"It's all the running you make me do. Three miles each day, rain or shine, will definitely do it," Randi retorted as she rushed to the door.

"I saw Janice and Mike in the grocery store tonight. I can't believe that they've been married for six years. It feels like only last year that we went to their wedding," Joni called from her bedroom door.

"No, last year Virginia and Todd got married, and the year before that it was Patrice and Ed."

"I didn't realize so many of our friends had gotten married. I guess we're among the last holdouts," Joni commented, pulling on her shoes.

"We've been too busy to notice. Besides, I'm not ready yet. I haven't had time to kiss enough frogs."

"That's the problem. I've kissed a few frogs, but I haven't found the prince. Actually, the last frog I kissed turned into Don. So much for fairy tales," Joni said, laughing.

The doorbell interrupted their happy banter. "Ah, there they are now," Randi exclaimed.

Everyone arrived at the same time carrying in platters and trays of food. The dining room table was soon groaning under the weight of sliced ham, hot macaroni and cheese, smoked turkey, steaming greens, buttery rolls, and every imaginable condiment.

"That looks like enough food to feed an army," Joni commented as she added her huge bowl of salad to the center of the table.

"We'll eat most of it before the first trick falls and the rest in about two hours. We always do when we get together. It's every woman for herself and let the diets be damned!" quipped Jan.

"I brought some candy for each table. We'll have plenty to

keep our hands busy between plays," Rick added as he poured the multicolored goodies into the bowls Joni handed to him.

"It sure is nice being together again. I don't think we ever see one another unless Joni has a party. That's a shame, too. We should do more to keep in touch," Grant commented as he piled his plate full of food.

"You're right. I remember when we used to play together as kids," Kristin added as she patiently waited her turn.

"I'm sorry that I've been out of touch. I promise to do better," Joni replied from the kitchen door. She carefully carried a tray heavy with glasses of wine and iced tea.

"It's not your responsibility to keep us connected. All of us enjoy these sessions. We aren't getting any younger. We should be more conscientious about being good to each other," Peter said as he accepted one of the glasses.

Randi chimed in as she sliced the bread, "Even those of us whose history in the group isn't ancient could host one of these evenings. Let's make a promise that we won't place the burden on the shoulders of one person."

Munching on a slice of kosher pickle, Frank retorted, "We can promise, but you know we won't keep it. Something always comes up. Before you know it, a year has passed. We're just so busy we hardly have time to breathe. But I agree that we should do this more often."

Amidst murmurs of agreement, the friends devoured their meal. Between bites, Rick said, "Frank is right; we would promise to do better. But the truth is that as soon as we leave here we'll become so involved in our own lives that we'll put our good intentions aside. The time will pass and we will forget to keep in touch."

Jan added, "That's what makes these card parties so special. We use them to catch up on the lives of old friends. We're all single, successful, professional people with stories to share. We're doctors, attorneys, schoolteachers and administrators, and union officials during the day. At night while playing cards, we just want to be ourselves and let our hair down."

"I agree, but we should still do better about keeping in touch. Bottom line," Randi replied.

As usual, the banter around the card tables was lively. "What do you mean trumping my ace? That's the only winner in my hand," Jan sputtered as her partner Rick threw a two of clubs on her card. She and Rick always paired up whenever they played spades. Their behavior led everyone to suspect that they had warm feelings for each other that they had not as yet realized.

"I thought the object was to win. Sitting here looking at this little nothing you threw down isn't going to win us the trick," Rick retorted.

"Are you calling my ace 'a little nothing'? You better think again. You'll remember this play when we don't make our bid. I was counting on that card for a trick," Jan pouted with feigned bad temper as she scooped up the tricks that fell from her partner's hand.

"Must you two start bickering this early in the evening? Someone would think you're married to each other from the way you fuss and carry on," Joni commented. She and her partner Grant had not managed to take a single trick. She hated starting out the night with her opponents running a Boston on her.

"Married? To him? Never!"

"What makes you think that I'd want to spend my life with you? You're bossy and quick-tempered."

"Me, bossy? Just because I have to tell you how to play doesn't mean that I'm bossy. It just says that you need assistance," Jan rebutted as she shuffled the extra deck. Her body language added extra punctuation to her sentences.

Grant suggested quietly, "Do you think you could stop haranguing this man long enough to deal? We've eaten dinner, now it's time to play. I didn't come here to listen to you browbeat Rick."

Laughing, Jan asked Joni as she dealt, "Why do you invite

people like this to your house? Don't you know anyone else? Why don't you invite some nice people for a change?"

Shaking her head, Joni replied, "I don't know why I do it. I guess it's because I don't know any better or maybe it's for the same reason that you come here every time. I know I'll have a good time with my friends."

"Humph!" Jan muttered. Turning to Grant, she spat, "For rushing me so much, I hope that I dealt you a hand as miserable as this one. Pass."

"Don't worry, you didn't," Grant responded. "Nine."

"Show-off!" Jan proclaimed.

The other table of friends was only slightly less noisy. They slammed down their trumps when they won and table-talked their bids. They laughed when they lost a trick and applauded when they were victorious. They were no more serious about the game than the people at Joni's table. Everyone just wanted to have fun.

"Damn it, the phone is ringing," Joni said as she laid down her hand. "I'll be right back. Don't look at my cards while I'm away, Jan."

"Would I do a thing like that? Just because you bid a six and I know you only have a two doesn't mean that I'd stoop to cheating. I'll find out soon enough that I'm right," Jan teased as she inched her fingers closer to Joni's carefully folded cards.

"Maybe you should take your cards with you," Rick suggested as he frowned at his partner.

"Whose side are you on anyway? You should want me to look at her cards. The ones that have been falling from your hand haven't been that great. We need all the help we can get," Jan retorted with her hand on her hip and her head turned to the side for emphasis.

Laughing, Joni rushed toward the kitchen. "Hello? Yes, this is Dr. Forest. May I help you?"

Joni could barely hear over the laughter coming from the living room. Closing the kitchen door with the toe of her tennis shoe, she listened carefully as the caller spoke. When she hung up, Joni no longer felt like playing cards.

Her friends read her expression as Joni returned to the room. A strange pall descended over their enjoyment. The cards seemed to freeze in midplay and the forks stopped on the way to open mouths.

"What happened? Has there been an emergency at the hospital? You don't have to go back to the ER tonight, do you?" Randi asked, thinking that someone had not reported for work and that Joni as the chief of the emergency room would have to cover.

"No, everything's fine in the ER."

"I hope it's not bad news about your parents," Grant said. All of them had older parents and always listened expectantly for emergency telephone calls.

"No, they're in Florida. That was Robert Brown, the chair of the facilities subcommittee of the board. Bob Turner died in a plane crash late this afternoon," Joni responded sadly.

"Oh, no! How did it happen? I thought he was on sabbatical resting on a beach somewhere," Randi asked as the sadness descended over her face.

"He was on leave," Joni replied softly. "One of the things he had always wanted to do was to fly a plane. Robert Brown says that Bob was taking flying lessons during his sabbatical. Anyway, he was in the process of taking the fifth lesson when the plane simply dropped from the sky. A large section of the wing fell off, and the plane careened out of control. Maybe a more skilled pilot would have been able to prevent the crash, but I doubt it. The instructor had duplicate controls. I guess it was simply their time."

No one spoke or moved for a long time. Randi was the only other person in the room who knew Bob Turner, yet they all felt the loss. They reflected on their own dreams deferred because of work or personal responsibilities. Life was so short and unpredictable.

The doorbell rang jarring them out of their trance. Slowly,

Joni rose and walked the short distance to the foyer. Opening the door, she jumped back in surprise.

"Sorry to barge in like this, but I wanted to be sure that you heard the news about Bob Turner," the voice said from the hallway.

"Yes, Robert Brown just called. Come in, please," Joni replied as she held the door wide.

Don Rivers stepped into the silence that filled the familiar condo. Immediately memories of happier times flooded his mind. He had spent wonderful evenings planning a future with Joni in that living room. She had served him delicious meals in the dining room. They had lain sexually spent in the queen-size bed in the bedroom. The good times had ended, but the condo had remained unchanged. The tasteful prints still repeated the colors of the sofa and chairs. Floral arrangements decorated each table. Joni's perfume lingered in the air even over the aroma of food. And fresh flowers decked the foyer table just as they had when he brought them to her. Don longed to pull Joni into his arms, but he refrained for fear of frightening her away. He had to remain on his best behavior.

"I see you have company. I won't stay long. Did Robert give you all the details?" Don asked without removing his lightweight jacket.

"Yes, I believe he did. He explained that Bob died as the result of a plane crash. That's such a loss for the hospital and for each of us personally," Joni replied with her arms folded tightly around her body. She remembered the time, too, when she would have sought solace from news like that in Don's arms.

"Yes, a terrible loss."

"You didn't have to come all the way here to tell me. You could have phoned," Joni suggested as they lingered in the foyer.

"I know, but I guess I needed to be here to tell you. We worked for the man for years. He was a mentor to both of us. It felt natural for me to come here in person," Don replied as he shifted his weight from one foot to the other like an uncertain schoolboy.

"Well, thanks. Would you like to join us? There's plenty of food left. You could take my place at the table if you're up for a hand of cards," Joni offered as she motioned toward the dining room.

"If I'm not intruding, I'd certainly enjoy something to eat. I've been at the hospital all day and haven't had anything since breakfast," Don replied as he followed her gaze and the aroma.

"I'll introduce you to everyone. You already know Randi," Joni replied as she hung Don's coat in the hall closet with the others and led the way into the living room. Making the introductions, she directed him to the dining room and handed him a plate.

"Thanks," Don said as he began to serve himself from the food that Joni brought from the refrigerator. "Your place looks great but a little smaller than I remembered."

"That's probably because the card tables take up a lot of space," Joni replied as she spooned some of the chicken and pasta salad onto his plate.

"My favorite," Don commented as he studied Joni's face.

"I know," Joni replied as she avoided his eyes. She could feel the color rising in her cheeks. "This is not the time for rehashing old memories. I'm going back to the game. Pull up an extra chair and join us when you're ready. Put the salad back in the fridge when you've finished."

"Will there ever be the right time?" Don asked as he eased his arms around Joni's shoulders and held her close.

"Maybe," Joni conceded as she slipped away.

Returning to the living room, Joni tried to shake off the effects of the news about Bob Turner and the closeness of Don. She cast a quick glimpse at Randi and smiled. She wanted her friend to know that she was okay with the unexpected turn of events and visitor.

Slowly, the evening regained some of its gaiety, although

the laughter never totally dissipated the gloom. As Joni cleared away the dishes, Don played a few hands in her place. She caught him watching her as she moved around the room. He touched her hand lightly whenever she stood near him and drank in her every move with his eyes.

By midnight, everyone had left. Randi stayed behind to help with the final cleanup. Drying the last platter, she asked, "Why do you think Don came over?"

"He told me that he wanted to share the news in person rather than simply dropping it on me. Hearing about Bob was rather shocking and upsetting. Over the past few months, I had worked closely with him," Joni replied as she wiped down the counter and turned out the light.

"I don't trust him. I saw the way he was watching you. The expression on his face was much more than simply friendship."

"I know."

"Joni, you're softening toward him, aren't you? I don't believe it," Randi exclaimed with something akin to frustration on her face.

"I'm not really changing, I'm just watching him closely. He really is putting forth considerable effort to show that he's different now. I think I'm taking a new, open-minded stance," Joni replied, hoping to end any further questioning by Randi.

Pulling her keys from her sweatsuit pocket, Randi said, "Well, maybe the board will name him the permanent chief of staff. If that happens, he'll be so busy with the hospital that he won't have time to continue his pursuit of you. You'll return to your senses, too."

"Bob Turner's death could certainly change things for Don and for me. But I won't allow myself to think about it yet. Too many things could still go wrong. There's no promise that the hospital would appoint Don as the chief of staff. The board might decide to go outside. They tried to do it for the ER chief's spot. We'll have to wait and see," Joni replied as she stretched and yawned. She was tired from the long day and the stress.

"Are we going to run tomorrow morning?"

"Sure. The weather should be perfect. I'll meet you at the elevator at nine. We'll grab some bagels on the way back."

"See you in the morning," Randi called as she walked down the hall toward her condo. "You'd better get some rest this weekend. You don't know what you'll have to face on Monday from Don and the board."

Even after she was in bed, Joni could not sleep. Bob Turner's death and its impact on City General kept her awake, although she was extremely tired. She played out the different scenarios and combinations as she waited for the quiet of the night and the purring of her cat to lull her to sleep. Randi could be right about Don's appointment to fill Bob's shoes, but then again, the board might look outside and bring in a new person whose leadership would take the hospital down a different path. She would just have to wait and see what happened.

And then there was Don. Joni wanted to believe that this new persona he exhibited would be a permanent one, but she would have to wait and see. Her long-denied feelings for Don were growing stronger by the day. Joni reminded herself that, if she was not careful, he would break her heart again. She had traveled that road already and did not want to do it again.

Thirteen

The better part of three months passed with only speculation regarding the permanent appointment of a new chief of staff. Everyone appeared to think that Don Rivers had the job pretty much sewn up. The board conducted a halfhearted candidate search, which produced no one with credentials strong enough to oust Don. The board continued to look, but no one thought that they would ever find anyone. The members of the emergency room staff were too busy to allow hospital politics to enter their lives. Even Joni felt confident that her job as chief of the emergency room was finally secure, although the board had not made an announcement about her position either.

One day at the end of June, Robert Brown brought around one of the many candidates they had met since Bob Turner's death. He had toured the rest of the hospital with interest and had specifically requested a lengthy visit in the emergency room. He had heard of the reputation of City General's clinic and emergency facility.

As soon as he entered the emergency room, Joni saw that Stephen Clay was different from the other hopefuls. She had read his résumé and knew that he had been the chief of staff at a medium-size hospital in Washington, D.C., for the past five years. The move to City General would be a promotion for him and a logical step in his career progression.

"Delighted to meet you, Dr. Forest. I've heard great things

about your work here at City General. I've watched the progress of the clinic you started with great interest," Stephen Clay commented enthusiastically as he shook Joni's hand.

"Thank you, Dr. Clay. We've been most fortunate to receive quite a bit of positive press. My staff is dedicated to making the clinic a successful profit center like its ER counterpart. In a few more weeks, we hope to have a clear handle on our success," Joni replied as she returned his firm handshake.

"I'll be here visiting for a few days. I'd appreciate it if you'd have lunch with me during my stay. I'd like to hear all about the funding, obstacles, and the benefits of such a massive undertaking," Stephen suggested.

"I'd love to share everything I know with you. In the beginning I offered seminars to any hospital administrator who wanted to hear about the conception of the idea. I've been too busy to do that since opening the clinic. However, I'd be happy to speak with you personally. You might just give me the impetus I need for getting my act together and taking it on the road again," Joni agreed with a warm smile.

"Great. How about this afternoon? I don't believe the board has anything in particular planned for me."

"Fine. How's noon for you?"

"Perfect, Dr. Forest. I'll see you then."

Joni and Randi watched as Robert Brown and Stephen Clay left the emergency room. Turning toward her friend Randi commented, "I think Don should be a little bit worried right now."

"I agree. I think the board has found a winner this time. Don should have felt a little concerned when he saw how good Stephen Clay looked on paper. After meeting with him, if I were in Don's shoes, I'd start to sweat. He's professional, polished, and capable of influencing the staff with his sincere approach. Don might just have some competition for the chief of staff spot after all. Does he remind you of someone?" Joni asked as the elevator door closed, blocking out the sight of their visitor.

"I can't think of anyone. Who?" Randi replied as she knitted her brow in concentration.

"Parker Fielding," Joni answered as she busied herself adding notes to an already complete chart.

"You're right. I don't know why I didn't see the resemblance. They have the same penetrating eyes and direct gaze and a very up-front manner. Stephen seems to be the same kind of honest guy. Maybe . . ." Randi commented casually as she watched Joni's agitation.

"Don't even go there! I don't have time," Joni stated as she handed Randi the chart and hurried to her office leaving the sound of her friend's laughter behind her.

Stephen Clay was not a physically imposing man. Unlike Don Rivers who stood more than six feet tall, he was a relatively short five-foot-nine, yet he carried himself with grace and ease. Unlike other short men, he seemed content with his stature. Although on a job interview, he had chosen to dress casually. His sports coat, sweater, open-neck shirt, and trousers were of good quality and suggested a country gentleman more than a hospital administrator. His dark-brown hair was slightly disheveled as if he had been caught by a gust of wind and had been too busy to care about his appearance. Unlike the other administrators who dressed in impeccably tailored three-piece black or dark-blue suits, Stephen was a pleasant breath of nonconformity.

Over lunch in the busy cafeteria, Joni delivered a casual but professional presentation to which Stephen listened with rapt attention. He took no notes, but from memory fired off questions, recited figures, and dug for additional depth of analysis. Joni was very impressed with his grasp of City General's emergency room function, his understanding of the connection between the emergency room and the clinic, and his comprehension of and agreement with her conservative approach to the issue of splitting the clinic from the emergency room. Joni was also moved by his sincere interest in her dreams and aspirations. It had been a long time since she had shared her thoughts with a man who appeared genuinely interested in her as a valued professional.

"Well? How was it?" Randi asked as soon as Joni returned.

"Stephen Clay is definitely head and shoulders above the other candidates we've seen. He makes Don look like a neophyte. I don't know how the other department chairs felt when they met with him this morning, but I was most impressed. He made me look at my figures in a totally different way. His past experience as the chief of staff of a big-city hospital has given him insights and experience that the other candidates, including Don Rivers, lacked," Joni replied as she carefully filed the latest set of figures she had prepared for the meeting with Stephen.

"What do you mean?"

"I've been studying the issue of separating the clinic from the ER. That still has merit and Stephen agrees with my analysis. However, he asked me if I'd given thought to an even larger issue that could give us incredible freedom to practice medicine. He asked if City General had ever thought of turning the management of the ER over to an outside firm so that we could really focus on expanding the clinic's functions. He thinks that the ER, as a sound profit center, could be managed by an outside organization with ease. We'd have more time to enjoy the medical side of our work because we'd spend less time on the administrative responsibilities."

"Are you saying that we'd actually get our lives back?"

"Exactly, Randi. I don't think the change would fly at City General, but what excites me isn't just the idea. It's the fact that he asked me to think beyond the here and now. From his experiences at the hospital in D.C., where administrative paperwork of the hospital has been turned over to a management company, he knew which questions to ask and in which direction to push my analysis. I'm excited about the concept. I can definitely see that Stephen's presence could do much to reshape the status quo of City General. I don't know if we're ready for his innovative ideas, but at least we'd have something to contemplate and consider."

"How is he as a person? Don's kind of a cold fish. He never seems comfortable with new people," Randi asked as she began to catch Joni's enthusiasm for the candidate.

"We chatted as if we'd worked together for years. I didn't feel any of that newness that keeps people locked up within themselves. He was great. Stephen's a very open, receptive kind of guy. He encourages people to think, to explore, and to reach for the impossible. The similarities between him and Parker are uncanny," Joni replied as she slipped into her jacket.

"Married?"

"No, he said that he never had the time. He sounds a lot like us. Too busy with the job to think about a serious personal life. He's dedicated. I like him already."

"Personally or professionally?"

"Definitely professionally. The jury is out on the personal issue."

"I think I can hear Don returning to Greece now."

Laughing, Joni responded, "I don't know if I'd go that far. But I do know that if I were Don Rivers, I wouldn't start moving my stuff into the chief of staff's office. I'd also make sure that my résumé was current."

Randi said tossing a new chart at Joni, "Everyone needs a little competition to keep them humble. By the way, the gentleman asked for you by name, and says he's been a patient here before. I couldn't find any previous records on him in the computer. Maybe he came here a long time ago. He looked strangely familiar to me, but I couldn't place him. We treat so many people. They remember us, but we don't remember all of them. He's waiting in the clinic for you now."

Frowning slightly, Joni accepted the chart and hurried across the waiting room to the clinic. She enjoyed her daily rotation and looked forward to her time with the patients. She had met many interesting and unusual people while treating their ailments. Joni wondered if one of those patients had returned.

Following Randi's direction to room two, Joni knocked lightly on the door and then entered. She looked carefully at the man sitting on the examining table in his underwear and short examining gown. He looked fit. She could not imagine what he needed from her.

"Hello, I'm Dr. Forest. I understand you requested my services. What seems to be the problem today, Mr. Jones?" Joni asked as she studied his face. A nagging memory tried to surface but failed.

"You don't remember me, do you, doctor? I guess I do look different although it hasn't been that long since I was here. However, I'll save you the discomfort by identifying myself. My wife brought me in here during the fall. I had experienced an unpleasant close encounter with an angry robbery victim, if I remember correctly," the man explained in a soft, Southern accent.

"I'm sorry, but I see many gunshot wounds, too many actually. I'm afraid I don't remember your specific treatment. How may I help you today?" Joni replied as she scanned her memory for recall of the man's chart.

"Well, perhaps this will help jog your memory," the man continued. "My wife and I 'borrowed' your friend. I'm surprised she didn't remember me. I admit I wasn't at my best with blood all over my clothes and my face an ashen disaster, but we did take an enjoyable ride together."

For an instant, Joni could not move. Her mind had connected with the image of the husband-and-wife team, the bullet wound in the man's shoulder, and Randi's abduction. Staring at the man, she suddenly remembered his face. He had indeed changed. His cheeks were rosy and his eyes sparkled with good health. When she had first met him, he had been drained of color and barely able to keep his eyes open from loss of blood and the ensuing weakness.

"Yes, I remember you now. I thought the police had arrested

you. Didn't I hear on the news that they had caught up with you and your wife when your wound became infected?" Joni asked incredulous that an admitted thief was sitting in the clinic as a free man rather than spending time in jail.

"You did indeed," the man replied, clapping his hands like a child. "Good job, doctor. I knew you'd remember if I mentioned my involvement with your friend. We were arrested, but the police couldn't make the charges stick. It seems that the older gentleman whom we robbed preferred not to press charges. You see, some of his wealth had been acquired through questionable means. To accuse us of stealing his treasures would have put him in jeopardy and under scrutiny for his own dealings. He decided that the safer route would be to ignore our little heist. As embarrassing as it was for him to have his security system breached, he would rather lose face with everyone to whom he had bragged about it than report us. The irony of life is sometimes nothing short of astounding. We robbed a robber."

"I don't understand what any of this has to do with either me or the hospital. Are you in need of medical attention? What can I do for you?" Joni asked as she struggled to understand the reason for his visit.

"I wanted to share my good fortune with you. When I was in need, you and this hospital took care of me. I felt terrible about repaying your kindness by kidnapping your friend and wondered what I could do to make amends for our behavior. The kind nurse had been very good to me, and we rewarded her by scaring her out of her wits. You had performed admirably under stress, and we treated you shabbily. When I read in the paper about your thriving operation, I knew just what to do. I'm here to make a contribution to City General's clinic," the man beamed.

"I can't believe what you're saying. You're expecting me to accept money from the man who kidnapped my best friend. You seem to think that I can act as if . . . as if that never happened, as if you're a regular person who wants to make a donation. Have you lost touch with reality? You're a criminal, a thug, a very bad man," Joni sputtered angrily as she searched for the right words with which to banish Mr. Jones from her life and the hospital.

"Great idea, isn't it!" the man continued mistaking Joni's stunned silence as her reaction to his generosity rather than the shock of seeing him again. "My wife and I made more money on that little theft than we will ever be able to spend. We've bought a couple of investment homes, an apartment building, and vacation property in the islands and in Europe. We've sheltered the money in bank accounts and stocks and bonds. We're set for life. Our kids will never have to work a day in their lives. We always wanted to be the rich, idle, gentrified people we pretended to be, and now we are. We can afford to be generous to others. We're looking for charities. Let me help you. Besides, we didn't hurt your friend."

"I don't know how to answer you, Mr. Jones. I've never had an offer like this one. City General could definitely use the money, but I don't know about the legality of accepting your support while knowing the circumstances of your acquired wealth," Joni replied.

"I've already checked with my lawyer who assures me that neither you nor the hospital would be placed in jeopardy by doing business with me," Mr. Jones stressed as he explained his position. "There's no taint attached to this money. The gentleman from whom we stole the art didn't press charges, as I told you. Art investors do the same thing with treasures every day. I sold the items through an auction house that didn't feel any qualms about taking its commission."

"But you stole the art. You didn't purchase it," Joni protested as she argued against accepting the much needed gift.

"Ah, that's a matter of little consequence. What makes you think that every item of art that's auctioned by the major auction houses was legally acquired? Dr. Forest, your naïveté is very refreshing but sadly misguided. Why do you think that so many secret Swiss bank accounts exist? I'm definitely not the only person to make money from under-the-table acquisitions. The gentleman from whom I stole the art has a houseful of masterpieces and first editions. I know that he did not acquire all of them in honest dealings. He would have pressed charges against us if he had," Mr. Jones explained as he tried to convince Joni to accept his offer even if it was acquired from illegal means.

"Mr. Jones, please give me a minute to think. Won't the man from whom you stole the art make a connection between City General's benefactor and his treasures?" Joni asked as she continued to digest the information.

"Probably, but there's nothing he can do about it now. I no longer have any of the pieces. I've sold everything. I will never divulge the source of my good fortune any more than you need to identify yours. If it makes you feel more comfortable, you can say that an anonymous benefactor turned all of your dreams into realities. I'm not doing this for the publicity. As you can imagine, Jones is not really my name. The clinic could use the money, couldn't it? I haven't been misinformed by the press on that score, have I?" Mr. Jones asked. As he tilted his head a little to the right, he looked like a leprechaun waiting for someone to dip into his pot of gold.

"You're definitely not mistaken. The clinic could make good use of your contribution. All right, Mr. Jones, you've convinced me. But don't think that you've cleaned the slate or bought your way into heaven. Kidnapping my friend and stealing the art was a crime for which you deserve punishment. On behalf of City General's clinic, I accept your generous offer," Joni replied although she could not bring herself to extend her hand in friendship to this man.

"Wonderful! You've made me a very happy man. I'll have my attorney draw up the papers and send over the check immediately," Mr. Jones bubbled as he kissed Joni's hand with a grand flourish. He looked rather silly in his current attire as he danced around the room in his excitement.

"Might I ask you another question, Mr. Jones? Why did

you decide to masquerade as a patient to make this offer?" Joni asked as she watched him resume his seat on the table. His cheeks glowed rosy pink from the exertion.

"I was afraid that you wouldn't see me if I didn't look like one. It would have been impossible for me to make an appointment with you if I identified myself as the robber you treated months ago. You might have been afraid of me," Mr. Jones replied. "You might have thought that I was up to my old tricks and planned to kidnap you this time. Besides, I wanted to get a feel for the clinic experience. The last time I was here, I received very personal and unique care. I wanted to see how the regular person would be treated if I came into the clinic with an unspecified ailment. I'm delighted to report that I received the same great attention as an ordinary person that I did as a gunshot-wound victim. The nurse on duty took my vital statistics promptly and wrote up my chart. I'm very satisfied. My money will be well spent here."

Chuckling at his behavior, Joni commented, "I'm glad your experiences here have been to your liking, Mr. Jones. We work hard to make sure that we give all of our patients quality care."

"Well, I'll be getting dressed now. I have an appointment with my attorney in thirty minutes and I don't want to be late. So that you know that I'm on the up-and-up with this offer of assistance, I'd like to leave a small contribution to the clinic with you now. I hope this will help to assure you that I'm sincere in my offer. I'm not some crackpot looking for attention and a bed in the psychiatric wing of the hospital," Mr. Jones stated as he reached into his trouser pocket and extracted his wallet. He smiled broadly as he handed a folded white envelope to Joni.

"This isn't necessary, Mr. Jones. I believe your intentions are purely honorable," Joni replied as she tried to return it.

"No, you must accept it. The statement from my attorney will show this as a partial payment of the full amount. You may open it at your leisure. I must hurry. I have to travel all the way across town in this wicked traffic," Mr. Jones responded as he pushed the envelope more securely into Joni's hand and closed her fingers over it.

"Thank you, Mr. Jones. I'm very grateful. I'd like to dedicate the clinic's face-lift to you, however, I don't know how that would be possible," Joni stated with a smile.

"I'm content knowing that the money is in your capable hands and will be well spent helping others. My name and public recognition are not important. The work that you do here is what matters. Once this transaction has been finalized, even my attorney will not be able to contact me except through my blind trust and e-mail address. My wife and I will become residents of the world," Mr. Jones replied as he started to pull on his trousers.

"In that case, good-bye. If you ever need any medical care, you'll know where to find me. Again, thank you for your contribution to City General," Joni stated as she left the room and closed the door.

Crossing the nearly empty waiting room, Joni returned to Randi where she stood at the nurses' station. "What took you so long? His chart didn't state that there was anything of a serious or complicated nature wrong with him," Randi demanded as soon as Joni dropped off her report.

"There wasn't anything the matter with him. Mr. Jones wanted to make a contribution to the clinic's expansion fund, and that's the way he went about it," Joni explained with a grin.

Looking at her incredulously, Randi queried, "You're telling me that a grown man decided that he would like to dress in a paper gown and his underwear to make a donation to the hospital? You don't see anything wrong with that behavior? Should I call for a psych consult for both of you?"

Laughing, Joni replied, "You don't grasp the entire picture. I thought he was a nutcase, too, when I first met him. However, he managed to convince me that he's totally serious and quite sane."

"How did he do that?"

"He introduced himself. Actually, he reintroduced himself and made our previous working arrangement known to me. You see, he's the robber who kidnapped you," Joni explained.

"What?" Randi exploded, "I thought he was in jail."

"Apparently not. He explained that the victim would not press charges against him for fear of his own illegal dealings coming under investigation. Anyway, our Mr. Jones wanted to see me so that he could make arrangements to give a generous sum of money to the clinic in appreciation for the outstanding treatment we gave him. It would appear that he has sold the stolen articles for an astronomical amount of money. He's secure for life and wants to spread the wealth," Joni explained as she slowly opened the envelope.

"What's in there?" Randi asked as she stepped closer for a look inside.

"He said that this is a good-faith deposit on the money that we'll receive from his attorney later today. He wanted us to have it so that we wouldn't think that he was a neighborhood nutcase," Joni said as she extracted the bills.

"How much is it?"

"Give me a chance to count it. It's in one-thousand-dollar denominations. Twenty, fifty, no—one hundred thousand dollars! I've never seen so many pictures of Grover Cleveland," Joni pronounced as she carefully counted the bills.

Staring incredulously, Randi exclaimed, "Did he say that this is only the down payment on a larger sum?"

"That's what the man said. It's hard to believe, isn't it?" Joni replied.

"Just think of all the supplies we'll be able to buy with this money. Even if the clinic never splits into its own entity, we'll be so much better stocked than we are now," Randi offered.

"I'm going upstairs to PR. They're the ones who handle all the donations to the hospital. I don't want all this money lying around down here," Joni said as she returned the money to the envelope and stuffed it into her pocket.

"Take Ralph with you. I'd feel better if you weren't alone," Randi suggested as she motioned for one of the hospital's security police.

"Good idea," Joni agreed as she motioned to Ralph and led him upstairs.

When she returned, the entire emergency room and clinic staffs were abuzz with excitement over the contribution. They could all envision the improvements, the new furnishings, the new equipment, and, if possible, a larger space.

"Joni, do you think we'll be able to expand into the other storage room? The clinic space is so much smaller than the ER's, and we see the same number of patients every day. We could really use the space," Alberta asked. She was one of the clinic's two PAs and knew its patient load intimately.

"I don't see why not, Alberta," Joni replied. "First, however, I want to see the full extent of Mr. Jones's generosity. We need to know how large a vision we can have. Right now, I see new equipment so that we don't have to stand in line to use the ER's. That will help tremendously. This money might not stretch far enough to purchase the machinery we need and expand our space."

"I'm ready to move boxes whenever you need me," Alberta responded as she hurried back to the clinic.

Leaning closer, Randi asked, "What exactly did Mr. Jones steal? He must have gotten his hands on some gold bars to have this kind of money."

"I don't know. He didn't volunteer the information, and I didn't ask. All I know is that he's set for life," Joni responded dreamily.

"Imagine how much the man from whom he stole this fortune must be worth. That kind of wealth just boggles my mind," Randi replied as she handed Joni a cup of coffee.

"He must be very lonely, too. Mr. Jones mentioned an extensive security system. Just imagine having so much wealth that you had to secure yourself from life in order to protect it. I wouldn't like to live that way," Joni said as she sipped the steaming brew.

"I don't think I would either, but I'd certainly like the chance to try. I could handle that kind of misery for a few months or even years," Randi added with a chuckle.

As they stood enjoying the momentary silence of the usually busy emergency room, Don Rivers appeared through the elevator doors. "I heard a wild rumor about a patient's generosity. Is it true?" Don said as he looked from Joni to Randi and back again.

"Sometimes hard work and dedication to duty pay off. News certainly travels fast in City General," Joni answered with a laugh. She had been expecting his visit since leaving the public relations office.

"Do you have any plans for the money?" Don asked.

"Not yet. I'm waiting to see if there really will be a check for a larger amount coming later this week. I don't know if I can completely trust him. It's kind of hard for me to put my faith in a thief and a kidnapper," Joni replied with skepticism.

"I can understand that, but you know how I feel about expanding the scope of the clinic. This might be just the right time to do it. If his donation is large enough, we'd be able to build a new wing for the clinic and totally separate it from the ER," Don stated as he mentally spent the contribution.

Randi added with a little smile, "Aren't you putting the cart before the horse a bit? That sounds like a good idea, Don, and one I'm sure Joni would support if the figures showed that the clinic would continue to treat the same number of patients every year. However, one hundred thousand dollars is all we have so far. It won't stretch far enough to cover building costs."

Interrupting the exchange, Joni smiled and said, "There will be plenty of time for making changes if the check arrives. By the way, what was your reaction to Stephen Clay?"

Stiffening, Don answered, "He comes highly recommended. I'm not privy to any more information about him than that since we're in consideration for the same job."

"I thought he was quite impressive when I had lunch with him. He was very interested in my thoughts on the ER and the clinic. He thought my decision to move slowly on the issue of separating the clinic from the ER to be a very reasonable one," Joni commented with a mischievous little grin. A little jealousy, professional and personal, would do Don good.

"I'm glad you were so favorably impressed. I suppose it's all in the hands of the board of directors now," Don replied. His face was tight with emotion.

"You've got to admit that the man knows all aspects of the hospital. He won't have to learn the ropes. He'll hit the ground running if he's selected by the board," Randi added with a merry smile at Don's discomfort.

Changing the subject Don said without waiting for a response, "Let me know when the check arrives. I'll be in my office this afternoon and tomorrow morning."

Watching the elevator door close, Randi commented, "I'd say that Don is beginning to feel the breath of competition down his neck."

"I think Don's worried that the board might have found a better candidate for the job. With Stephen Clay in the candidate pool, Don should be worried about his future. We'll have to be nicer to him the next time he visits us," Joni commented as she started toward her office.

"I couldn't agree with you more about the job. I'll take the other issue under advisement for your sake," Randi replied with a crooked smile.

"Don't be so hard on him, Randi. Don is really trying to do better and to be more people-oriented. He's come a long way," Joni defended him almost by habit but definitely from the heart.

"Look, Joni, you can forgive and forget if you want, but I

can't. He was not nice to you. Anyway, it looks as if he might not stay here long enough to work his way back into your heart," Randi replied as she turned her attention to her nurses' time cards.

Pushing thoughts of checks, Don, and the expansion of the clinic from her mind, Joni concentrated on the work piled on her desk. Slowly she made her way through the patient charts, reviewing each one with care for thoroughness of preparation. Where necessary, she wrote questions on sticky paper for the attending physicians to answer before closing the files. She did not want anything to fall through the cracks. She had to be careful in the litigious society in which the hospital did business.

In her tenure as chief of the emergency room, Joni had been able to respond to every lawsuit with ease due in part to the careful preparation of charts she demanded from the physicians. Regardless of their fatigue or the number of patients they treated in a day, the doctors knew that Joni required detailed notes on patient care. She wanted to be able to open any file and know exactly what care the physician had administered.

Joni was so engrossed in her work that she did not hear Randi enter the office. *"Ahem,"* Randi signaled as she stood beside the desk. "Aren't you ready to go home yet? It's after six."

"One more chart to review and I'll be ready. Give me five minutes," Joni replied without looking up from the paper on her desk.

"Fine, I'll wait right here. I don't want you to start anything else. I'm hungry. I thought we'd stop at the pizza place around the corner for dinner," Randi said as she lowered her tired body into the chair.

"Sounds good to me."

"Has the check arrived yet?" Joni asked as she opened the last chart.

"Not yet. Maybe Mr. Jones didn't make it to his attorney's office in time. Maybe there is no check," Randi commented running her hand over the worn upholstery.

"No, it'll come eventually. I don't think he was lying."

Looking around the dull, little room, Randi commented, "I certainly hope you take some of that money and buy paint for this office. It's so depressing I don't see how you can stand to work in here."

"It's not so bad. I don't even notice it anymore."

"Well, it needs some bright colors on the wall, new carpet, and new furniture. This carpet is almost threadbare, and the desk looks like something from surplus stock."

"It is. You should have seen the one Don used. It was even worse than this."

"Speaking of Don. . . ."

"No, let's not, at least not while I'm trying to finish my work. We can talk about him over dinner if you'd like."

"I just wanted to say that I think it takes a lot of nerve for him to try to tell you how to spend the money Mr. Jones donated to the clinic. He specifically left the money in your care, not in Don's."

"Randi, please, just a few more minutes of silence."

"Doesn't the gall of the man bother you? Don't you get angry whenever you see him?"

"No."

"But he's so sure of himself."

"It's all a front. He's just as insecure as the rest of us. The only difference is that he doesn't have a friend babbling away in his office and distracting him from his work," Joni said as she glared at Randi.

"Okay, I won't say another word," Randi sulked.

For a few seconds, she was silent. Unable to sit still, she paced the room. When she tired of that, she toyed with the latest bouquet of roses from Don in the window and rearranged the few books on the shelf. A discreet knocking at the door broke the silence.

"This just arrived for you, Joni," Alberta announced as she excitedly waved the big, white envelope.

Opening it, Joni pulled out the single slip of paper. "Alberta don't just stand there. It's time to move some boxes," she announced with a big smile.

"Fantastic!" Alberta shouted as she darted off to share the good news.

"Wow! I've never seen so many zeros," Randi said as she looked over Joni's shoulder.

"We can certainly buy a lot of equipment and build a lot of walls with this," Joni commented as she thought of the opportunities the money afforded them.

"I'll take the check upstairs while you finish your work. We can really celebrate now," Randi said as she left Joni to her work.

Enjoying the silence, Joni found it hard to push the thought of expansion possibilities out of her mind as she returned to the chart. Mentally, she drafted a proposal that she would present to the board. Mr. Jones's contribution had placed everything she wanted for the clinic within reach.

"Joni, I just have to say one more thing about Don. . . ." Randi began as soon as she returned.

Swiftly, Joni raised her hand and said, "Only a few more lines. Finished. Let's go. My work for the day is done. You can talk about Don as much as you want over dinner."

As Joni slipped out of her white jacket, Randi said, "I think you still have feelings for him. That's why he doesn't annoy you. You still care for him. I see the way you look at him since the night he crashed the card party. You can't hide it from me. That's why you won't date other men."

"Look, I'll admit it. I still care very much for him, but there are obstacles. When we've settled this hospital business, maybe there will be time to work on a relationship with Don,"

Joni quipped as she turned out the light and locked the office door.

"Would you take him back if he crawled?"

A large weather front had swept through Baltimore bringing with it oppressive heat and humidity. Pushing open the door and feeling the blast of hot air against her cheeks, Joni stuffed her sweater into her bag. Looking at Randi, she replied, "He has crawled, and I have rejected him for the time being."

"Wow. I didn't know you two had talked."

"Since when do I have to tell you everything?" Joni snapped tartly as they braced against the heat.

"We're best friends. You're supposed to tell me all of your business," Randi replied as her words hung in the moist air.

"Do you tell me everything?" Joni asked as she opened the heavy restaurant door.

"Yes, I always do. Well, maybe I keep a few little things to myself, but not the big ones," Randi replied as she slipped into the booth.

"Well, this time it's different," Joni commented as she scanned the menu.

"So, you do think about him," Randi said as if making an astute observation.

"I think of him often. I sometimes find myself wishing that we could be together again. But then I remember the past and I put the thoughts out of my mind. There's a lot of healing yet to be done by both of us," Joni replied as she picked up a crumb from the last diners' meals.

"You probably think about him most when you're alone," Randi added as she poured the contents of a sugar package into her steaming tea.

"When do I have time to be either lonely or alone?" Joni rebutted as she ordered a small pepperoni and sausage pizza.

"When you're not at the hospital, you might feel lonely," Randi offered. She ordered the chicken and pineapple pizza.

"You're not going to like it. It's too sweet."

"I'll eat some of yours if I don't."

"When I'm not at the hospital, we're together."

"Not all the time."

"Randi, the only time we're not either at work, going to work, or talking about work together is when we're asleep. City General consumes our lives and you know it," Joni replied, munching a bread stick.

"You certainly shot him a zinger today about Stephen Clay."

"You're right, and I shouldn't have. It wasn't a kind thing to do. He was obviously very worried about his position. I only did it to show him that he's not the only candidate with possibilities for the position."

Tasting her pizza, Randi announced, "You're right. It is too sweet. I should have listened to you. I'll trade you a couple slices of yours for two of these."

"Fine."

They ate in silence until Randi said, "I guess you're right. We are either at the hospital or together. That's the way it is with best friends."

"You're right. I rest my case."

The ate the rest of their meal without feeling any pressure for small talk. Tomorrow, Joni would face the demands of the hospital and her feelings for Don Rivers. For the rest of the evening, relaxation and dinner were her only concerns.

Fourteen

For the next two weeks, the conversation around the lunch tables and the coffee machine centered on Stephen Clay and the huge contribution the mysterious Mr. Jones had given to Joni for use in the clinic. Everyone spoke warmly of Dr. Clay's interaction with them and voiced their preference for him over Don as the chief of staff. When they spoke of Mr. Jones, they wondered who he was and what Joni had done to make him feel so generous toward the hospital.

Joni was so busy that she only heard snippets of their conversation. With Mr. Jones's money, she purchased the equipment that would make the clinic's operation more efficient. No longer would any member of its staff have to wait in line for shared X-ray facilities, the copy machine, or medical supplies. She replaced any tattered or frayed furniture with new fixtures and arranged to have another underutilized closet removed and the clinic's facility enlarged. She proposed the construction of a clinic wing to the board, although she still resisted the idea of splitting it from the emergency room.

Joni was so engrossed in her work in the clinic that she did not hear Stephen Clay enter. She almost tumbled off the step stool when he asked, "I'm in town for another meeting with the board and thought I'd drop by to see you. Have you given my suggestion about turning the ER over to outside management any further thought, Joni?"

"Oh, Stephen, you startled me. I didn't know you were

visiting the ER today," Joni replied as she regained her composure. "I honestly haven't had the time to think about it yet. However, I am inclined to say that we're not ready for that kind of change here. We're a big hospital with a small-hospital feel. This clinic is our first major innovative step. We need to move slowly with any other changes. I'm not rejecting the suggestion because it certainly has merit. It would give us so much flexibility to practice medicine rather than being the paper pushers that we are now. However, with the changes in administration still looming over us, I think we need to wait for a while."

Smiling, Stephen commented, "Fair enough. You have a very valid point about the managerial upheaval. There will be time for examining my suggestion when the dust settles."

"By the way, has the board decided on who will assume the chief of staff position? I haven't been in the loop the last few weeks. Have I missed something?" Joni asked as she descended the ladder and returned it to the small storage area.

"Nothing yet, but I heard that they will make the announcement later this week. Regardless of their decision, I've thoroughly enjoyed my visits to City General," Stephen responded as he helped her carry the last of the boxes into the little room.

"We always enjoyed having you with us. Thanks for the help. I'll keep my eyes open for the announcement," Joni said as she waved good-bye.

As usual, a line of patients awaited the opening of the clinic's doors. Waving to Sally, Joni signaled that she had finally finished the work she had started at seven in the morning. She had not wanted to disrupt the smooth flow of the clinic by being in the way with the ladder. More importantly, Joni had not wanted to deprive patients of treatment by closing the clinic so that she could do the necessary work. She had gladly come in early.

Squeezing past the waiting patients, Joni returned to the ER. "Glad you're here," Randi greeted her. "We're about to be swamped with patients. There's been an accident in the harbor. I'm not sure just how many patients we'll see, but I bet we'll get the bulk of them."

"Do you know what happened?" Joni asked slipping into her white jacket and donning her stethoscope as she brushed the dust from her hair.

"According to the radio, two barges carrying cargo and workers collided. It's taken a little time to rescue everyone from the water, but the newscaster said that no one drowned. I understand that there've been quite a number of really bad injuries. It could have been worse if this had been winter," Randi explained.

"Looks like they're here already," Joni exclaimed as she pointed to the ambulances pulling into the driveway. From where she stood, she could count five of them.

The first of the paramedics entered pushing a stretcher carrying a man in a neck brace. He was covered in slimy harbor water and blood. His face looked battered. His breathing was shallow and his lips appeared blue.

"Roll him into number one, John," Joni ordered as she followed. She read the hastily prepared chart as she walked.

"He stopped breathing twice on the way over. Right now he's holding his own, but we had to bag him for a while. He hasn't regained consciousness since the divers pulled him from the water," John said as he pushed the stretcher into position.

"All right, on my count. One, two, three. How many more do you think we'll get?" Joni asked as she opened the man's wet shirt.

"I couldn't say for sure. They're sending the less serious injuries to the other hospitals, but it's a madhouse down there on the wharf. Bodies are everywhere. It was a bad accident. I have to go right back for more. See you later, doc," John replied as he pushed the stretcher out of the exam room door.

"What have we got here?" Joni asked as she turned her attention to the assembled nurses who worked to get the man's vital signs.

"He has a badly lacerated forearm, bruises to the face, neck, and chest. His identification says that he's a local man. I'll contact his family," Christina recited as she made the entries on the man's chart.

"Let's stop that bleeding and transfer him immediately to surgery. I'm concerned about the facial swelling. Handle him gently, folks," Joni ordered as she quickly applied pressure to the site of the wound on the man's arm.

"This is a bad one," Christina commented as the blood continued to flow.

"It runs the length of his arm. Let's work fast, people," Joni replied.

"His pressure is falling," Ben interjected. "He's stopped breathing."

"I'm clearing the airway and putting in the tube. Got it. Okay, Ben, you push, and I'll bag him as we go. It's time for the transfer. There's nothing we can do for him down here," Joni ordered as she hopped onto the gurney as Ben and Christina pushed it toward the waiting elevator.

When she returned, Joni rushed into room two to help out. Barely through the door, she stopped short. To her surprise, Don stood beside the gurney. He had heard about the accident and had left a meeting in geriatrics. In the past, he never would have joined in the fray unless dragged into it. He always felt that an administrator should leave the practice of medicine to his staff. Now, however, when Don saw that the emergency room was short-handed, he rolled up his sleeves and jumped in to help. He was examining the badly mauled leg of a seaman. The man had become trapped under the debris and had been dragged by the leg along the rough beams of the pier.

"Don, I'm surprised to see you down here. I'll relieve you of this," Joni said as she stepped closer.

"No way, you need every pair of hands you can get. I wasn't doing anything vital upstairs. This is where the action is. I'm fine. Go get your own patient," Don replied with a smile as he returned to the raw flesh.

"We could definitely use the help. Thanks," Joni said as she left the patient in his care. She was too shocked by the change in his behavior to think of anything witty to say.

The triage staff had increased its number to three as they sorted the patients according to the extent of their injuries. Those patients who were not rolled in on stretchers occupied the area in the center of the waiting room. Randi had set aside a section of the room for the nurses to treat and release the least critical of the patients. At least twenty people waited their turn to have one of the staff clean cuts, apply butterfly strips to the more serious ones, and administer tetanus shots against infection from puncture wounds. The four physician's assistants worked in another section. They treated patients whose injuries required stitches. The paramedics on the site of the accident had provided the preliminary treatment for their wounds, but their injuries still required more.

The doctors treated the most critical patients in the five packed examining rooms, each of which could handle four patients in separate areas. On Randi's direction, Joni entered room four where the captain of one of the vessels moaned in agony. His hand had been smashed after becoming stuck between two falling beams while he tried to steer the vessel. The fire department had used chain saws to free him from the wreckage of his boat.

"Let me look at that hand, captain. We'll give you something for the pain and transfer you to surgery as soon as possible," Joni said in a calm, soothing tone.

"How are my men?" the captain asked in a strained voice.

"We're working on them now, but I don't know any specifics as yet. Too many injured people," Joni replied calmly as she inspected the hand. Even without the benefit of X ray, Joni could see that the captain's hand had suffered multiple fractures. Laying it gingerly on a splint, she immobilized it as much as possible.

"I don't know how this happened. One minute, we were sailing out of the harbor without a hitch and the next, another vessel had crashed into us. I couldn't steer away from it in time," the captain fretted.

"Lie still, captain. Don't worry about that now. I'm sure it wasn't your fault."

"My chest! There's an awful pressure on my chest," the captain groaned as he reached with his free hand to pull away his gown.

"What's happening, Martin?" Joni asked the nurse who was monitoring the captain's vital statistics.

"He has developed an arrhythmia. He's going into arrest," Martin replied, as he reached for the paddles.

"Two hundred. Clear!" Joni shouted applying the paddles to the captain's chest.

"Nothing."

"Three hundred. Clear!"

The examining room filled with the smell of scorched flesh. Red imprints developed on the man's chest as they waited for the monitor to register the return of a normal heartbeat.

"He's back," Martin announced. "His BP is stabilizing."

"Let's transfer him to the coronary ICU. His hand will have to wait," Joni instructed as she slipped the chart under the foot of the bed.

Throwing her soiled gloves and blood-spotted gown into the hamper, Joni returned to the nurses' station for another chart. The nurses had treated and sent home all of the patients with minor injuries and were now helping the PAs work on the others. The steady hum of voices had replaced the roar of the past hour.

As Joni hurried to examining room three, she caught a quick glimpse of Don working on another patient. The furrow on his brow showed his level of concentration as his fingers gently administered the needed treatment. He did not look up as she rushed past.

"Doc, do something about my leg. I have to get back out there to help my mates. They need me," one of the crewmen begged as Joni entered the room.

"What seems to be the problem, sailor?" Joni asked as she surveyed his chart.

"I was trying to help one of my buddies. He had been trapped under a beam and couldn't get up. His head was bleeding badly. When I lifted him, I must have twisted my leg the wrong way because I heard something in my knee pop. My leg gave way; it just wouldn't hold my weight. You gotta fix me up. I gotta go help my mates," Norman Christian begged.

Manipulating the leg, Joni stated, "I'm going to put some pressure on your knee. Does it hurt as I shift it to the left?"

"No, doc, nothing. The skin feels tight from the swelling, but my knee doesn't really hurt," Norman replied.

"Fine, Norman. Do you feel any discomfort when I move the kneecap?"

"No. What's the matter? What did I do to my knee? That popping really scared me."

Patting Norman on the shoulder, Joni replied, "I don't think you'll be doing much on that knee for a while. I suspect that you injured the anterior cruciate ligament. You're going to need to ice it, give it rest for about two weeks, and see an orthopedic surgeon. We have several great doctors on staff. I'll send you for an MRI, and then arrange for you to see one today."

"I can't be laid up for two weeks. I have work to do. No, doc, we've got to do better than that. My mates need me now," Norman protested as he tried to get up.

Pressing him into the mattress, Joni replied, "Don't worry about your mates. Everything is under control at the harbor. Besides, your knee won't hold your weight right now. There's nothing you can do for anyone else. This was a freaky accident, that's all. The surgeon might be able to suggest ways to shorten your recovery time. For now, let's just wait and see. At least you're in good company. President Clinton had the same injury."

"Yeah, but he doesn't make his living by working on the water. I can't give up that much time and money. Get me that

MRI and call that surgeon. As much as I hate the idea of being cut, I can't sit around waiting for the knee to heal on its own. I've never missed a day of work in my life. What's the chance you're wrong, doc?" Norman stated with a disgusted shake of his head.

"It's possible, and it has happened before. However, from what you've told me and from the amount of swelling and the feel of your knee, I'd say that I'm about seventy percent right. The MRI will confirm my diagnosis. I'll send in a technician. You'll be fine, Norman. Let's look at the bright side. The orthopedic surgeon might want to try a noninvasive regimen of therapy rather than surgery. You'll be back to work in no time at all if he does. You'll just have to wait and see," Joni responded.

"Okay, doc," Norman replied softly. Joni left him angrily pounding his fist into the palm of his hand.

All morning, Joni moved from one patient to the next. As she treated one of the harbor policemen for a badly lacerated leg, he said, "I've been on the harbor patrol for ten years. This is the worst accident I've ever seen. That captain really caused a mess."

"I treated the captain whose vessel he hit, but he wasn't sure how it happened. He said that one minute the harbor was clear and the next he was broadsided. He said he never had a chance," Joni commented as she carefully sutured the wound.

"From the looks of it, I'd agree with him. One vessel was sailing out of the harbor. The other on its way across the water careened into it. The captain of the second one was drunk. I could smell it on his breath. He said that he didn't even see the vessel he hit. He claimed that the fog blocked his view," the officer replied with a sneer.

"I didn't see any fog on the harbor this morning. My condo has a great view of the water," Joni commented as she made the last stitches and applied the gauze bandage.

"I was on the water when the accident happened," the officer stated bluntly. "There wasn't any fog. The man's just trying to cover his ass. Anyway, there are investigators from both companies and the Coast Guard all over the area right now. I know they'll ask me what I know. I didn't see the accident, but I did smell the man's breath. He couldn't have walked a straight line if his life depended on it. After the collision, there were men in the water everywhere. I just knew we'd have a lot of casualties, but the rescue effort started so fast that I don't think we lost any of them."

"All done, officer. You're free to go. Your leg will be sore for a while. You did a good job. You're right; there weren't any casualties. The injuries would have been a lot harder to treat if you guys had not been there. You made our job easy," Joni said as she helped the officer sit up.

"Thanks, doc. You're right about it being sore, but I'm going back to work. I don't want to miss my chance to be on the evening news. There were cameras and reporters all over the place when the paramedics brought me in here," the officer replied as he picked up his slicker and limped away.

Chuckling, Joni threw away the bloodied gauze and cotton swabs. Counting the instruments, she deposited them in the appropriate bins for disposal or sterilization. Tossing her soiled gloves and cover into the hamper she joined Randi in the hall.

"What's so funny?" Randi demanded. "Share it with me. I could use a good laugh after a day like this."

"I just treated a man with a gash in his leg that required more than fifty stitches. As he left, he said that he would return to work so that he wouldn't miss the chance for publicity and an appearance on the evening news. I was just chuckling at the way people react to disaster. The last thing I'd think about would be the evening news if I had a leg that looked like that," Joni explained as she scanned the almost empty waiting room. The clinic had reopened in the lull following the accident and treated the usual walk-in traffic.

At that moment, Stephen Clay joined them at the desk. "You two have some team here. I don't know if I've ever seen people pull together like this. Incredible. You've done a great job of turning this into a dynamic operation."

"Thank you, Stephen. We do seem to thrive on the excitement and the urgency," Joni replied modestly.

"I was really impressed at the way everyone fit into their slot without direction. I didn't see any patient suffer from lack of care. No one gave instructions. Everyone just knew what to do. Thank you both for an informative morning. Joni, when you have time to give my suggestion some thought, I'd appreciate the chance to go over it in depth with you. From the way this ER practices medicine, I'd say that this is the ideal department for an outside management firm to take over the paperwork. You would have much more time for doing what you do best," Stephen offered.

"Aren't there some down sides to having outside management step in to do the scheduling and payroll?" Joni asked as she made the final notes in the last chart.

"Sure, but there are for anything. You'd have to stipulate the boundaries and see to it that the firm operates to your requirements. I know of too many hospitals that turn things over and then wash their hands of all responsibility for the successful implementation of the policy change. Then, when something goes wrong and there are too few physicians and nurses on rotation to manage a disaster, they panic and blame the management firm. I see an outsider as a tool, not as the whole ball of wax," Stephen explained as he tried to allay her fears.

"I still don't think that an outsider's presence would work here at City General, but thank you for the suggestion," Joni replied as she waved good-bye.

"Let me know if you change your mind," Stephen nodded and disappeared into the elevator.

Turning her attention to the pile of paper before her, Joni ignored Randi's steady gaze. Finally when she couldn't stand the pressure of her friend's eyes boring into her head, Joni looked up and said, "Well, say it. I know you're dying to make a comment."

"I am, and it's that I'm really proud of you. Being an administrator hasn't made you change your ways. I'm glad to see that you stick up for the little guy. He would have implemented changes that would have torn apart all of our longstanding teams. However, I still like his management style. He knows when to drop a subject," Randi said with a quick smile that turned into a wicked grin as she added, "I forgot to tell you that Don is waiting to see you in your office if you have a minute."

"Did he say what he wanted?"

"No, he only said he'd wait. Maybe he has heard something and wants to be the first to share the news with you," Randi offered as she carefully filed away the first of many charts.

"I'll let you know. I'll come to get you for lunch as soon as I can. Could you finish with Norman while I go to my office?" Joni asked as she handed Randi the chart.

"Gladly. You'll know where to find me," Randi called after her.

Although she was tired and would rather sit down for a few minutes than speak with Don, Joni hoped that the board had finally decided to make the long-awaited announcement. "Good afternoon," she intoned as she entered her office. "Randi said you wanted to speak with me. Sorry to keep you waiting, but I was rather busy. What's up?"

Turning from the window from which he had watched the arrival of the ambulances, Don replied, "I have something important to talk over with you. I had hoped to find a better time, but I don't think there will ever be one."

"I'm listening. Fire away," Joni said as she sank into the faded leather of the old sofa.

"I've done everything I can to prove to you that I've changed. I don't know what else to do. I need you back in my life. Is there any chance for us?" Don asked. His expression showed neither hope nor a sense of impending rejection. He appeared open to accepting Joni's decision.

"We're different people from the ones we were then. I don't know that we can go back to being the way we were," Joni answered honestly and without any hesitation.

"I thought that's what you'd say. That's why I have a proposition to make," Don replied softly. "I watched you in action today. You're a dynamo. No wonder the ER is functioning more efficiently with you as its chief than it ever did under my management. You're everywhere at one time motivating the staff and pitching in beside them. It's your ER now, and the clinic is a wonder. You pulled that together all by yourself, including securing the funding and the gifts. You never asked anyone for help. You've built quite a name for yourself in the field because of it."

Smiling Joni said, "Thanks for the words of praise, but I didn't do it alone. I've had a very dedicated staff behind me every step of the way. If it hadn't been for Randi's support and her rapport with the nursing staff, I don't know how I could have done it. Randi and her nurses pitched in to make the ER and the clinic work. Everyone here knows that we had to become a team in order to survive. We're lean and mean by necessity. The other choice was to lose jobs, and no one wanted that. We pulled together because we had to, and we're stronger for it."

"I still know that you were the driving force behind the changes. I tried to motivate those same people without much success. They wanted to follow your lead. Anyway, this is what I want to propose. I don't want us to go back to the way we were. There were too many kinks in the fiber of our old relationship for me to want to relive that life. What I propose is that we go forward. I'd like for us to get to know each other again with the intention of getting married in the near future. You're a formidable opponent in business and I'm not exactly a slouch myself. We'd be a dynamite team, if you'd just give us a chance," Don stated as he placed his hands on Joni's shoulders.

"I've watched the new you, and you have changed. The old Don Rivers never would have joined us in the ER today. I was most impressed. I haven't been blind to the merit of some of your suggestions for modifications in the ER either. There's always room for improvement, even in an organization that's in good shape. Professionally, we'd make a good team," Joni conceded with a smile as she gazed into Don's eyes and saw the love and respect reflected there.

"And personally?" Don asked with an earnestness that almost made Joni's heart break.

"I think there might be a chance for us in that area, too. However, we'll have to see how that works out. It's still too early for a definite commitment," Joni replied with a smile as Don pulled her closer.

With a chuckle, Don said, "I'll take what I can get. I'll just have to work harder."

Don's lips pressed tightly against hers and spoke of the happiness that would one day be theirs. Wrapping his arms around her lithe body, he held her with special tenderness for all the lost days. Joni melted against him as the unspoken promises overwhelmed her.

Looking into Joni's eyes, Don said, "There's one more thing that I should tell you. Before coming down here, I officially withdrew my name from the candidacy for the chief of staff position and for the ER chief spot. I don't want anything to come between us. As long as we work in the same hospital, there's always room for gossip and competition."

Concerned Joni asked, "What are your plans, Don? You're a damn good physician and administrator. I don't see why we can't work together. We can ignore the talk."

Jingling the coins in his pocket, Don replied, "As a matter of fact, I'm taking a position in D.C. I'll be the new chief of staff at Ward Circle Hospital. I won't be far away if you ever need me. We can discuss the day over dinner every night."

"Isn't that Stephen's hospital?" Joni asked as she straightened Don's tie and allowed her fingers to linger on his chest.

"Yeah, funny how things work out, isn't it?" Don answered as he pulled her into his arms once again.

Hating to part from the comfort of his arms, Joni pushed away gently and said, "I think we should break this up, if you're worried about gossip. Someone could come in here any minute."

Rising and pulling Joni up with him, Don replied, "You're right. Besides, I have a meeting at my new hospital in two hours. I'll see you at dinner tonight."

Accompanying Don to the door, Joni asked, "Should I drive into D.C.?"

Giving her one last kiss, Don responded, "No, our usual place. Only this time, we won't need a table in the corner."

For a while, Joni stared at the closed door. She had not anticipated Don's departure. With the knowledge that Don was out of contention for the job and with the revised productivity figures firmly in hand, Joni rushed upstairs to the conference room. She knew that the board was in session again to decide the fate of those who had waited so long for the announcement. She hoped she would not be too late. In her haste, Joni forgot all about her lunch with Randi.

By late afternoon, the board had made its decision. Memos arrived at every department chair's desk. Standing with hers firmly in her hands, Joni lingered beside the nurses' station.

"Hey, you stood me up. When you didn't return, I went without you. What's that you're holding? Is it the announcement? Well, open it. You've waited all this time. Open it," Randi urged impatiently.

"No, you read it to me," Joni demanded as she thrust the envelope toward Randi.

"You're a nutcase. If I had worked as hard as you have for something, I'd want to see it in print myself," Randi chided with a laugh as she opened the interoffice mail envelope that contained the sheets of paper that announced the appointments.

Looking over her shoulder, Joni mused with a wicked little grin, "There're three sheets in here. That's odd. I knew there would be two of them but not three. The third one must be the announcement of a celebration party."

"Probably. Now be quiet while I read this," Randi ordered as she cleared her throat dramatically. " 'The Board of City General proudly announces the appointment of Stephen Clay as the new chief of staff. Dr. Clay comes to City General from his position as chief of staff at Ward Circle Hospital in Washington, D.C.' I wonder how Don will take this?"

"He already knows. He told me earlier that he's taking Stephen's old job. He wants to give us a professional separation while we work on our personal lives. Don has asked me to marry him again. I think I might just say yes this time," Joni replied with a little smile.

"So that's why he wanted to see you. Well, as you know, I never really liked him, but I guess I'll have to get used to him if he's to be my best friend's husband," Randi commented matter-of-factly.

"He'll grow on you. Actually, Don's a lot of fun. Now that he has changed, he'll be even more enjoyable to be around," Joni replied with a laugh at Randi's continued dislike of the subject.

"Anyway, now the next appointment. 'The Board of City General proudly announces the appointment of Joni Forest as the chief of the emergency medical services and clinic. Dr. Forest has been serving dutifully and efficiently as acting chief of the emergency room. Under her direction, the service has become one of City General's leading profit centers. The newly opened clinic has gained local and regional recognition.' It's finally official. That's great, Joni!" Randi said as she hugged her best friend.

"Yeah, I'm really happy about it. What's on the last sheet?" Joni responded as she beamed at her friend.

"It's probably just the reception announcement," Randi replied as she tossed the sheet onto the messy desk.

"No, read it. If it's this afternoon, we'll miss it if you don't," Joni protested with her hand on Randi's arm.

Looking her friend over from head to toe, Randi said, "If it's that important to you, I'll read it. Geez! 'The Board of City General proudly announces the appointment of Randi Timberlake as the new cochief of the clinic. Nurse Timberlake will assume the position along with Dr. Forest until such time as they complete the expansion of the facility into an independent unit. Her replacement as head nurse of the emergency room will be announced at that time.' "

As Randi looked at Joni, her expression changed from shock to one of disbelief. "You did this for me?" Randi asked as the tears glistened in her eyes. "Thanks, Joni. You don't know how much this means to me."

"Don't ever say I never gave you anything. Besides, you deserve it. You've put as much sweat into this clinic as I have. Thank you for being such a great partner," Joni responded in a whisper as they hugged each other.

Suddenly, the emergency room filled with the sound of noisemakers. Confetti floated everywhere. Streamers interlocked and landed on the charts that cluttered the nurses' station. "Hip, hip, hooray." Sylvia led the chorus of cheers.

"We've been saving this stuff since the end of December. It's about time the board made its decision," Christina shouted over the noise.

"Let's hear it for the greatest ER team in the state!" Bob yelled.

"What do you mean in the state? We're the best in the whole damn country!" Mary challenged.

Everyone took up the call. Soon the room was so noisy that no one could hear the phones if they rang. "Okay, everyone. Let's settle down," Randi ordered as she dried her eyes. "The ER is still open for business. Let's remember that we're the best because we give the best care to our patients. Let's clean up this place and look as if we're an emergency room staff."

"Party pooper!" Joni proclaimed under her breath as she rounded the corner to her office.

"Did you say something, doctor?" Randi demanded with a broad smile.

"Not a word, nurse. Never would I be foolish enough to challenge you," Joni replied with a salute.

Reaching the familiar door, Joni stopped short. While the staff celebrated the announcements, the manager of the hospital's print shop had removed Don's name. In its place, he had carefully stenciled JONI FOREST, MD, CHIEF OF EMERGENCY MEDICAL SERVICES AND CLINIC.

Pushing it open, Joni felt that she had finally realized her goal. Inside the office, the walls were still gray. The furniture was still worn. The desk was still battered and scarred. However, the office looked different. For the first time, it was really hers. Joni was the chief of the emergency room.

Joni walked to the window and looked out at the empty driveway. A vase of bright yellow roses and a little, black velvet box sat on the little braided hospital-gown rug. A large, handprinted card that read, MARRY ME. SAY YES! leaned against the vase. Opening the box, Joni took out the diamond ring and slipped it onto the third finger of her left hand. A big smile illuminated her face as she folded her arms across her body.

Cramming the card into her pocket to share with Randi later, Joni sat in the rickety desk chair and opened the first of many patient charts demanding her attention. The sound of voices, rolling gurneys, and rushing feet greeted her ears from the busy hall. The telephone rang off the hook in the bustling ER. Joni still had much to do before she could meet Don for dinner at their special place.

Arabesque Romances
by *Roberta Gayle*

__MOONRISE **0-7860-0268-9** **$4.99**US/**$6.50**CAN

When beautiful art dealer Pascale de Ravenault and Captain Jack Devlin meet, an undeniable spark of passion is kindled . . . but the two must battle scheming revolutionaries intent on capturing a legendary masterpiece in order to save a love that has captured them both.

__SUNRISE AND SHADOWS
0-7860-0136-4 **$4.99**US/**$6.50**CAN

Navajo raised Roses Jordan had both grit and goodness—yet no man had ever touched her heart. Then a handsome, restless man named Tobe Hunter rode into town—searching for a way to stop running, a place to make a new life, and a woman to love . . .

__WORTH WAITING FOR
0-7860-0522-X **$4.99**US/**$6.50**CAN

Attorney Eliza Taylor had her life under perfect control until she was enlisted to help a friend's handsome brother, Ely, keep custody of his son. Suddenly, Eliza finds herself in the middle of a case loaded with legal curves and falling for a man who ignites her deepest hungers . . .

__BOUQUET **0-7860-0515-7** **$4.99**US/**$6.50**CAN
by Roberta Gayle, Anna Larence, & Gail McFarland

Spring is the time to celebrate the women who gave us the precious gift of life—and the irreplaceable love that sustains us. Cherish the power of a mother's love—and a mother in love—with these heartwarming tales. . . .

Call toll free **1-888-345-BOOK** to order by phone or use this coupon to order by mail.

Name______________________________
Address____________________________
City__________________ State ________ Zip ______
Please send me the books I have checked above.
I am enclosing $__________
Plus postage and handling* $__________
Sales tax (in NY, TN, and DC) $__________
Total amount enclosed $__________

*Add $2.50 for the first book and $.50 for each additional book.

Send check or money order (no cash or CODs) to: **Arabesque Books, Dept. C.O., 850 Third Avenue, 16th Floor, New York, NY 10022**

Prices and numbers subject to change without notice.

All orders subject to availability.

Visit our website at **www.arabesquebooks.com**